The Moonl

The Moonlight Sonata

Book Two of the Beethoven Trilogy

by
Tess Alps

YouCaxton Publications
Oxford & Shrewsbury

ISBN 978-1-913425-38-8
Published by YouCaxton Publications 2020
YCBN: 01

YouCaxton Publications
enquiries@youcaxton.co.uk

Dedication:

For Tim, Tom and Joanna
And in memory of my Mum, Kay

Contents

Acknowledgements

A chance encounter with Kate and Greg Mosse at a party led to me sharing with them my early drafts of the first novel in this trilogy, The Harp Quartet. They kindly gave me lots of encouragement, helped me believe that I had some skill as a writer and told me to persist.

Through them, I was introduced to the literary agent, Felicity Bryan. I had no idea who Felicity Bryan was back then, but she took me under her wing and generously gave me her time and a heap of expert advice without which I could never have embarked on this endeavour. When Felicity sadly died earlier this year, I read the many tributes to her and realised that I had been in the hands of a revered legend who had helped many writers start out on their journeys. How lucky was I. Felicity loved music herself and I will think of her and count my blessings whenever I listen to The Moonlight Sonata.

I must also thank the friends and family who read it in its less polished state and shared their thoughts, particularly my Irish relatives who did their best to keep me on the straight and narrow.

I read widely as background to the story but I would like to acknowledge the debt I owe to three books in particular that I came to depend on:

Modern Ireland 1600-1972 R.F. Foster

Founded on Fear Peter Tyrell edited by Diarmuid Whelan

*The Collected Poems of WB Yeats WB Yeats
(Wordsworth Poetry Library)*

The Moonlight Sonata

Chapter 1 - July 1951

Cathy got off the bus about half a mile outside Rowanbridge. It was twelve years since she had last done that, since she had left the village where she had been born and spent the first sixteen years of her life. She could have stayed on until the bus had reached the Post Office in Main Street, a mere five hundred yards from her family home, but she needed more time - to breathe in the country air and to unclench the knots in her stomach.

The hedgerows looked exactly as she remembered them, the sheep and cows too. Over those twelve years away, she had often dreamed of walking along this road from Kilkenny into Rowanbridge and picking honeysuckle for her mother, Hannah. And, sure enough, there it was, winding through the hawthorn, seemingly so delicate but standing up bravely to the strong summer gusts.

Should she gather some now for her mother? When she was little, her Daddy often used to bring her walking here and they would always pick a bunch of something pretty to take back home: violets and primroses in spring, wild roses and honeysuckle in summer, or perhaps just hips and haws in autumn, the stems wrapped around with trailing ivy.

Sometimes, these fairy bouquets - as her Daddy called them - would be accepted with a delighted kiss and hug for Cathy. Her mother would ask Aggie, their housemaid, to pop them into a tiny jug to sit on the study desk while Hannah worked at the accounts. At other times, the little bunches would be ignored and left to wilt on the kitchen table. It just depended how her mother's day was going.

As the village came into view, Cathy suddenly felt panic in her throat. She was scared of how she was going to find her mother, scared of what her mother would say to her, scared of seeing other people who would remember her. Above all, she was scared of seeing Tricky again.

Cathy arrived at the crossroads with Main Street. On the opposite corner, McLoughlin's bar was looking very smart with new blue paint, scarlet pelargoniums on the sills and white-and-blue painted signs in Celtic lettering indicating the separate entrances for the 'Lounge' and the 'Bar'. Cathy knew that the McDermotts' pub, as her family's pub was still popularly known, was unlikely to be in such good repair but at least it wouldn't look like a pub that didn't know whether it was British or Irish.

Cathy could see a couple of old women limping along the pavement towards her. Was one of them old Mrs Magee? Despite carrying a fairly heavy case, Cathy decided to avoid Main Street and its inhabitants and crossed over to go along the back road, past the school and church, over the bridge, past her Aunt Stasia's house and then up Mill Lane to get round to her old home, even though that meant going past the ruined Cromwell's Tower and the memories it held.

A large black car sped past her. She recognised Nicholas Byrne at the wheel but she was confident he wouldn't have a clue who this skinny young woman was, lugging a battered demob case along the road. She knew that Nicholas Byrne, of the landed Byrne family, had once proposed to her mother so he might easily have been her father, except that 'she' – the very particular cocktail of McDermott and Fitzgerald genes that Cathy was composed of - would never have actually existed.

As a child, Cathy was always being told she was just like her father. That made her very happy, not just because he had gifted her her beautiful golden hair, now hidden under her silk scarf, but because of all the other qualities they shared: their love of music and books, their delight in nature and their belief in fairness and kindness. Cathy was pleased that her sixteen-year-old mother had so firmly rejected Nicholas Byrne all those long thirty-five years ago. Her mother had always known what she wanted - and it wasn't Nicholas

Byrne, despite all his family's land and wealth. Hannah had wanted John Fitzgerald and she had made sure she got him.

When Cathy reached the gate into the churchyard she stopped, put down her case and sat on the wall for a rest. In the corner of her eye she saw Father Stephen come out of the presbytery, lock his front door and set off towards the village. His one-time head of unruly black curls was just as unkempt but was now steely grey. He glanced back at Cathy and she thought maybe a shadow of recognition crossed his eyes. But he didn't stop. Cathy knew where he was heading: to see her mother.

Cathy looked over the wall into the churchyard and wondered about going in to find the familiar graves she had tended lovingly all those years ago. But oughtn't she really get home to her mother as soon as possible? Sure, she would only be a couple of minutes. She picked up her case and the bunch of honeysuckle and walked through the churchyard gate over to the shaded graves.

Chapter 2 - May 22nd 1924

Cathy blew as hard as she could and made a wish, just like her Daddy had told her to, but it took three goes to extinguish all four candles on the cake. Then she snuggled back into her Daddy's arms as everyone sang 'Happy Birthday' to her again.

'Well, Cathleen, what a big girl you are now. And, of course, it is my wedding anniversary too today. We shall always share a special day, you know.' Her Aunt Stasia was dandling baby Andrew on her knee while toddler Peter played at her feet with the wooden farm animals Cathy had just been given as a present. 'I'll never forget the day you were born. You were at least two weeks early but Hannah had decided she was going to be the centre of attention on my wedding day after all.'

'Here, Stasia, let me just take that cake away and cut it up for everyone.' Aggie leant over the table to reach for the cake-stand, kicking Stasia as she went. 'Oh, I'm so sorry, Stasia. I didn't want to step on little Peter there.'

Cathy watched from her Daddy's knee as her beautiful, smiley Mammy, wearing a new blue dress and shiny beads, handed out plates of the birthday cake that Aggie had cut.

'Stasia, can I give Peter a piece of cake?' Hannah bent down to the little boy and stroked his hair.

'No, no. Not until he's eaten his tea. Agnes, could you wrap up a couple of pieces for us to take home. Edmund, maybe you should wait until after supper too.' Her husband froze with a slice of cake just an inch from his mouth.

'Nonsense, Stasia. Let the poor man have a bit of cake on Cathy's birthday.' Grandad James was tucking heartily into his cake.

'Yes, go on, Edmund. You can just leave off the soup tonight before your dinner if you're too full.' Hannah stood at Edmund's elbow defying him not to reject the cake and gave him a wink out of the eyeline of her sister.

'Ah, go on now, Edmund. It's absolutely delicious and I, for one, am going to have another piece. So there.' James held up his plate defiantly for Aggie to deposit another slice on it. 'Look at Cathy. She's enjoying herself.' James chuckled to see his beloved grand-daughter's face smeared with chocolate icing.

'John, be careful. Cathleen is dropping cake all over your best trousers.' But John had no intention of taking Stasia's advice to interrupt his daughter's pure joy at eating chocolate cake.

'It's good isn't it, Cathy, macushla. Made with six eggs from the finest hens, reared by your clever Mammy, and the very best Bourneville cocoa from the shop. Not made by her - or me of course - but by the birthday girl herself. OK, with a little help from the very talented Aggie. Come on now, Edmund, how could you refuse cake made by a four-year-old on her birthday?' Cathy looked at her Daddy's mouth as he said these words. Yes, it was true she had helped make the cake. She had cracked the eggs one by one into the mixing bowl and she had licked the bowl clean afterwards.

Edmund finally surrendered to John's entreaty and took a bite to cheers from the Fitzgerald camp. 'Very nice,' was his verdict, mumbled while avoiding his wife's eyes.

Cathy slid off her father's knee and knelt down beside her cousin Peter.

'Agnes, Agnes! Get those hands wiped before she gets chocolate over Peter's best shirt,' panicked Stasia. Aggie dutifully took a linen napkin to Cathy's hands and did her best with a lick or two of spit. When released from Aggie's kindly grip, Cathy picked up the figure of a cow from the floor but Peter snatched it away from her. Then the same thing happened when she tried to take the little wooden sheep.

'Come on, Peter. Come with me.' Cathy stood and took the toddler's hand. 'Can I take Peter to see the chicks, Mammy?'

'Yes, of course, my angel. Look after him now. He's not even three years old yet, you know. Aggie, will you go down with them please and keep an eye on them out in the yard.' The children ran to the stairs pursued by a harassed Aggie.

'Well, now we're all here with no servants listening in, can I ask how the business is going? Stasia adopted her best conspiratorial whisper. 'I hear the pub isn't very busy most nights and I went into the shop two days ago and you had run out of bread when it was only half past eleven.'

'It's actually none of your business, Stasia. You stick to running your own affairs. We can run our own shop perfectly well thank you. We've managed perfectly well for the last five years for heaven's sake.'

'We're fine, thank you, Stasia.' John, ever the diplomat. 'Your father is a great help to me and, of course, Hannah has an excellent head for business. I know I don't - it's probably not what I should be doing – but we're getting along okay.' Hannah and her father exchanged a glance. John had no idea that James was subsidising the accounts each month, albeit modestly, to avoid them going into the red.

'Suit yourselves. I am only thinking of you. I don't want to see my sister and her family in any difficulties. Jimmy Boyle has been heard saying a few things.'

'Has he now? Maybe if he moved his arse a bit and put his energies into managing the pub properly, the business would be in better shape.'

'Hannah, such language. I know he's inclined to swing the lead but he needs a strong master watching over him.'

'Leave it to me, girls,' James was well used to diverting the McDermott sisters from their habitual scrapping. 'I'll have a quiet word with him. Now then, Stasia, have you resolved your friendly dispute with the Byrnes over access to the west field?' He had been keeping the McDermott peace ever since his wife had died ten years previously, leaving him with two relentlessly competitive teenage daughters. Stasia was only two years older than Hannah but, following the loss of their mother in 1914, she had instantly assumed the role of mistress of the household, a position that Hannah had never accepted.

'It's ongoing, Father. But we shall win of course. Edmund has prepared all the documents. Maybe you could run an eye over them when you're next over at the villa. Actually, I was going to ask whether you'd like to come and live with us for the next six months, Father. You haven't been back to live for nearly a year. I'm sure Peter would like to spend more time with his grandfather. And I don't like to think of you in such close proximity to the temptation of that wretched pub.'

'And there we have it. Stasia's mission to keep you away from the Guinness, Dada.' Hannah laughed and patted her father's hand. 'Stasia, can you come down to the study for a moment please? I need you to sign something.' The two sisters went downstairs leaving the three men alone in the drawing room. James was already dozing off leaving John and Edmund in awkward intimacy.

'So then, we seem to be heading towards a Home Rule solution now there's a Labour Prime Minister in London. Who'd have thought it? But I'm guessing it won't be the sort of Home Rule you'd like, John.' Edmund would normally never dream of talking about politics but he couldn't think what else he could make conversation about with John. It wasn't like he could talk about the price of grain to him. He knew that John's fervent desire for an independent and united Ireland would not be delivered by the latest political events. John gave a rueful laugh.

'And what do you reckon de Valera will do next, John? It's been a year now since the civil war ended. Are you still as involved with the Republicans as before?'

'Well, it's one thing fighting the English and, like Dev, I was incensed when Griffith and Collins caved in to Lloyd George. But I hate to see Irishman fighting Irishman. I suppose some sort of political compromise has to be the way forward. For now at least. De Valera might look like he's out of the game today but he's smart, and you can be sure he'll work out a way to get back into power. One day we *will* have a united Irish Republic, Edmund. It's not just a dream. I truly believe it must happen.'

'I find it all such a terrible waste of effort. Why can't men just get back to work rather than arguing and playing around with guns. You'd think the war would have finished anyone's interest in violence.' Four years fighting in the trenches had effectively turned Edmund Hughes into a pacifist, though he would have been shocked to hear himself described as one.

Down in the study, Hannah sat on the small cane chair to face her sister, who had taken the squashy leather armchair as if it were her divine right to sit in the comfiest seat. 'Hannah, you need to get Agnes to use some beeswax on that desk. It's looking very shabby and it's a shame because it's a fine piece of furniture. Are those cat scratches down the side? You really shouldn't let that wretched cat in here.'

'Her name is Aggie and she has more than enough to do, Stasia. She does everything in the house and she helps out in the shop and the pub when we need her to. And, as for where I let my cat go, that is entirely my business.'

Honey had been given to Hannah by Tricky Byrne, Nicholas's taciturn elder brother, when it was just a tiny kitten and the ginger moggy enjoyed the privileged status of being the only cat allowed into the house.

'Well, perhaps you need to do some of those things yourself, instead of asking Agnes. There's no point you wasting so much time practising your violin any more. It's not as if you still have ambitions to be a concert player, is it.'

'Who knows? I could still become a professional violinist. I'm only twenty-four, after all. And John tells me my playing is better than ever.' It was true. Hannah's musical talent was exceptional. She had garnered considerable admiration on the few occasions she had played in public in Dublin during her years at the Maple Academy. Playing music together had fertilised the soil in which the budding romance between Hannah and her then teacher, John, had germinated, taken root and blossomed.

'Well, that would be just like you. You demand that Father divide up the land and businesses between us only for you to run back to a glamorous Dublin life when you get bored, leaving us to pick up the pieces. Mind you, it would certainly be a good idea to get John Fitzgerald away from here, messing everything up.'

'John doesn't pretend to be a farmer or a businessman, but he's doing his best and working hard.' Stasia shrugged at her sister's testy defence of her husband. 'Anyway, let's not argue.' Hannah breathed in deeply. 'I wanted to ask you something in private. You know we each took one of Mammy's rings – you the diamonds and me the emerald one.'

Stasia nodded and held out her left hand. 'I wear it every day, unless I'm doing something really messy. It made a beautiful engagement ring. And I always think of her when I look at it.'

'It's lovely. But I never wear the emerald ring. I just never have occasion to. And it's better not to have rings on when I'm playing. So…I'm thinking of selling it, but I thought I should tell you first. As it was Mammy's.'

'Hannah! How could you think of such a thing? That's sacrilege.'

'For heaven's sake, Stasia, it's just a ring. I don't need a ring to remember Mammy. It's silly for it to stay in a drawer. I could use the money to get the barn repaired.'

'I can't believe that you would sell something so precious to buy timber and plaster.'

'I was thinking something more like corrugated iron, actually.'

'Well, I can't stop you I suppose. It's yours. But can I ask you to sell it me, at least?'

'I can't ask my sister to give me money for a ring that belonged to her own mother.'

'Better that than a stranger buying it.'

Hannah stared at the floor for some moments before replying. 'Well, OK then. But you mustn't tell Daddy.'

'He'll see it when I wear it. But I doubt he'll remember it. Not something men take much notice of, is it. Just a risk we'll have to take if you're sure you want to part with it. You don't want to save it for Cathy when she grows up?'

'Stop it, Stasia. Of course, I'd rather *not* sell it, but needs must.'

Hannah and Stasia climbed back up to the drawing room in time to hear John extolling the virtues of Eamonn de Valera to a clearly sceptical Edmund.

'Why do you only talk about politics when we women are out of the room?' protested Stasia. 'Our votes count just the same as yours now. I have stronger political views than Edmund you know and probably know more about what's happening too.'

'You talk about women's votes, Stasia. But if we were back under the yoke of the English, which I know you'd like - you want handsome King George and that nice Queen Mary to rule over us still – you'd have to wait until you were twenty-eight. Whereas we Irish women have finally achieved equality.' When Hannah started talking politics, John was never totally sure whether she was expressing genuine conviction or just grabbing another chance to needle Stasia.

There was a clattering on the stairs. John went over to open the drawing room door. 'Who could that be coming up the stairs, I wonder? I hope it's not some naughty leprechauns.'

He whipped open the door to reveal Cathy, cradling a tiny day-old yellow chick, and behind her was Peter, an egg triumphantly held in each hand and the yolks of a few more dripping down his best shirt.

Chapter 3 – June 1925

Cathy always knew when she was allowed to get up and go into her parents' bedroom because she would hear the sound of the gramophone coming across the landing from the drawing room.

Her Daddy's early morning routine was to go silently downstairs at about seven o'clock and make a tray of tea, with a glass of milk for her, and bring it upstairs for her Mammy, usually followed by Honey. Before he woke Hannah, John would choose a shiny black disc to play and start up the gramophone so that his entrance into the bedroom was always accompanied by some beautiful music – usually happy music but occasionally sad. He would wake his wife gently with a kiss and seconds later Cathy would arrive and jump onto their bed, clutching some of her favourite books. John knew from experience not to pour the tea until this minor earthquake had taken place.

Today, the music was very jolly with lots of trumpets and drums and with people singing which seemed to match the bright sunshine blazing through the gap in her curtains. Cathy swung her legs out of bed, grabbed her newest book and ran over the landing through the drawing room and up onto the magic ship. That was her Daddy's name for his and Mammy's big bed.

Cathy bounced up and down on the mattress in time to the music.

'Stop it now, Cathy, you'll break the springs and you might hurt Honey.' Morning was never her mother's best time.

'Ah, she's OK. Now macushla, maybe calm down a little, eh? Come and drink your milk and I'll read you something.' Cathy dived under the covers between her parents sending Honey scampering off to the drawing room where she took up peaceful residence on the sofa. This was one of Cathy's favourite parts of the day, when her Daddy read to her as Mammy sat and sipped her tea.

'This one, Daddy please.' Cathy couldn't read this book – *Pollyanna* - herself but she had many others where she could understand all the words. John had been teaching her to read since she was two and she would never have her fill of stories. She liked the ones about fairies or animals or girls like herself. Her Daddy began reading.

'Miss POLLY HARRINGTON entered her kitchen a little hurriedly this June morning. Miss Polly did not usually make hurried movements; she specially prided herself on her repose of manner. But to-day she was hurrying, actually hurrying.

Nancy, washing dishes at the sink...' '

'Nancy is like Bessie, Daddy, and Miss Polly is like Aunt Stasia.'

'Ha-ha! I love it. Yes, they are exactly like them. You're a very perceptive Countess indeed.'

Cathy had no idea that when her Daddy called her Countess Cathleen he was invoking Yeats's selfless aristocrat - who had sold her soul to the devil so that she could save her tenants from famine - but she liked its imposing sound well enough.

Hannah drained her cup and put it down. 'John, we need to decide soon about Cathy's school, you know. She could start at the village school in September. I'm not having her anywhere near the convent in Kilkenny.'

Hannah's unhappy experiences and battles with Mother Veronica at Our Lady's convent, coupled with her husband's militant atheism, had turned her into an unrepentant lapsed Catholic, but Hannah was also a pragmatist and the village school offered her daughter a reasonable education, plus the prospect of making friends.

'I don't want her going near any school at all. They all push religion at the children. She's learning just fine here with us.'

Cathy had already started doing simple sums and could write her letters and numbers out, guided by her adoring father. John had shown her how to play the recorder a little and sometimes, when he was playing his cello, he would let her hold his bow and play on just one string while he did the fingering for *Twinkle, Twinkle Little Star*. Her mother had never let her touch her violin, mind, but she would often play to Cathy who would dance around the drawing room to the lovely sounds. But Cathy wasn't only keen to do scholarly or artistic things; she loved to help Aggie in the house and she would feed the hens every morning and do her best to set the table for breakfast.

'We haven't the time, John. Not to teach her properly. There's far too much for us to do with the shop and the pub. Keeping Jimmy Boyle in order is a job in itself. Then there's the land. In fact, look at the glorious weather today. You need to get out there and cut the hay field before the rains come back.'

'It doesn't have to be today, Hannah. I promised Thomas Derrig I'd help him write an article for the *Kilkenny People.*' Derrig was the local prospective Fianna Fáil candidate whom John dearly wanted to see elected to the Dáil; he was doing what he could to help the cause. 'I'll cut the hay later this week. I might be a reluctant farmer but I'll get there in the end. I promise.' John took Hannah's cup from her, kissed her and poured her more tea.

'I don't want Cathy at a school where there are priests hanging around. I just don't like any clergy having anything to do with education. I'm not saying Father Stephen can't be trusted – he's seems a decent enough man and I know he's not at the school all the time - but it shouldn't be any of the church's business. Aoife's last letter was all about what's still going on at the Letterfrack school, all the latest punishments that those evil priests manage to dream up. Christian Brothers? What a joke.'

Cathy had never met Aoife but she knew the name well. She knew that she was a teacher who lived by the sea with her parents and that she was the sister of Daddy's first wife, Ailsa, who had died after only a few years of marriage. Aoife's letters came all the way from Cleggan out in Connemara to Rowanbridge at least once a month. Her Daddy had shown her where Cleggan was on the big map in the study, exactly where he had lived and where Letterfrack School was where he had worked for a time until his protests at the Brothers' tyranny had earned him his dismissal. He had promised to take Cathy to Cleggan one day. She had never seen the sea and it was a promise she knew her Daddy would try to keep if he could, but she never reminded him just in case he couldn't.

Sometimes, her Daddy smiled or even laughed at what Aoife had written but more often the letters made him run his fingers through his golden hair and put him in a dark mood. John would read out the more shocking passages to her Mammy, who would nod her agreement at his outrage.

'Ruari and Shawna are still sheltering one boy who ran away after a terrible beating and what he told them about the way those so-called Christian Brothers abuse the boys is just horrifying. The de Bhailises can scarcely afford to feed another mouth but there's no way they are letting this poor boy go back to Letterfrack school. I should send them a little money actually.'

'Can he not go to the Gardai?'

'Do you think they'd take the word of a twelve-year old rough Cork lad against the word of the Christian Brothers?'

'Well, something needs to be done. Could you not go and tell the authorities your story too? And there must be other adults who could all give evidence.'

'You'd think so, wouldn't you? There are plenty who know all about the shameful goings-on but there's a fearful conspiracy to hide it all. Maybe I should do something…'

Cathy had stopped listening to this boring grown-up talk and was now jumping up and down again on the bed, falling over and laughing. John grabbed her and pushed the tangle of blonde hair off her face.

'Cathy, Cathy macushla, be careful. Don't jump up and down near Mummy's tummy. You know there's something precious in there.'

Cathy had been told about the 'precious thing in Mummy's tummy' a few times. But she had been told that last year as well and nothing had come of it. Her mother's stomach had swelled up and then gone down again. She wasn't even sure what it was supposed to be.

'Stasia's pregnant again you know. I couldn't bear for her to squeeze a third one out before we manage a second.'

'Don't be silly, Hannah. It's not a competition.'

'Now that's where you're wrong, John. Stasia is breeding her way to world domination. Not over me so much, but you should just hear her gloating about Nicholas and Louisa Byrne. She's a proper bitch, my sister.' After Hannah had rejected Nicholas Byrne's proposal nine years ago, he had passed over a hopeful and devoted Stasia in favour of a bank manager's daughter from Kilkenny, but the union had so far proved barren.

'Sssh, Hannah. Cathy, don't listen your mother. Why don't you go downstairs and Aggie will give you your breakfast while Mummy and I finish listening to this music.'

Cathy ran down the stairs to the kitchen. The door to the yard was open and Aggie was sitting on the back step, enjoying a cigarette in the sunshine.

'Oops. Don't look, don't look.' Aggie stubbed out the cigarette and put the end in her apron pocket. 'Are you ready for your porridge my sweetie? What a lovely day it is. You can come with me for a walk up to your Auntie Stasia's this afternoon. Bessie has some sausages waiting that I need to collect. Then we can have them for tea.'

'Yum-yum. Sausages are my favourite. '

'Me too, sweetie, with some lovely buttery spuds.'

Cathy sat at the table looking at the pictures in *Pollyanna* as Aggie stirred the porridge.

'Aggie, what's the precious thing in Mammy's tummy?'

'Ah. Now then. I think that is for your Mammy or Daddy to tell you, not me.'

'I think it's a baby because Mammy's tummy is getting fatter and that's what happened to Auntie Stasia before cousin Andrew was born - and Eileen before her baby arrived.'

'There's no fooling you Cathy, is there? Yes, it is a baby - but don't tell your parents that I told you. OK?' Aggie turned and tapped the side of her nose. 'Our secret.'

******

A week later, Cathy sat at the kitchen table drawing. She picked up the wooden sheep and stood it on her drawing pad so that she could better copy the shape. Then she took the cow and horse and finally the cockerel. She was going to draw a whole farmyard and then colour it in to take up to Mammy who had been in bed for the last three days.

Cathy suspected that the 'precious thing' was gone again because Mammy had been crying and Daddy had looked very sad and hadn't wanted to read to her for very long or do any sums. He'd been playing his cello a lot downstairs in the study, away from everyone. They couldn't even go outside for a walk because it had been raining for days now. She heard her Mammy shouting at Daddy yesterday that the hay was all gone because of the wet, but Cathy thought she would go and check it was still there when the sun came out. Where could hay have gone off to on its own, after all?

She could hear Daddy out in the road talking to the men delivering the beer. She went and looked out of the study window; there he was on the pavement in the pelting rain, with his sleeves rolled up and his sopping wet shirt stuck to his back, shifting crates inside with Jimmy Boyle. He was quite strong really, even though he didn't look it. He could lift her onto his shoulders in a trice and still run around the field chasing Mammy. Not today though.

Aggie came downstairs carrying some sheets. They had lots of red stains on them. Cathy knew it was blood.

'Come on now, my sweetie. Your Mammy has suggested that we go and see if your Auntie Stasia can look after you for a couple of days until she's feeling a bit better. We'll wait until after your lunch. That'll give you time to finish your picture and hopefully the rain will have stopped by then.'

But the rain didn't stop all day. Cathy took her Mammy her picture after she'd eaten. Hannah was sitting up in bed reading, with Honey curled up asleep at her feet; she smiled faintly at the sight of her daughter.

'Cathy, how lovely this picture is. Thank you so much.'

'I put in lots of hens because I know they're your favourite.'

'No - only my favourite animals. You, my angel, are my favourite.' And Hannah's eyes filled as she hugged her golden child. 'I'm sorry I've not been very well, but I'll soon be up and about. Until then, I'm sure your Auntie Stasia will welcome you for a little break and you can have fun playing with your cousins. And your Grandpa will be very excited to have you to stay.'

'Baby Andrew can't play. And Peter can't read yet. But he can do jigsaws. I quite like jigsaws. I'll take *Dr Dolittle* for Grandpa to read to me. He's a bit like Dr Dolittle because he talks to the cats and to Lady all the time.' Lady was the brown Labrador in the Hughes household.

'Yes, you do that. He will love reading to you. And ask him to show you some of his magic tricks. He used to do them for Stasia and me when we were little and I still don't know how he does some of them.'

It was still raining after lunch but Aggie and Cathy wrapped themselves up, put up umbrellas and walked through the village and on up to the large house - the villa as Stasia liked to call it - that the McDermotts had built right in front of the Byrnes' graceful old Georgian farmhouse, to the Byrnes' great annoyance. Bessie opened the back door to the bedraggled Aggie and Cathy and immediately put the kettle on the range hob as the two visitors struggled out of their dripping wet coats and sodden shoes. Cathy drank her milky tea and ate a biscuit and the two maids exchanged whispers and nods, before Aggie got up and knocked on Aunt Stasia's study door.

'Cathy, why don't you go up to the nursery and find your Grandpa and Peter up there,' said Bessie. 'They'll be so excited to see you.'

'I'll get my book. I've drawn a picture for them too.' Cathy clutched *Dr Dolittle* and the drawing pad in one hand while Bessie took the other and led her to the foot of the stairs.

When Grandpa, exhausted from pretending to be a Pushmi-pullyu and giving his grandchildren rides on all fours, brought Cathy and Peter downstairs half an hour later, Aggie had already gone back to Main Street. Stasia was taking tea in the drawing room.

'There you are, Cathy. I hope you've been playing nicely with Peter. He's younger than you, you know, so you must look after him. Here's your tea, Father.'

James collapsed into an armchair. 'Ouf. I don't think I'll be able to keep up with all these grandchildren soon. Once Andrew can walk properly and the new one arrives it'll be pandemonium in this house.'

'Do you really think I'd allow that sort of chaos? As soon as the boys are old enough, Edmund will be keeping them busy out on the farm or, if they're inside, I'll be making sure they do their work for school. The Christian Brothers expect very high standards.'

'My Daddy says that the Christian Brothers are savages and beat children in their school.'

Stasia put her cup down and gave Cathy a hard stare. 'What are you talking about, Cathy? Your father knows nothing about the Brothers' school in Kilkenny.' Stasia kept up her glare. 'Off you go to see Bessie, you two, and she will give you some tea. Then it'll be bedtime soon after.'

Bessie made them some very tasty sardine sandwiches, and then they were passed over to Nanny Maud for a bath and some bedtime stories. At half past six, Stasia walked into the nursery where Andrew was in his cot and Peter and Cathy were arranged head to toe in the same bed.

'Now you two, I don't expect any silliness just because you're in the same bed. Straight off to sleep after prayers. Out of bed now.' Stasia knelt down beside the bed and Peter slipped from under his sheets and knelt by her side. 'Come along Cathy. I hope you say your prayers every night, like a good girl.'

'I don't know any prayers, Auntie Stasia. I'm sorry.'

'Well, well. I can't say I'm surprised. But for as long as you are in this house you will behave like a proper Christian child. No wonder your mother is having so many troubles if she never confesses her sins or asks God to look after her. Come and kneel here beside Peter and me. Come on now.'

Cathy wondered what her Daddy would say but she sheepishly crept out of her bedclothes and knelt down.

'Now, see how Peter is holding his hands. That's what we do when we pray.'

'Why?'

'So that we can concentrate on speaking to God, rather than fidgeting.'

'Does Grandpa pray?'

'Of course he does. Do you think he's a heathen or something? All respectable people pray, don't they Peter. Now, repeat after me: *Hail Mary, full of grace…*'

Chapter 4 - November 1925

James didn't wait for Stasia's new baby to arrive before moving back into Main Street at the start of October. It was lovely to visit his new grandson, Matthew, and even to hold him for five minutes maybe, but he relished the relative peace of Main Street. Aggie let him sit in the kitchen all morning and she would even pop down and put a few bets on for him after he'd read the racing pages.

And he loved to hear Hannah playing her violin in the afternoon – perfect to have a little nap to – and then there was little Cathy who would always run and find his spectacles or his book for him if he had left them in his bedroom. And, of course, it was grand to be able to slip next door into the pub and enjoy a glass of Guinness a few times a week, and chat to old friends.

Most of all, he felt he really needed to be on hand to help John Fitzgerald. The man meant well and could work hard when he got around to it, but he was no businessman in James's opinion. Not that he would ever say such a thing out loud, and particularly not to Stasia who never seemed to stop saying it. This afternoon James and John had arranged to review the October accounts. The turnover of the shop and the pub had been sliding downwards, slowly but relentlessly. James couldn't understand it; something needed to be done sooner rather than later. Hannah did her bit – in fact she was down at the shop right now helping Eileen unload some of the special Christmas stock – but James didn't think it was right that she should do this sort of manual work. Stasia would never dream of being seen in a shop, though she worked very hard behind the scenes at the paperwork and the ledgers and suchlike, but please God she would never get to see Hannah behind a counter.

James could hear John and Cathy up the hallway in the dining room, talking and laughing. John spent so much time with his daughter in the mornings, not just doing the basics of reading and writing but painting or playing music together too. She and her father would often go out for walks and bring back flowers, feathers or unusual stones. Cathy had amassed a whole collection of twigs in her bedroom that she said looked like people dancing. This was all very charming, but how was the work going to get done?

The dining room door opened and Cathy ran down to the kitchen. 'Bonjour, grand-père.'

'What's that now?'

'Daddy is teaching me some French. It means "Hello, Grandpa".'

'You clever girl.'

John stuck his head around the door. 'I'm just off into Kilkenny to meet up with Thomas Derrig and his team. We need to be ready for an election any day. Could you please just keep an eye on Cathy until Aggie gets back, James? She's no trouble and will just read her books quietly. Look after your Grandpa, macushla, and I'll be back this afternoon.'

'Are we not going to do the October accounts then, John?'

'Oh, blast it. I forgot. Tomorrow will be OK though, James, won't it? Bye now.'

Cathy fetched this week's favourite book - *Irish Fairy Tales* by James Stephens - from the dining room and settled at the kitchen table. She couldn't read all the words but she knew the stories off by heart and she loved to look at the Rackham illustrations and imagined herself flying through the magic forests.

'Do you believe in fairies and the little people, Grandpa?'

'No, I don't, Cathy. I wish I did. Do you?'

'I'm not sure. But I like reading about them. I wish we had a dog so that I could call it Bran, like Fionn's dog.'

'That would be a grand name. Will your Mammy and Daddy not let you have a dog? Peter and Andrew have Lady after all.'

'No. Mammy doesn't like dogs.' Cathy continued with her reading as James leafed through the paper. 'Grandpa, do you believe in God and Mary and Jesus?'

'Of course I do, and I go to mass most Sundays.'

'Aren't they the same as fairies though? That's what Daddy says.'

'Not at all. We might not be able to see them but they are looking after us all the time.'

'Do you say your prayers? Auntie Stasia told me that if I said a prayer every day, like the one she taught me, Mammy wouldn't get ill so often and I'd be able to have a brother or sister.'

'Well, it doesn't work like that, sweetie, I'm afraid. I say a prayer every night for your Mammy and for all the family. Your Aunt Stasia maybe has too simple a way of looking at things.'

'But if I said the prayer every night, do you think it would help Mammy?'

'Cathy, my love, it can't hurt, though I think you should only do it if you believe in God. It's up to you.'

There was a faint knock at the front door. 'I'll go, Grandpa. You stay there.'

Cathy needed to stand on tiptoes to reach the front door handle, but she knew she could manage it, even though the door was quite heavy to pull open. She stepped back in shock at the sight that greeted her. Standing there in the pouring rain was a dirty tramp, drips running off the end of his nose. She had seen this man once before, standing in a field when she and her father had gone for a walk to Cromwell's Tower. She hadn't liked the look of him then and she liked him even less close-up.

'Hannah? She there?'

'No, my Mammy and Daddy are out - but I can get my Grandpa if you like.' Cathy was backing further away from the doorway ready to escape from this horrid man if need be into the safety of the kitchen.

23

The man shook his head and walked away. Cathy shut the door with a loud bang and ran back to the kitchen.

'Who was that then?'

'He didn't say. He was very dirty with torn clothes. And he had funny boots on.'

'Maybe a tinker looking for some work.'

'No, he knew Mammy's name.'

The back door opened and Aggie staggered in carrying sodden bags of vegetables. She sat on the step and took off her muddy boots. 'What did Tricky want? I saw him walking off just now.'

'Ah, Tricky. That makes sense. Cathy thought it was an old tramp and I assumed it was a tinker.'

'You'd be hard pushed to tell the difference, Cathy. Though of course on paper he's the wealthiest fella in the village with the biggest farm for miles around.'

Tricky Byrne was talked of as 'the odd one' around the village, though in theory he was the richest man around having inherited the big Georgian farmhouse and all the extensive land that went with it on the death of the father. In practice however, Nicholas had immediately assumed the role of land-owner and Tricky had let him, happy just to continue doing what he was best at - dairyman and hands-on farm labourer – leaving Nicholas to run the estate and manage all the business affairs.

'I know that legally he owns all the Byrnes' land, but I'm sure he and Nicholas will sort out some arrangement between them that's fair. Can you imagine Tricky trying to deal with that huge estate on his own? He's fine with the cows and the sheep but not with all the money.'

'Well, it's his to give away. Maybe I should be flirting with him more in the pub of an evening before I turn into an old maid. I could just about tolerate being married to Tricky Byrne and his squint if it meant I never had to dig up another fecking carrot.'

It was raining again the next day. John and James were locked in the study, going over the October accounts. So, no lessons for Cathy this morning. But at least her Mammy was still here. Cathy could hear her practising her scales upstairs and she told herself she must be as dedicated to the piano as her mother was to the violin.

Aggie was doing the laundry which meant the kitchen and scullery were hot and steamy, full of wet clothes drying around the range on clothes horses in the absence of a breezy, fine day outside. It also meant Aggie was very grumpy so there was no way Cathy was going in there for a while. Maybe her Mammy would read to her or play a game with her if she asked nicely. Cathy decided to wait until the big hand on the clock reached the number three and then she would go upstairs and ask her Mammy to spend some time with her.

Cathy assembled the necessary items: dominoes, a pack of cards and her *Irish Fairy Tales*. She knew Mammy liked those very much too. The instant the clock chimed the quarter Cathy climbed the stairs to the drawing room, opening the door very gently so as not to disturb her mother. Hannah continued to play as Cathy sat down on the edge of the sofa.

'Oh, hello you, my angel. I didn't see you come in.'

'That's OK. I like listening to you. But Daddy is busy so I wondered whether you'd like to play with me or read with me.' Cathy held out her book and the dominoes as peace offerings.

'Come on then. I've got about a half-hour before lunch and then I have to go back and finish the Christmas displays with Eileen. She has no idea how to make the goods look attractive enough to entice the customers.'

Hannah loosened her bow, packed away her violin and sat next to her daughter, pulling her close to her. 'It's lovely to have a cuddle, isn't it?' Cathy nodded. 'The reason I'm trying to do more practice is because my schoolfriends from Dublin, Maisie and Eamonn, are getting married next spring and they've asked me and Daddy to play at the wedding. We were all at school together you see, at the Maple Academy, and Daddy was a teacher there. His mother, your Granny, still owns the school. It's lovely to be asked but I want to make sure that my playing is up to scratch because there will be lots of sophisticated Dublin people there who know what good playing sounds like.'

'Will I be able to come to the wedding?'

'Maybe. I don't see why not. I'll ask Maisie and I doubt she'd say no to me. You've never been to Dublin, have you? It's a very beautiful and exciting place. And you could meet your great-aunt Lily who was my Mammy's sister. She's great fun and has a wonderful big, posh house.'

'If I go, will I be able to meet my Granny?'

Hannah took a deep breath. 'We'll see. It depends on her, really.'

'She's my only Granny alive and I'd really like her to know about me.'

'Ah, she knows about you right enough. Your Daddy writes to her regularly and he's even sent her a couple of photographs. But she chooses not to write back.'

'That's a bit rude isn't it, Mammy?'

'It's complicated, darling. Now, which story shall we read today?'

Letitia Fitzgerald, John's mother and owner of the Maple Academy, would probably not relish being called Granny even by a grand-daughter as adorable as Cathy. She had not spoken to her son since he had announced in 1918 that he intended to marry one of their pupils and she was not a woman who easily changed her mind. The senior Mrs Fitzgerald had banished John from the Academy and vowed never to set eyes on Hannah again. It was, after all, the second time he had presented her with an already pregnant teenage fiancée.

At a quarter to one, Aggie shouted in the hallway for everyone to come and get their lunch in the dining room. It was just cold meat, potatoes and pickles like it was every Tuesday when she was so busy scrubbing clothes. But Cathy really liked it because she didn't have to eat any cabbage or other stinky green vegetable. Hannah and Cathy went downstairs and started serving themselves. They waited several minutes but there was no sign of James or John.

'You start, Cathy. I'll just go and call them again.'

Cathy sat alone, eating some potato and ham, wondering where her family had disappeared to. Eventually, the three grown-ups walked into the dining room and took their seats but Cathy could tell there was something wrong. They all ate their food in near silence with only requests for water or the mustard breaking up the tension. Hannah put her knife and fork together and pushed her plate away.

'I must be away to the shop. God knows what sort of abomination Eileen will have created without me. When I get back, let's hope you two have sorted out what's missing. And I think I should take Cathy with me as neither of you can spare any time with her and Aggie is much too busy with the laundry. That's why she needs to be at school. Would you like to come with me, my angel?'

'Yes, please, Mammy. I love being in the shop. I can bring a book - but I'd like to help if I can.'

'We'll see. Off you go and pop your mackintosh on. The rain is very heavy now.'

There were two customers in the shop when Hannah and Cathy arrived. Their baskets were already full of groceries and they were now deep in some juicy gossip with Eileen, who looked startled when Hannah and Cathy walked in.

'Oh, you made me jump, Mrs Fitzgerald. Mrs O'Connor here was just telling us that her husband found Tricky Byrne in the field the other day underneath one of his cows, sucking milk directly from its udder.' The three women sniggered.

'That's the nearest *his* mouth is ever going to get to a female breast.' The three women broke into cackles at Mrs O'Connor's great wit.

'Mind your language please. There's a child present.' With that rebuke, Hannah bundled Cathy into the back of the shop.

When the two women had left, Eileen popped her head round the curtain that separated the shop from the storeroom. 'I'm very sorry Mrs Fitzgerald. That May O'Connor has a very crude mouth on her. You'd never think she was a doctor's wife.'

'I don't like to hear gossip about people who are doing no-one any harm. I know you can't stop her, Eileen, but please don't take part in any of it.'

'Right you are. Now, shall I finish washing down the shelves ready for the Christmas preserves?'

'Yes, you get on with that and I'll start arranging the confectionary.' Hannah picked up a roll of red crepe paper and cut enough to line a shelf, folded it into eight and then cut the bottom edge into a scalloped pattern.

'I could do that, Mammy, I'm sure.'

'Well now, why not? You have a try and I'll see if it's good enough.'

Cathy spent the next hour making shelf liners and then she moved on to opening various exotic looking crates, full of boxes of sugared almonds, candied dates and other treats which she handed up to her mother, who was standing halfway up the set of wooden steps. 'Be careful, Mammy - just in case there's a precious thing in your tummy.'

Hannah laughed. 'No need to worry about that, Cathy. No baby in there just now. But it's very sweet of you to worry about me.'

'I've been saying a prayer every night for you before I go to sleep, like Auntie Stasia told me to. Grandpa says it can't hurt. But don't tell Daddy.'

Hannah gave a rueful smile. 'It'll be our little secret, my darling. No, it can't hurt and who knows what magic it might do. It's good to have hope and I'm very touched that you have been thinking about me.'

Hannah came down the steps and took a box of candies into the backroom. 'Come in, Cathy, and have a rest. You've worked very hard. Read your book. And here, have some jellied fruits as a little treat while I make us all some tea. I know you like them. Just don't eat them all at once.'

The shop doorbell tinkled from time to time, but Cathy was oblivious to all the comings and goings as she marvelled at *Alice's Adventures through the Looking Glass*. Five o'clock came around quickly and Eileen came to say goodnight to her before she left for the day.

'Miss Cathy, you've made the shelves look really lovely. Thank you for your help. You can come and work in the shop any time you want as far as I'm concerned.'

Hannah bolted the shop door behind Eileen and turned the sign to 'Closed'. 'I won't be too much longer, Cathy. I just need to bag up the till.'

After about five minutes there was urgent knocking on the shop door. Cathy could hear her mother unbolt the door and open it to someone. Low mumbling followed. She stood up and gently made a tiny gap in the curtain so she could see who it was. Her heart jumped when she saw it was the same horrid dirty man who had come to the house yesterday.

'Seen him. Hand in the till.'

'Gracious, Tricky. Are you sure? We can't go accusing people without some proper evidence.'

'Seen with these eyes. Every night.'

'Well, let me talk to my father and John about it. We'll have to think what best to do. But thank you for letting me know your suspicions. I'm very grateful.'

'OK. Off now. Good night, Hannah McDermott.

'Fitzgerald! Goodnight Tricky.'

After supper later that evening, Cathy brought out her jellied fruits and offered one to everyone.

'Yum yum. I'd love a strawberry one. Thank you, my treasure. You're very generous.' Her grandpa's fat fingers dived into the tin and then held up a glowing red jelly as if he had discovered a rare jewel.

'A lemon one for me, please.' Her Mammy took a sweet and blew Cathy a kiss.

Cathy offered the sweets to her Daddy.

'Not for me, macushla. You keep them for yourself. And I don't think your Mammy thinks I deserve one today anyway. Save it for Aggie.'

'I'm going to take Aggie one - but I want you to have one too, Daddy. Then the tin will be nearly empty and I can keep my crayons in it.'

'In that case, I shall have the green one, of course. That's the very best colour of all. It's a Sinn Féin sweetie!' John popped the jelly into his mouth and gave Cathy a kiss.

Chapter 5 - April 1927

'Turn around so I can see how it looks from the front. It's very pretty, Cathy, but I know just the thing that will make it perfect.' Lily went over to her chest of drawers and pulled out a long cerise silk scarf. 'Pink is all very well, but if you're not careful it can look a little insipid. Always take your Auntie Lily's advice when it comes to fashion.'

Lily wound the scarf around the new frock's dropped waist and tied it into an extravagant bow at the side. Cathy knew that this glamorous woman was really her great-aunt but her Mammy had advised her that would not be a welcome title; plain 'Aunt' would be as much as Lily could accept. 'That's better. Now you could pass for a princess or a fairy queen.'

Cathy, her parents and her grandpa had journeyed from Rowanbridge to stay with Mammy's Aunt Lily in her luxurious home in Dublin two days before. It was a very exciting, unusual house which didn't look that big on the street and was joined to the houses either side, but it seemed to go on and on forever inside, room after splendid room, and was full of silky rugs and lavish drapery.

Cathy was fascinated by the way her Great-aunt Lily spoke – quite loudly - and waved her arms around, like she was acting in a play all the time. Lily had been an actress in her youth, Cathy remembered. Cathy couldn't quite understand everything the grown-ups kept talking about but she listened as hard as she could. She got the impression they were discussing serious matters - about the government and music and books.

The Rowanbridge contingent had arranged to stay with Lily for the long Easter weekend, having left the shop and pub completely in Jimmy and Eileen Boyle's hands. It was the first holiday of any sort they had taken since Cathy had been born. The chief purpose of the trip was to attend and

31

play at Maisie and Eamonn's wedding, but Lily had kindly sent her driver, Slattery, down to Rowanbridge to drive them up to Dublin so James had decided to tag along too.

It was hard to believe that James and Lily were from the same generation; James with his white whiskers and lumbering gait while Lily, with her vibrant pile of auburn hair, porcelain cheeks and scarlet lips, was as vigorous as a twenty-year-old. But then only one of them knew how to employ all the tricks of the theatrical profession. James and his dear sister-in-law – he called her the Merry Widow, even to her face - were not coming to the wedding but would instead spend Easter Saturday eating rich food, drinking fine wine and chatting about old times and lost loved ones.

But there were also new loved ones to talk about. Lily was amazed - and slightly appalled - that Stasia was soon to have her fourth baby. 'Who would have thought, James, that it would be Stasia who would turn out to be the more fertile of your daughters. Three sons already to help Edmund with the farm, so she must be hoping that this one will turn out to be a little girl to help her in the house.'

'Don't let Stasia or Hannah hear you say that. They'd bite my head off if I were to suggest such a thing. As far as they are concerned, girls can plough fields and boys bake cakes.'

Lily wasn't very eager to meet Stasia's brood. She really didn't understand little boys whereas she had always loved looking after her nieces, Stasia and Hannah, and now her great-niece, Cathy, was proving to be an utter delight.

'Let's go downstairs, Cathy, and have breakfast. Best take off the dress in case you drop something on it. Then we'll get you all dressed up before it's time for Slattery to take you to pick up your Mummy's friend, Ellen. She's going to take care of you while your mother and father are busy playing at the wedding.'

Yesterday, Hannah and John had met up with the other two members of the string quartet at the home of Felix Brennan, Hannah's old violin teacher. The quartet had some history; it had been formed when Lily had asked her talented niece, then studying at the Maple Academy alongside Hannah's viola-playing friend, Seamus, to come and play for one of her literary soirées. Hannah had led the quartet with Felix, leader of the orchestra at the Gaiety Theatre, happily playing second fiddle to his star pupil. The cellist of the quartet was John Fitzgerald, of course.

At the Maple Academy, Seamus had observed at close quarters the romance emerging between Hannah and John, fed by the strong emotions that playing Beethoven's *Harp Quartet* aroused. As he had watched their attachment grow, Seamus had chosen to suppress his own deep feelings for Hannah and had quietly withdrawn from the contest, without even declaring himself to her. But Hannah had anyway guessed all along.

Hannah and John came to kiss Cathy goodbye as she finished her scrambled eggs at the breakfast table, her Grandpa raking over the racing pages at her side. Cathy had never seen her parents looking so elegant, her mother dressed in pale grey barathea with crimson embroidery and a grey cloche hat with a big crimson rose on the side that she had borrowed from Lily, and her Daddy dressed in his hired morning suit with a silk cravat. How handsome they looked as a couple together.

'So, my angel, Auntie Lily will get you dressed and then Slattery will pick you up at ten thirty and take you to my friend Ellen's. She's my very best friend and she's going to look after you in the church while your Daddy and I are busy playing. She's lovely. Then we'll be there at the end of the service.'

Ellen was watching out for the familiar green Ford from her cousin's front window when Slattery drew up, Cathy nervous in the back seat. She came out of the front door and walked to the pavement using a cane while Slattery held open the car's back door.

'Good morning, miss. Nice to see you again.' Slattery had witnessed several of Ellen and Hannah's high jinks when she and Hannah had been at the Maple Academy together.

'Morning Slattery. Good to see you again too. It's been a few years. Don't worry. I'm not drunk today, not yet anyway. Jeezus, it's a bit fresh out here but at least it's not raining.' Ellen joined Cathy on the back seat and gave her a smacking kiss on the cheek. 'Hello, Cathy. I met you when you were just a toddler but not since. I'm guessing you don't remember me.' Ellen nudged Cathy and smiled. 'But your Ma tells me all about you in her letters, and what a clever and kind girl you are. I'm honoured to accompany you to the wedding.'

'Hello, Ellen. Mammy has told me about you too. And she told me to say she sends her love and will see you soon.'

Ellen laughed and put her arm around Cathy and pulled her close. 'Ah, your mother and I had such a great craic at school together. And we had loads of other friends too. So many laughs. Even though there was a war going on at the time, we were completely oblivious to it, all wrapped up in own little dramas and intrigues. I'm hoping that lots of our schoolfriends from those days will be at the wedding today.'

The two sat in cheerful silence as Slattery wound his way through central Dublin.

'Have you hurt yourself, Ellen?'

'My stick do you mean? I have a gammy leg, Cathy. I've had it a very long time. When I was about your age I got a disease called polio. It left me with a weak and bent leg. I used to wear a metal brace on it when I was young and when we all wore long skirts it was OK. I try to manage without anything most of the time now the skirts are so much shorter, but it's going to be a long old day, so I reckoned I should come prepared. And I can always use my stick to whack people on the head if they annoy me.'

Cathy blushed and wished she hadn't said anything about Ellen's limp. 'I like your hat, Ellen. I like blue ribbons. They're my favourite.'

'And you look pretty as a picture in your pink dress, Cathy. I love the bright pink sash.'

'My Great-Aunt Lily gave it to me.'

'Ah, I thought I detected the theatrical hand of Aunt Lily there.'

Cathy had rarely been inside a church. In fact, she had only been to the Rowanbridge church for the christenings of her cousins. This church, with its white pillars and statues on the roof, was very different from the dark and cramped one in Rowanbridge. More like a Greek temple. There was coloured light coming through the semi-circular window above the altar and the church was filled with gleaming candles, reflected in the brass, and huge vases of white flowers, ready for Easter Sunday.

Cathy always avoided looking at the crucifix in Rowanbridge church – it made her feel distinctly queasy - but this one looked less like a poor starving man nailed to a cross and more like an oriental god housed in his own miniature golden palace.

Ellen seemed to know almost everyone at the wedding. She introduced Cathy as 'Hannah and John's girl' and everyone remarked how much the little girl looked like her father. Everything was smiles and kisses and hugs.

Ellen led Cathy to a pew near the front where she was able to see her Mammy and Daddy seated at the side waiting with Mr Brennan and a very tall, apple-cheeked man – Seamus she assumed. She gave them a little wave which her Daddy returned along with a blown kiss. Cathy knew all about Seamus, how he had been to the war, played in special concerts with her Mammy, was now a solicitor and was maybe going to marry Ellen one day.

Organ music was rippling underneath the excited hum of the congregation as Cathy looked all around the church at the smartly dressed men and women. Ellen pointed out Eamonn, the bridegroom, sitting at the front with his best man, Daniel.

'That's Eamonn on the front row who is getting married to Maisie. He's now Dr O'Toole because he's just completed a PhD in Economics. He's very clever and so is Daniel sitting next to him. He is now a mathematics tutor at Cambridge. He always left us all behind at school. He's Eamonn's best man, though Lord knows what sort of speech he's going to make. At least you can trust him not to have lost the ring. Eamonn could have picked someone better at public speaking for all our sakes but he is so very loyal. We were all at your Granny's school together, you know. Maisie used to be one of our room-mates.'

'Yes, I know. Mammy has told me lots of the names and lots of stories too.'

'Has she, indeed? Well, you should probably hear our side of the story some time.'

The organ stopped and the string quartet began playing some Handel, as the bridal procession moved down the aisle. Everyone stood up. Cathy moved to the end of the pew so she could get a good view. She thought Maisie looked exquisite, just like the picture of Delvcaem in her book of *Irish Fairy Tales*, with white flowers around her head and a lace veil over her face which then trailed down her back and far behind her.

When the wedding party moved into the vestry for the signing of the register, the string quartet moved themselves to the centre, in front of the altar, and began playing. It was the second movement of *The Harp Quartet*. Cathy had never seen her mother and father looking so happy and in love. They kept looking at each other and smiling and the music smiled too.

Afterwards, at the wedding reception, Cathy sat at a table between her parents who kept holding hands behind her back. This made her feel warm and soft inside. In fact, everyone seemed to be holding someone's hands and hugging or kissing someone. Cathy marvelled at how the bride and groom at the top table held hands throughout the meal, managing to eat with just a fork. Eamonn kept lifting Maisie's hand to his lips and then kissing her on the mouth.

'How blissfully happy Maisie and Eamonn look,' said Hannah. 'They really couldn't look more in love. I wish I'd had a proper wedding in a church, with flowers and a beautiful dress and all my friends around, instead of in a drab registry office with a few disapproving relatives. Though I wouldn't swap my bridegroom for anything.' Hannah leant over Cathy's head and kissed John.

Hannah turned to Ellen and Seamus. 'So, when will we be back in Dublin to see you two get wed?' Hannah had been expecting Seamus to call off their now embarrassingly lengthy engagement after he returned from the war – she really wished he would for everyone's sake - but he hadn't yet plucked up the courage to break Ellen's heart.

Ellen looked at Seamus and both shuffled uneasily in their seats. 'Seamus wants to wait until he has completed all his qualifications and is properly set up. And that's very sensible really as a wedding would be a big distraction for him.'

The conversation moved on and, as the meal neared its end, people began moving around the tables to talk to other friends. Cathy turned and watched her father go to chat with Visha and Sourja, the sister and brother whose parents had left them at the Maple Academy for the duration of the war while they went to manage their factory in India, making shirts for the British army. Visha was now a doctor in the East End of London and Sourja had stayed on in the Royal Navy when the war finished. He looked very splendid in his uniform, medals glinting on his chest. Next to them were Roisin and Maeve, the sisters with their famous blazing red hair. John was fascinated to hear them talk of their work cataloguing traditional Irish myths and songs, alongside their parents. All these people had existed in Cathy's head, shaped by what Hannah had told her about them, but it was wonderful to have her sketchy outlines of them turned into real flesh and blood. She turned back to the table to finish her dessert. Her mother and Seamus were in an intense, whispered conversation.

'I saw you, you know, you big soppy old thing, Seamus. Great big tears in your eyes in *The Harp*. I didn't think a wedding would get to you like that.'

Seamus took up his wine glass and took a long slug. 'It's not this wedding that bothers me, Hannah McDermott. That music – *The Harp* - was the first time I realised you were in love, but that it wasn't with me.'

Seamus pushed back his chair and walked away from the table into the throng of guests. Cathy watched as her mother took several deep breaths, shook her head and then finished her own glass of wine.

******

That night, Cathy fell asleep the instant her Daddy tucked her in. It had been a very exciting day but also very tiring. Ten hours later, she awoke in a grand and unfamiliar bedroom and remembered that she was in Dublin in her Great-Aunt Lily's house. The dress she had worn the day before was hanging on the door with the cerise silk scarf draped over the back of a chair. Cathy crept out of her bedroom and went to stand outside her parents' room, making sure she woke no-one else, but she could hear that they were already awake and talking quietly. She was old enough now to know that it was sensible to knock before she went in, so she tapped gently.

'Come in…?' Her father sounded curious to see who the knock was from but laughed when Cathy ran in and jumped onto the magic ship of their bed.

'Good morning, macushla. Happy Easter Sunday. I was just reading your Mammy a poem about Easter. One that has nothing to do with the resurrected son of some god in a mythical heaven but a famous one about the Easter of 1916 and some other young men who fought for our freedom and who were sacrificed to save us all. Without people like them we wouldn't be where we are today with a free Irish State.'

Hannah was leaning against John's arm and flicking through the book. 'It's all very well to have Yeats in the Senate, you know, but he hasn't published anything since 1921. I think I'd rather have him writing than governing. Here, read this to our own lovely young girl,' said Hannah passing the book back to John and opening her arms for Cathy to come and cuddle up.

'OK then. Cathy, this is by our greatest poet, William Butler Yeats, who is my favourite writer and one of your mother's too. You're a bit young and some of his poems are quite long and deal with serious topics. But this is a very short poem called *To A Young Girl* and it was published just before you were born. See what you think.

My dear, my dear, I know
More than another
What makes your heart beat so;
Not even your own mother
Can know it as I know,
Who broke my heart for her
When the wild thought,
That she denies and has forgot,
Set all her blood astir
And glittered in her eyes.'

John leant over to kiss his wife passionately on the lips as Cathy looked on. She didn't understand the poem – and it hardly rhymed at all – but if it made her Mammy and Daddy want to kiss each other rather than shout and sulk then it was fine by her. And she liked the sound of her father's voice saying those words.

'Come on now, shake a leg,' Hannah threw back the bedcovers, 'We mustn't be late for breakfast at Aunt Lily's.

There was a bowl of pastel-coloured boiled eggs for breakfast with hot cross buns and tea. Just as her Mammy had taught her, Cathy played the upside-down empty eggshell trick on James and Lily.

They both fell for it very dramatically, to laughter all round, and Cathy suspected that maybe they were just pretending to be fooled - but who cared? After breakfast, Aunt Lily presented Cathy with a chocolate egg and told her not to eat it until after dinner.

John folded his napkin and stood up from the table. 'Hannah, I have decided that I shall go down to Dalkey, after all. If I don't take this opportunity while I'm in Dublin it could be years before there's another chance. And she's not getting any younger.'

'She might turn you away.'

'That's possible of course. But I don't think she will. And especially not if I take Cathy with me.'

Cathy looked from her father to her mother. Where was she to be taken?

'Well, don't let me interfere, but Slattery is at your disposal this morning if you do want to go to the Academy. James will only need to walk just around the corner to mass and I shall go too to keep him company. It must be more than twenty-five years since I was at a mass.' Lily rested her bejewelled hand on James's and gave it a squeeze.

'Thank you, Lily, that would be very helpful. Cathy, we're going to go to Dalkey this morning and introduce you to your Grandmother.'

******

It was a while before anyone came to open the big green front door of the Maple Academy, despite John's brisk knocking. He had seen the front window curtains twitch a little. Mrs Fitzgerald was clearly having to think hard about this encounter.

'John, how very unexpected.' Mrs Fitzgerald presented a forbidding figure to Cathy as she looked up at the tall, straight-backed, steel-haired woman. Was this really her Granny?

Mrs Fitzgerald instantly turned and walked down the hallway, assuming they would follow. John held Cathy's hand as they entered the Maple Academy and shut the door behind them. He took off his overcoat and Cathy's jacket, hat and scarf and hung them on the familiar oak stand, leading her then into his mother's crimson sitting room. Mrs Fitzgerald was standing in front of the fireplace with her back to the door but she turned as they walked in and flung her arms silently around John. They stayed locked in an awkward embrace for some time before Mrs Fitzgerald dropped her arms and turned to look at Cathy.

'So, Mother, let me introduce you to Cathy.'

Mrs Fitzgerald bent down and shook Cathy's hand. Cathy could see that she was crying.

'How do you do, Cathy. You must be seven years old now, I think. It's very nice to meet you and I am sorry we have never met before. You can call me Grandma if you wish.'

Mrs Fitzgerald rang a bell for tea and milk for Cathy. All the students were away on their Easter holidays so there was just old Lizzie in the kitchen but she couldn't hide her excitement at seeing Mr John back at the Academy.

'I'm glad to see you looking well, Lizzie. It's been too long.'

'Oh, Mr John, sir. You're looking mighty fine yourself. And this is your little one, is it? The apple hasn't fallen far from the tree there, I see. God bless you all.'

While Cathy drank her milk, her grandmother went out of the room, returning with a pile of books and a solitaire board. She explained patiently to her grand-daughter how to play it. Cathy soon mastered it and happily played away as the adults talked quietly.

'Why did you never answer my letters, Mother?'

'I wanted to - of course I did - but I couldn't. I didn't know what to say. I forgave you instantly of course, despite you causing me so much heartache. But I cannot forgive her. I will not forgive her.'

'But I was the one to blame, Mother. I was the mature adult. She was still a child in many ways. I should have known better though.'

'No. I do not accept that. She was old way beyond her years when she arrived here. I always suspected she had an immoral streak in her. Her sister more or less said as much when we first met, but I was too stupid to listen - or perhaps too desperate for another student. And you ... you have always been powerless when some young girl has set her sights on you.'

'We shall just have to agree to disagree. Look, never mind about the past. Let us start over again, Mother. Can I bring Hannah to see you or maybe you would like to come and visit us in Rowanbridge?'

'Never. Never. I shall never let that woman into my house nor enter hers. She stole my son away from me and broke my heart. She nearly brought this business to ruin too. Thankfully I managed to keep the scandal confined to a few people.'

'She is my wife, Mother, and I love her. You must find it in yourself to forgive, Mother, or you will always be unhappy.'

'I am less unhappy now that you have come to see me, my son. And I see your daughter looks just like you and not like her. I should very much like you both to come and stay here with me - for a holiday, or maybe for longer. Surely you would prefer to come back and work as a teacher rather than try to lead a life as a farmer or a shopkeeper. You're totally unsuited to that sort of work. It must be soul-destroying. And I could teach Cathy myself, until she was old enough to join the Academy properly. This place needs you, John. It is waiting for you to come back and take charge.'

'I'm sorry, Mother. That's impossible.'

Mrs Fitzgerald dropped the subject and they moved on to discuss less tortured topics: what had become of some of the students that John had known, what was on at the Abbey Theatre and the need for new guttering on the Academy.

After an hour or so, John rose and told Cathy to come and put on her coat.

'Will you not stay a little longer and have some lunch with me, John?'

'I'm sorry, Mother. I promised we'd be back for Easter Sunday lunch at Lily's and Slattery has been waiting for us all this while. Next time, though, we'll make proper arrangements. Today's visit was a spur of the moment decision.'

'Thank you for coming. Truly.' Mrs Fitzgerald kissed her son on the cheek. 'You're a bigger person than me.'

John went out to the hall to fetch their outdoor clothes while his mother started to collect up some books.

'Here Cathy. You might like this book of piano pieces. They are all by great composers – Mozart, Haydn – but are not too difficult. Maybe you can play them to me next time we meet. Never waste your time playing inferior music. And when you're ready, you can start studying this.'

Mrs Fitzgerald held out a well-used copy of Beethoven's *Moonlight Sonata*. 'I taught your father the first movement when he was just nine, so I'm sure you would enjoy it too. It's very beautiful but quite simple to play.'

'Yes, I thought I was very grown-up indeed when you taught me that, mother.'

'And take this book with you to read, Cathy, and then we can talk about it when I next see you. It was always one of my favourites when I was about your age.' Mrs Fitzgerald handed a leather-bound copy of *Jane Eyre* to her grand-daughter.

'It's a little old for her mother.'

'Never say that. Children find their own level. When she's ready she will read it and love it.'

******

John and Cathy arrived back at Pembroke Street just in time for lunch. Lily, James and Hannah were already seated in the dining room, chatting happily and drinking wine.

'Well, how did it go?' Hannah was eager to hear a full report.

'We'll talk later. She is well enough - looking a bit older of course - though missing me ... missing us. She was very, very pleased indeed to meet Cathy. And Cathy was pleased to meet her too, I think.'

Cathy nodded. 'My Grandma gave me this music and this book.' Cathy passed the pile of great works over to her mother.

'That's ridiculous. Angel, you won't be ready to read *Jane Eyre* until you are fourteen, at least.'

'But I can look at it and make sure I understand all the words. And she gave me this piano music too.'

'*The Moonlight Sonata*? Good heavens. What is she thinking of? You'll get very frustrated trying to play it, my angel.'

'I don't think so, Hannah. The first movement at least is well within her capability. It's good to stretch children and I played it myself when I was not that much older than Cathy.'

'Letitia Fitzgerald. Always the teacher, you know. That's what makes her so extraordinary, in my opinion.' Lily's admiration was obvious.

John took all the volumes from Hannah and placed them on the side table. 'They are the first presents Cathy has ever had from her Grandma so they're special. Let's not get any food on them. Now then. How was your morning? Probably not quite as emotional as mine. What did you get up to, my love, while Lily and James went off to mass? Did you go to meet Ellen?'

'Hannah came with us after all.' James was pouring everyone a glass of red wine. 'It was a real treat to go all together to mass. Of course, neither Lily nor Hannah went up to communion with me. But they can make up for it here with the bread and rather better wine on the table.' James laughed and clinked his glass with Lily's.

'Happy Easter, everyone.'

Chapter 6 - September 1927

Cathy loved the big orange dahlias on the altar. They didn't grow flowers at home – there were just a few scrubby old bushes in the back yard growing above the expanse of weeds - and she wondered whether her Mammy would let her sow some seeds next year. Flowers were just one of the things she enjoyed about coming to mass; she liked the candles, the smell of incense and the singing. And she got to meet other children from the village, which was a treat, as her home-schooling meant she knew very few other children, apart from her cousins.

Cathy and Hannah had started coming to mass every Sunday soon after Easter. Cathy knew her father did not approve at all, but he had been so busy with the forthcoming general election he could hardly object.

'Do you really want to go with your mother to mass, Cathy? There is no right answer. You are free to choose either way and I shall respect your decision.'

'I think … yes. Yes, I'd like to go, Daddy. Is that OK?'

'Of course. It's fine, if that's what you really want.' And John stroked her golden hair.

A similar conversation had taken place over whether Cathy would like to start attending the village school this coming term. Hannah pushed hard, saying that neither she nor John could afford the time Cathy's education demanded, and she would be able to make friends of her own age. John conceded those points and Cathy confirmed, when asked, that she would also like to start school, please Daddy.

'Just keep asking questions, macushla. Don't just accept what teachers tell you. That's all I ask.'

The June election had seen great successes for Fianna Fáil under de Valera, but Cosgrave and Cumann na nGaedheal had scraped home nevertheless. The government never looked stable so, by aligning Fianna Fáil with the Labour

Party against Cosgrave over the summer, de Valera had forced another general election, coming up next week. Cosgrave was not going to fight Carlow-Kilkenny this time but was moving to Cork. This was the best chance yet of getting John's man, Thomas Derrig, elected to the Dáil.

John threw himself into the campaign, writing speeches, printing leaflets, canvassing on the streets. The fields were left untended, the shop left unstocked and Jimmy Boyle left to have free reign over the pub. Cathy missed seeing her father so much too, but at least she could read everything herself these days. And there was less time for her parents to argue.

Cathy looked along the pew. Her mother was sitting next to Grandad. Then, across the aisle, were Auntie Stasia, Uncle Edmund and the three young Hughes boy cousins. Peter, Andrew and Matthew had been joined by a fourth boy, born to Stasia only last month and left back home with Nanny Maud. Stasia had named the new baby Paul, causing Aggie to comment that she didn't think Stasia Hughes would stop having babies until she had recreated the full set of Christ's apostles. Hannah laughed and remarked that she had a sneaking suspicion that Stasia enjoyed flaunting her excessive fertility in front of the still childless Nicholas and Louisa Byrne.

Cathy was fascinated by people taking communion. Stasia, Edmund and James would shuffle out of the pew following the ringing of bells by the server, young Sam McCarthy, and when they returned to their places, Cathy could see that they were discreetly trying to move something around in their mouths. Was this really the body of Christ? It sounded a bit disgusting. Cathy wondered why her mother didn't go up to communion. Hannah simply answered that she wasn't ready yet, and that she would need to make a confession first. All in good time.

Father Stephen was standing by the church door as they left, shaking hands and chatting. Cathy could hear old Mrs

Byrne and Stasia discussing the state of the church with him, cobwebs everywhere and the brass unpolished. Father Stephen blushed and said he would see what could be done but turned to greet Hannah and Cathy with some relief.

'Good morning Mrs Fitzgerald. You look very well. Blooming in fact. And Cathy, tomorrow will be your first day at school. That's a big adventure. Are you excited?'

Cathy liked Father Stephen. His sermons were always interesting and sometimes even funny. He seemed much happier conversing with children than with grown-ups.

'I am quite excited, Father, but a little bit scared too.'

'Well, let me tell you a secret. I get a bit scared every time I say mass or when I have to come into school to talk to all the children. It's better once you've started. Good luck tomorrow. I'll see you there.'

Uncle Edmund had brought the car to the church gate so that James would not have far to walk. He was becoming increasingly wobbly and frail, though still as sharp as ever in his wits. Stasia helped her father into the car.

'Hannah, will it be OK if you walk the boys and Cathy back to the villa? I'll take Matthew but we won't all fit in the car. I would normally happily walk with you in the lovely sunshine but Paul was a very big baby and I'm still a bit sore *down there*.' Stasia's voice dropped to a whisper as she pointed a finger to the ground.

Hannah held Andrew's hand as they walked down towards the river from the church, leaving Peter and Cathy free to run back and forth, kicking stones and swishing the hedgerow weeds with their bare hands. It was slow work making a four year-old walk quite so far. They all paused on the bridge to throw some leaves and berries into the river below and watched them bob downstream.

'Where will they end up, Mammy?'

'I have no idea, Cathy. The sea, I guess.'

'A fish will gobble them all up.' And Peter mimed being a big fish.

Tricky was sitting on the wall as they approached the villa. 'Good morning, Tricky. How are you?'

'No husband?'

'No, not today. He's in Kilkenny working to get Thomas Derrig elected on the 15th. That's why Cathy and I are coming to have lunch with Stasia and Edmund. Aggie has the day off.'

'Your fields. Mess everywhere.'

Cathy bridled at the implied criticism of her father from this horrible dirty man. 'Yes, I'm afraid John had no time to cut the hay this year, and we've let the weeds take over the vegetables.'

'Blight on the spuds. Need burning.'

'Oh dear. I'll tell John. We won't be popular if we don't get rid of that fast. Thank you for keeping an eye out for us, Tricky.'

Cathy, Peter and Andrew ran up to the nursery as soon as they arrived, the boys to play with their trains and teddies. Cathy liked playing with those too, but she was more interested in humans. Baby Paul was awake and gurgling happily in his cot. Cathy put her finger into Paul's tiny fist so that he could grab it. Cathy wished they could have a baby in their house, one she would be allowed to pick up and feed and look after.

The smell of roasting beef was becoming irresistible and, soon enough, the gong sounded for them to gather in the dining room.

After Stasia said grace, Edmund carved the beef deftly. Everyone was silent as they tucked into the delicious spread, even the normally rowdy boys.

'Peter, use your knife and fork properly. You're six years old for heaven's sake. Hannah, I've been wondering – now that you're back going to mass and everything – would you like to be Paul's godmother? Father Stephen will be christening him in three weeks' time. Don't worry if not - I can always ask Edmund's cousin. And I've asked Nicholas Byrne to be his godfather.'

Hannah smiled to herself. Oh, was there no end to the tiny acts of vengeance on Nicholas Byrne that Stasia could dream up.

'Thank you. I'd be honoured. And then, maybe next year, I can return the favour. We shall be having our own baby in February, God willing.' Hannah looked around the table; her father exclaimed, looking thrilled while her sister just looked shocked.

'Eat up Cathy. And I'd better tuck in too, if I'm eating for two.'

Chapter 7 - April 1928

Baby Rose arrived in February, the least rose-like time of the year, when there were deep frosts most days. But she spread sunshine all over the Main Street household. Rose usually woke up around six thirty in the morning for her first feed of the day. If she had been woken too, Cathy would jump out of bed to go and see to her, but her Daddy was usually already there by the cot, cradling his 'fairy child'. Her Mammy had stopped breast-feeding Rose a month before, when she was just nine weeks old, but this meant that Cathy was able to give Rose a bottle or sit with John while he did so, singing or talking to his baby all the while.

Rose was such a beautiful, sunny baby, with golden hair like Cathy's own, and she didn't cry too much, unlike her baby cousin Paul, who seemed to have been born grouchy. Cathy snuggled up to her Daddy as he sat on the bed and cradled Rose. She didn't mind getting fewer cuddles herself from John these days. She understood why he was captivated by the baby.

'Can I hold her and finish feeding her, please Daddy?'

'Of course, my Countess. You look after your sister so carefully, don't you. What a kind girl you are.'

'I love having a baby sister.'

'Well, we've all waited a long time for Rose to come along but she was worth the wait, don't you think?' Cathy nodded and looked into Rose's blue eyes as the baby contentedly sucked on the bottle.

'Maybe she was waiting until we had a Fianna Fáil TD for Kilkenny. What do you reckon, Cathy? Rose obviously has excellent taste when it comes to politics.' Thomas Derrig's election last September had given her Daddy another reason to celebrate.

Very softly, John began to sing a song that Cathy had heard him sing before to Rose, one with strange-sounding words she didn't understand. She knew it was in Gaelic but nothing else.

'What *is* that song, Daddy?'

John paused and put his arm around Cathy. 'The lullaby is called *Seoithín, Seo Hó*. To be honest, I've forgotten what all the words mean – I think white fairies dancing on the roof are in it somewhere. I used to sing it to you too, when you were a baby. I learned it from a wonderful woman called Shawna, Aoife's mother, when I lived in Connemara for a couple of years in my early twenties. I was trying to learn Gaelic properly back then but I'm afraid very little has stayed with me - apart from *macushla*, which I call you all the time. Did you know it was Gaelic?

'I guessed it was. No-one else calls me that.'

'Maybe we could learn Gaelic together.'

'I'd like that. What's Connemara like?'

'Aah…nothing like Rowanbridge. It's very dramatic with mountains and lakes and the sea on all sides. Wild but deep and exciting. I shall take you there one day.' Cathy didn't like to remind her father that he had made that promise to her several times already. 'The sea is beautiful but also treacherous. There was a terrible storm last year off the coast where Aoife and her family live. Forty-five fishermen were drowned. Thankfully Ruari, Aoife's father, had not gone out in his boat that day. But you must always be mindful of the power of the sea.'

'I will, Daddy, if I ever get to see it. Rose likes your singing. Do you think she'd like me to play the piano to her?'

'I'm sure she'd love it. You could play her the first bars of *The Moonlight Sonata* that you've learned so well. It's very gentle. Almost a lullaby. And it would be a sort of message from her granny.'

'Yes, it is gentle. But I think it's very sad too.'

Rose finished her milk and John took her from Cathy's arms to burp her. 'Thank you, *cuisle mo chroidhe*. That means something like 'beat of my heart'. Now, you need to get washed and dressed ready for your breakfast and then off to school.'

Cathy had taken to Rowanbridge school instantly. She found that she was rather further ahead in her reading, writing and numbers than the other children in her class but there were many things she had to learn from scratch, like the words to hymns and how to play hopscotch. The best thing about school was finding some friends of her own. Cathy had at first been rather shy to go up to other children in the playground but, luckily, they had no such qualms. In her first week, back in September, she had found herself surrounded by girls and boys at break-time wanting to know all about this girl who had only just started at the school even though she was nearly eight years old. Where had she been? Who had taught her before? Why was she so clever?

It didn't take longer than a couple of weeks before Cathy was just one of them. She had lost her special allure but in its place she now had two good friends: Bernie O'Rourke and Marion Magee. Bernie was short for Bernadette. Cathy was in awe that Bernie was the youngest of *ten* brothers and sisters - how lucky was she – but was curious as to why all Bernie's sisters had names that made them sound like boys: Gerry, Jo, Harry, and Bobby. Maybe that's what made Bernie so strong and fearless.

Marion was an only child and very prissy indeed. There were more dolls and stuffed or knitted animals in her tiny bedroom than Cathy could count, some made by her granny, the very Mrs Magee who had been a governess to her mother. The three girls made a diverse trio, but quickly formed a tight bond. Their favourite games were, in ascending order: Jacks, Robin Hood and his Merry Men (on account of Marion, of course, who always insisted on playing Maid Marion) and skipping. They always walked home from school together and usually spent some time in one or the other's house before tea-time. Marion always wanted to go to Cathy's house because of baby Rose, and Bernie liked to go there too so she could slide down the bales in the barn.

Today, they had decided to go home the long way, past the church, down along the river and then back up Mill Lane, past Cromwell's Tower to end up at Cathy's house.

'Let's pick some flowers for your Mammy, Cathy. These are pretty.' Marion scooped up a handful of the white blooms growing by the river bank.

'Poo! They stink. You can't give those to Mrs Fitzgerald.' Bernie knocked the wild garlic out of Marion's hand. 'Now you're going to smell awful.' The girls climbed up from the river and sauntered along Mill Lane.

'I reckon Sam McCarthy is sweet on you, Cathy.' Bernie linked her arm with Cathy's. 'He's always picking up your pencils and fetching you stuff.'

'You mustn't let boys kiss you though, my Mammy says. Not until you're married. That's how you get a baby. Who'd want to kiss them anyway?' Marion wrinkled up her nose.

'Don't be an idiot, Marion Magee. Have you not seen how the dogs and cats and rabbits make babies? Even dragonflies. The man has to put his willy inside the woman's tummy. My sister Gerry has told me all about it, so I wouldn't let any boy do that to me.'

The girls had reached the tower by now. 'Come on, let's go inside. They say there's a banshee in there. Wooo-hooo.' Bernie ran around Marion, wailing into her ear. 'But don't worry. I shall protect you. Come on. We just have to climb over the gate. No-one will see us.'

'It might be dangerous with all those crumbling stones.'

'Don't be such a baby, Marion.'

Eventually Bernie coaxed Cathy and Marion to join her in the field. The cows barely registered their presence, munching monotonously on the spring grass. One of the herd calmly ambled away as the trio picked their way through the field, avoiding the most vivid green patches where the cowpats lurked.

They came around the blind side of the Tower and stopped dead. There was Tricky Byrne, leaning against the wall, trousers round his ankles, tugging away at his penis. Marion gave a weak scream which made Tricky instantly bend over to hide himself from their gaze. The girls turned, ran back to and over the gate and on up the lane, not stopping until they reached the pavement outside Cathy's house.

'Oh God, that was disgusting. I think I'm going to be sick.'

Bernie was laughing loudly. 'Oh, grow up Marion. If you had five brothers like me, you'd have seen that sort of thing aplenty.'

'But it can't be right that he does it in public, surely.' Cathy was inclined to agree more with Marion than Bernie. Tricky Byrne was disgusting enough in her eyes without exposing himself like that.

The girls went around to the kitchen door. Aggie was sitting at the kitchen table feeding Rose. In the background, Cathy could hear her mother shouting and her father talking loudly.

'We've just seen Tricky Byrne playing with himself, Aggie, round the back of the Tower. It was horrible.' Cathy couldn't wait to share her disgust.

'Have you indeed. Best keep out of that field then.'

'My sisters have warned me about him,' said Bernie. 'They say he did it all the time when they were at school. But I don't think he wanted us to see him, like.'

'Can Bernie and Marion have some tea with us Aggie?' Aggie put down the bottle and handed Rose over to Cathy.

'I don't think today is a very good day, you know, Cathy. Your Mammy and Daddy are very busy with things for the business and they're very tired. I'm sorry girls, but you're best off home now. You can come and play another day soon.'

Marion gave Rose a little kiss on her head before she and Bernie said good-bye and sloped off out of the kitchen, leaving Cathy listening to her parents' altercation in the study.

Aggie made some bread and jam for Cathy and mashed a fresh pot of tea. 'Don't worry, my love. It's just your Mammy. You know how she is when things don't go just right. It's just a storm in a tea-cup. Now, look what arrived for you today. Looks like a parcel from your Granny in Dublin. You can open it after you've eaten, when your hands aren't sticky.'

Cathy ate her tea with Rose sitting up on her lap while Aggie busied herself with peeling potatoes. The raised voices stopped eventually. Hannah walked into the kitchen, clearly simmering with rage as she acknowledged neither of her children nor Aggie. She poured herself a cup of tea and sat at the kitchen table in silence. Soon, the sound of the slow movement of the *Moonlight Sonata* drifted down from upstairs. Hannah rose and went back out, slamming the door behind her.

Chapter 8 - February 1929

James had moved back into the Main Street house in November to escape the noise of his four Hughes grandsons. There was a baby here to contend with but Rose was altogether more serene than baby Paul, and Hannah's baby came with the benefit of a pint of Guinness at the pub and the company of his old drinking pals.

Cathy could see instantly that her Grandad wasn't very well; he was very forgetful and had trouble getting up from the dining table. He often fell asleep in the kitchen armchair, even while she was talking to him or showing him her drawings.

Then, the day after Boxing Day, he didn't come down to breakfast. Her Mammy found him unconscious on the floor by his bed. Her Daddy ran to fetch Dr O'Connor who pronounced that her Grandad had had a stroke and had then prescribed various pills. Dr O'Connor said there was no point taking him into Kilkenny Hospital; there was nothing better they could do for him there and James would be much happier kept at home.

James regained consciousness the same day but he couldn't walk and the right side of his mouth was so droopy that Cathy found it hard to understand him at first. Over the next weeks, her Mammy devoted herself to caring for her Grandad, feeding and washing him, even putting him on the bedpan - though Aggie was always left to empty it.

Through the Christmas holidays, Cathy spent as much time as she could looking after either her Grandad or baby Rose. She was more than happy to do either; she loved caring for people and making everything as good as it could be. Soon after New Year, when she was back at school, her Grandad started to sit up and then, a week later, he managed to get himself out of bed, with the help of her Daddy's shoulder and a walking stick, to sit in a chair.

James still only had the use of his left hand so Cathy would often be the one to cut up his food for him and even put it onto a spoon for him to transfer shakily into his mouth. But he never attempted to leave his bedroom or wear anything but a nightshirt.

Because James was more or less bedbound, people would come to visit the Main Street house which made for plenty of comings and goings in the house. Everyone had a lot more to do and Cathy was always ready to lend a hand: making cups of tea, dusting furniture, hanging out the washing.

With Hannah so occupied, John was left to run both businesses and the farmland entirely alone. Neither of Cathy's parents found much time to play their instruments for their own pleasure, though both would go up and play for James's benefit, whether popular piano music from John or traditional folk songs from Hannah's violin. Certainly, the morning gramophone sessions had stopped, both for lack of time and for fear of disturbing James's morning lie-ins.

That Sunday morning, they were all waiting for Stasia, Edmund and the four 'apostles' to arrive. Sunday was the day the Hugheses visited James and then they always stayed on to lunch. The fact that this made a lot of extra work for Aggie didn't seem to occur to Stasia.

Father Stephen had promised to come along after the eleven o'clock service to say a private mass for James and to give him communion. He did this most weeks and Hannah, Cathy and the entire Hughes brood had got into the habit of joining in. James's bedroom would be very packed; the fire in the grate, the heat of oil lamps and all the bodies would turn the room into a veritable Turkish bath.

Father Stephen was one of Cathy's favourite grown-ups. He came into school three times a week to give them religious instruction but he also knew lots about history and geography and he would relate bible stories to places and events in the Holy Land today. Cathy was part of the small group of children being prepared for their first Holy Communion. She was late to this initiation into being a fully-fledged Catholic, being a couple of years older than the rest of the group, who were all just six or seven years old. She appreciated just how patient Father Stephen was with them all. He was a relatively quiet man for a priest – Auntie Stasia said he wasn't really suited to the role - but he was always so kind to everyone and Cathy could detect a cheeky twinkle in his eye. He even made time to come and see her Grandad during the week if he could, when he would read him articles from the newspaper or even give him a game of backgammon if James felt up to it.

Cathy heard a knock at the front door. That would be the Hugheses. Stasia was not one to enter through the backdoor so Cathy dashed downstairs to try and save Aggie a trip down the hallway. Stasia shooed Edmund and the boys outside to go and find John in the farmyard. Cathy wasn't sure why her Daddy always kept out the way when the priest arrived. She knew he wouldn't take part in the mass but he seemed to want to get as far away as possible. Stasia followed Cathy upstairs to the drawing room. Hannah was sitting looking at a piece of music while Rose played with Honey contentedly on the hearthrug. Stasia ignored her sister and popped her head around James's door.

'Morning Father. I hope you're well today,' and, without waiting for a reply, Stasia went and joined Hannah on the sofa. 'How has he been this week? He looks very grey.'

'Much as last week. No better, no worse.'

'I can't help regretting that I let him come back here before Christmas, you know. All that drinking going on, and late nights. You really should have stopped him.'

'Stasia, he's a grown man. And he needs some pleasures in life.'

'Well, you would know all about that in this house. All play and no work, it seems to me.'

Normally, Hannah would have fought against her sister's slur, but today she needed to ask a favour and she was not looking forward to it at all. 'Maybe you're right. We think we work hard, but maybe not hard enough.'

Stasia picked up Rose and bounced her on her knee. 'Hello, you beauty. Hello, hello now.' Stasia blew her cheeks out and made some loud raspberry noises. Rose giggled and slapped her Auntie Stasia on the nose in joy. Cathy had never seen Stasia behave like this with her own sons.

'You don't know how lucky you are, Hannah, to have pretty girls. Boys are just so loud and dirty.'

'Yes, we are very lucky in our daughters, though less lucky in business. That's what I want to talk to you about. Things are not going too well.'

'Perhaps if you hadn't turned your backs on God for so long.'

'The pub's turnover has been sliding down and down, and the shop too is not making much of a profit. Tricky Byrne reckons that Jimmy Boyle has his hands in the till but it's impossible to prove anything.'

'Just ask him straight out. Of course, he'll deny it, but it'll make him realise you're onto him, if he is stealing. He was never to be trusted. John needs to be in there keeping an eye on him at all times. He might not like it but that's what's needed if you're going to get a grip on any business.'

'The thing is, Stasia, we find ourselves totally without ready cash. We don't have enough to pay the wages even. Daddy has always given me a little money every month, but since he's been ill of course it's the last thing on his mind and I'm not going to ask him when he's in a sick bed.'

'Well, if that useless husband of yours would do an honest day's work for a change, instead of parading the streets of Kilkenny handing out Fenian propaganda or playing his cello you wouldn't be in this state.' The way Stasia said 'playing the cello' made it sound like a deviant practice.

'Thank you for the advice, Stasia, but, yes, I know things have to change and they will. We just need some help to tide us over. Could you see your way to lending us some money for six months or so until we are back on our feet?'

'Neither a borrower nor a lender be.'

'I don't think that applies to your own sister.'

'I won't lend you money, Hannah. You and John have to learn from the consequences of your own actions – or inactions, I should say. But what I will do - and Edmund will agree with me - is buy one of your fields. The top meadow. It adjoins our land. The hay is going to waste anyway.'

Cathy kept her head down and focussed on stroking the loudly purring cat. Her cheeks were burning with shame that she wanted no-one to see. Was her Mammy really going to sell part of their farm without asking Daddy?

'So be it. I have very little choice, do I? Edmund and John can agree a fair price between them but can I please have some cash immediately so that I can pay the staff?'

'I shall go to the bank tomorrow morning. Come and see me after - about three o'clock.'

There were footsteps and chatter on the stairs.

'And that'll be Father Stephen now with the boys. It's Sunday and we're about to hear Mass. Let's turn our thoughts away from Mammon, Hannah, for the rest of today at least.'

Chapter 9 - August 1929

It seemed very weird to see everyone wearing black clothes on this balmy, sunny, summer day, Cathy thought. Like the black ribbons her mother had put in her golden hair that morning, they just didn't seem right together. But Cathy was glad that her Grandad was being buried with bright sunshine all around.

Rowanbridge looked as handsome as could be, with gaudy flowers on its windowsills defying the mournful procession pacing along Main Street to the church. Her Grandad wouldn't have wanted to be anywhere near the church on a day like today; there was a race meeting on at Gowran Park later and that's where he would have made sure he was in such glorious weather.

Her Mammy and Auntie Stasia, with black veils over their heads and arms linked, were at the front of the cortège walking side by side directly behind the coffin which was pulled by two magnificent black horses with black plumes on their heads. Cathy thought they looked a bit like the horses she had seen at the circus last year, only they had had scarlet feathers. Grandad would have preferred red, she thought. She and Peter walked behind their mothers, holding their Daddies' hands, followed by Aunt Lily and two elderly cousins of Grandad's from Wexford.

Cathy could hear Aggie blowing her nose loudly a couple of rows behind her. Her Mammy wasn't crying today; she probably had no tears left. And Auntie Stasia must have cried too, though Cathy hadn't seen her do it. Both women had stayed by their father's side for nearly two days continuously as he slowly slid away from them, united in their grief and love for their beloved Dada.

It was odd to see her own Daddy sitting in a church pew. She had only seen him in a church once before, but he had been playing his cello then, and the wedding in Dublin had seemed much more like a party than a religious service.

Earlier that morning, Cathy had retraced one of her Grandad's favourite strolls down to the river and had picked a bunch of orange montbretia which, on her return, she had put into James's open coffin before it was finally closed up ready for the funeral. There were grander flowers on top of the coffin, white carnations and roses, but she knew he would have preferred her simple offering.

She looked around the church. Just about everyone from Rowanbridge seemed to be there: the Byrnes, the McLoughlins, Jimmy and Eileen Boyle, Mrs Magee, her son and daughter-in-law and even her friend Marion. Cathy smiled at Marion but decided it would be wrong to wave. All the people who had ever worked for James, on the farms or in the shops, had turned out in mourning, along with many of his customers and cronies from the pub. Even some of the brewery delivery men from Kilkenny had made the effort to come along. Cathy was amazed that one person could have made so many friends in his lifetime.

Everyone stood up as Father Stephen led the pall-bearers up to the altar. Cathy knew that Father Stephen would be dreading this event: the whole of Rowanbridge out in force to hear him say mass and to deliver a tribute to the well-loved James McDermott. Afterwards, she couldn't remember everything that Father Stephen had said, but she had seen her mother smile and nod and shed a few tears as the priest recounted the many stories he had collected from people in the village. Apparently, her Grandad had been a very clever businessman, a generous employer, a fine judge of horseflesh and a cracking backgammon player.

When Father Stephen talked about James's devastation at losing his wife at such a young age and the strength he had found to bring up his daughters alone and then the joy at seeing those daughters become mothers themselves,

Cathy was surprised to find that she was crying along with her Mammy.

The sun was still shining down on them as they stood at James's graveside. It was a very familiar place. Cathy came most weeks with Hannah to put flowers on her grandmother's grave, right next to which the deep hole for her grandad had been dug. The oak coffin was lowered gently into it.

Cathy read the familiar headstone: *Evaline McDermott, 1876-1912, beloved wife of James, mother of Anastasia and Johannah. Rest in Peace with God and his Angels.* Cathy had never thought about her as a real person before, married to Grandad and living in their house, cooking on the range and sleeping in Grandad's big old bed. How young she had been when she died; just thirty-six, not that much older than her own Mammy today.

But now, as Father Stephen had said, she and Grandad were reunited in heaven. It was a comforting thought in many ways but it troubled Cathy a little. Would Grandmother Evaline have grown older, she wondered, as her Grandad had done, or would they be reunited at mismatched ages with James old enough to be his wife's father? Ah, well. God must be used to sorting these things out. Best leave it to him.

The crowd dispersed and a select group followed Edmund and Stasia to their home where they hosted a polite funeral breakfast for the 'respectable people' as she called them: members of the family, close friends like the Byrnes, James's professional and business contacts and Father Stephen. It was a very sober affair – just sandwiches and cups of tea - and Father Stephen on hand to dispense comforting words to anyone who looked in need.

As soon as she decently could, Hannah fetched Rose from Nanny Maud's care and rounded up John and Cathy to go back home where she knew the real wake was going on. Jimmy Boyle and Aggie were in charge of lubricating the villagers, the farm workers and the racing crowd before they headed off to Gowran Park for the afternoon.

'Come on you two. We need to get back before Jimmy Boyle gives away every last drop of drink in the place.' Hannah was setting a very brisk pace along the river bank.

'It's only for one day, Hannah, and it's what your father would have wanted.' John was carrying Rose on his shoulders.

'Will you never stop giving away every last penny we own, John Fitzgerald? You won't be happy until your daughters and I are begging on the streets.' John transferred Rose from his shoulders to his left arm so that he could take Hannah's hand.

'Come on, my darling. It's been a difficult day – difficult few months - for you.'

Hannah burst into noisy sobs. 'I miss him so much though.'

Cathy went to the other side of her Mammy and took her other hand. The noise of the wake was just discernible as they walked past Cromwell's Tower towards Main Street.

'Now, that is the sound of Guinness and Tullamore, pure and simple.' John chuckled. 'I think we should go in and have one glass with them, you know, Hannah.'

'That is the sound of money pouring down the drain, John. But, yes, let's go in for just half an hour. Cathy, can you look after Rose for just a little while, please? Your Daddy and I need to go and thank all the people who've come to pay their last respects to your Grandad.'

'Of course, Mammy.'

John set Rose down onto the lane and she toddled over to her sister's outstretched hands. 'Just watch her carefully, macushla. She can move quite fast now.'

Cathy stood watching as her parents walked through the front door of the noisy pub and then bent down to give Rose a kiss. 'Now, Rosie, I'm going to show you how to pick some flowers from the hedgerows to give to Mammy. She's very sad and it'll cheer her up no end.'

Chapter 10 - October 1929

The first time Cathy understood what the Depression was doing to ordinary people was when Bernie came into school with her toes poking out of the top of her shoes where the leather had been cut away. She had grown out of them over the summer but her parents couldn't afford to buy any new ones because her father had lost his job at the Kilkenny woollen mills the month before. And, with nine other children to compete against at the O'Rourke kitchen table, Bernie was always very keen to come home with Cathy after school to take full advantage of the bread and jam on offer from Aggie.

Almost the whole of Rowanbridge was starting to be touched by the economic gloom in some way, even if it was just having a bigger pool of casual labourers lining up at harvest time to work on the Hugheses' and Byrnes' farms. Stasia had even been heard to say that the Depression was a blessing; the Hughes had managed to drop the daily rate by more than a shilling, yet there were still queues of men and women at the farm gates looking for a day's work.

There was no silver lining for John and Hannah. The Depression just meant that business was slower at the shop and the pub. John would never consider dropping anyone's wages – and Hannah knew better than to suggest it.

In fact, John saw the growing misery around the village and took it upon himself to help wherever he could. If he knew that a family was in no position to pay their monthly account for groceries he would lose the invoice under a pile of other papers. If he ever found himself behind the till at the shop or the pub at the weekend he would give a couple of extra pence change or add an extra rasher into the package. Cathy saw her father's small gestures of compassion and loved him all the more for them, even whilst realising they were perhaps unwise.

Hannah's deep sadness at the loss of her father was lifting only to be replaced by extreme anxiety about money. 'John, listen to me. We have to do something. The money we made from selling the field is nearly all used up. I shall soon have to break into the little bequest my father left me and after that what will we do?'

'Don't worry Hannah. This Depression won't last forever.'

'Aggie hasn't been paid for the last two weeks, have you Aggie?'

'Don't worry about me. I can always go and sell meself on the streets of Kilkenny if I need to pay the rent, though I bet no-one has the cash even for that these days. Yes, even though I would be dirt cheap, before anyone else says it.'

Cathy listened to all this talk of financial straitening but there always seemed to be food on their table and her shoes were never too tight.

Cathy was excited when her grandmother's fortnightly letter arrived. She always enjoyed reading about what was happening at the Academy and about the concerts her Granny had been to. With her father's help, she would write a reply in her neat and chubby hand, giving her Granny a little news and informing her how she was getting on learning the sonatinas and gavottes in the book of piano music she had been given. It was a very proud day when she had written to her Granny to say that she had finished learning the first movement of the *Moonlight Sonata*. She added that she hoped she'd be able to play it to her sometime soon.

Sometimes her Granny sent more than a letter; she sent a package containing a book or some music maybe. But the best part of her Granny's letters was the money they always contained; usually it was a couple of sixpences but occasionally as much as half a crown.

Until this term, Cathy had saved the money in her piggybank, on her mother's advice. But these days she couldn't wait to take the money and go along to their shop to spend it on sweets and treats that she would share with all the children at school. Cathy calculated that the money was doing a better job being spent than by sitting inside a china pig; their own shop got the custom and her friends shared the spoils. But today, Cathy had decided she would buy a packet of tea, just for Bernie, something more useful than sweets, something that Bernie's whole family could enjoy.

Eileen was curious to see young Cathy open the door and come into the shop before school. 'You're up bright and early. And why, pray, are you buying tea, Miss Cathy? If Aggie needs tea, you can just take all you want, you know. Just write it in the book. It's your shop.'

'Oh no. This isn't for us. I'm just running an errand before school for … for Father Stephen. The tea is for him.' Cathy blushed at her own fib but hoped Father Stephen would approve of her motives when she eventually came to make her first confession.

Bernie was bemused by the packet of tea when Cathy produced it, on the walk home with Marion. 'Why are you giving me tea, Cathy?'

'Well, it was going to be thrown out at the shop – I'm not sure why – and I thought your Mammy might like it. She was saying the other day how expensive tea is.' Another fib. How they seemed to mount up once she had started.

'OK.' Bernie shrugged and popped the packet into her satchel. 'Can we come home with you, Cathy, and play on your piano?'

'Oooh yes, and can we play with Rose?'

The three girls trooped into the kitchen to shouts from Aggie.

'Oi, you three. Stop right there. Where on earth have you been, you girls? Walking home along the river again? I haven't the time to be sweeping up your mess so get those muddy boots off if you're wanting to go up to the drawing room. And here, take Rose with you.'

The girls messed about on the piano for a while, attempted to play dominoes without Rose sweeping everything off the table all the time, teased Honey with the tassels on the curtain and listened to the gramophone. Then they came back downstairs and put their boots on again.

'Where are you off to now, Cathy? It won't be long before it's tea-time, you know.'

'I won't be long, Aggie. Just taking Bernie and Marion to see the new chicks.'

While Marion was occupied cooing over the yellow bits of fluff, Cathy took Bernie's hand and dragged her off to the main hen house. She rifled through the straw until she had found three eggs. 'Here, take these for your tea. Go on.' Bernie looked at Cathy and then carefully took the eggs from her. She understood now.

Chapter 11 - May 1930

It took exactly eleven minutes to walk from the Main Street house to the church as long as Cathy was on her own and not having to take Rose with her. Those days, Cathy was making the journey at least sixteen times a week; back and forth to school, next door to the church, every weekday; to Holy Communion instruction on Saturday afternoons; to mass on Sundays with her mother; one more time on a Saturday - to help clean the church or to arrange flowers or wash the altar linen - at her mother's insistence.

But Hannah was making the short walk even more often. Following her James's death, Hannah had started to attend mass every morning, sometimes as early as seven-thirty in the morning, and often she would go for afternoon Benediction as well. Cathy knew that her father despaired of her Mammy's increasing devotion and religious observance. Even her Auntie Stasia had commented that one could take things too far and that Hannah would be better off putting some of that energy into doing the accounts but Cathy could see that her mother derived great solace from being in church, and Father Stephen was so sympathetic and would talk to Hannah for as long as she wanted after the service.

He was very kind to Cathy as preparations for her First Holy Communion drew to an end. She found her first confession surreal: kneeling inside the little cubicle speaking through the metal grill, pretending that Father Stephen didn't know it was her.

'Bless me Father for I have sinned.' Cathy had been rehearsing the long list of sins that she had amassed over her ten years alive and was now able to confess them and have the slate wiped clean. 'I have been lazy, I have been impatient, I have been selfish, I have been greedy,' - that was for yesterday's sausages - 'I have been angry, I have been proud,' - that was for when she had played the Schubert

Impromptu at school last month and had loved the applause - 'I have told lies.'

Cathy blushed behind the grill. Was telling lies the worst sin she had committed? Cathy didn't think they were as bad as when she had shouted at Rose for scribbling on one of her drawings and Rose had burst into tears and run to her Daddy. That was awful. But the word 'lies' sounded much more serious. Either way, as she recited the list of her wrongdoings to the priest, Cathy realised what a terrible person she had been and resolved never to sin again. The five Hail Marys Father Stephen had given as a penance seemed very inadequate.

Father Stephen gave her absolution and exhorted her to 'go and sin no more'. Cathy resolved to keep her soul shiny and pure until her First Communion the next day. She wanted to be able to wear the lovely white communion dress with a clear conscience. Surely, she could do that. But it turned out to be quite hard, especially when Rose was so annoying that night and wouldn't go to sleep. Cathy kept calm and just kept putting her back into bed with a smile and a kiss.

The next morning, Cathy got up and washed herself all over. Then she put on the communion dress. Her Auntie Stasia had made it for her with fabric left over from her own wedding dress. It was so pretty. There was also an exquisite veil she had to wear that had been kept in the family for generations. It had been worn by her Grandmother Evaline and Great-Aunt Lily - and by Stasia and Hannah - for their First Communions.

Cathy went into her parents' bedroom, carrying the veil. She needed her mother's help to arrange it properly. Hannah and John were still asleep, her father curled around her mother, their golden and chestnut hair mingled on the pillows. Cathy stood and watched them for a while, so peaceful for a change, until the alarm clock on the table beside them made her jump. It was just six-thirty.

Taking communion proved to be rather traumatic. Father Stephen placed the sacred wafer onto her tongue, as she and the other five children taking their first communion - one of them her cousin Andrew - knelt at the altar rail. The wafer immediately became stuck onto her upper palate. Cathy knew she was not supposed to bite into the host but she panicked when it disintegrated as she used her tongue to try and roll it free. No-one sitting in the church could tell, but God did, of course, and Cathy hoped that he would forgive her on her first go.

Auntie Stasia was hosting Sunday lunch for everyone afterwards, including Father Stephen. Her father hadn't come to the church. Cathy understood; it was enough that he had put his hands on her shoulders before she and her mother set off for church and told her that she looked like a real Countess or a white fairy and wished her a very happy day. But he was here now and seemed happy enough to be talking politics with Father Stephen with a glass of whiskey and water in his hand.

Cathy wasn't sure that she could eat any lunch. She had the body of Christ inside her now after all, and she didn't think it would be right to pile roast pork and cabbage on top of it. Perhaps potatoes would be acceptable though, as they were almost white.

'Why are you only taking your First Communion today? I took mine two years ago and you're older than me. Andrew's only seven and he took his today. Is it because your father's a heathen? That's what Mammy says.' Cousin Peter was talking with his mouth stuffed full of roast pork.

'There's no fixed date when you have to take it, Peter. You take it when you're ready.' Hannah came to Cathy's rescue.

'Okay.' Peter seemed quite satisfied with the answer. 'Are you leaving your meat, Cathy?' and he speared a slice of roast pork from her plate and carried it over to his, dripping gravy as he went.

'What's going on in your west field, John?' asked Edmund. 'I saw Nicholas and Tricky walking round it last week and then Tricky ploughing it up yesterday.'

'Not our field anymore, Edmund. Theirs to cut or plough as they think fit.'

'What's that you say, John?' Stasia's ears were attuned to any talk of land. 'Did you say your west field is now the property of the Byrnes?'

'I did, Stasia. Hannah and I decided to sell all three of our fields to them a couple of months ago. I think we all know that I'm even less of a farmer than I am a landlord and shopkeeper. And the money will see us through until this terrible Depression ends.'

'Perhaps if you didn't try and feed the whole village you wouldn't have to sell our father's land to the Byrnes. How could you have done such a thing, John?'

'It's just a commercial transaction, Stasia.'

'No, it's not. It's the McDermott family's land. Hannah, how could you have let this happen? You must have known how upsetting it would be. And to the Byrnes of all people. Do you want to see their farm get even bigger than ours?'

'Stasia, we really didn't care who bought it and I'm sure Daddy wouldn't have minded either.'

'We would have bought it off you, wouldn't we Edmund, if you had given us a chance. That way at least the McDermott land would have stayed in the family.'

'Well, the last time we sold a field to you, Stasia, we never heard the end of it. So there you have it. The deed is done.'

There was a long silence, until Hannah picked up the plate of meat.

'Father Stephen, can I give you a little more pork?'

Chapter 12 - July 1930

It was a shock for Cathy to discover that she had had another sister – half-sister to be precise – born eight years before her. She had just finished performing a Mozart minuet to her Daddy's delight, when he called her over, put his arms around her waist and sat her on his knee.

John had decided it was time to tell Cathy the whole story; how he had fallen in love with Aoife's sister, Ailsa, when he had gone to live in Connemara in his early twenties. Cathy heard about their golden-haired daughter, Mairé, who had never been well, but who had been loved ferociously by her parents and her auntie Aoife and her grand-parents, Shawna and Ruari. Cathy gasped when she heard that Ailsa had died suddenly, leaving Mairé to be looked after by her Daddy and her other relatives and she cried a little along with her Daddy when he told her that his first daughter had died not long afterwards. Cathy had often seen her father holding the lock of yellow hair when she walked into their bedroom unannounced, but he would quickly put it into the top drawer of the dressing table. She was always conscious of its existence when she was in that room but she had never dared ask about it; she knew it would be a difficult story for her Daddy to tell. Now she knew its significance.

'I want you to know about Cleggan and all the people there because I'm going to take you on a trip to meet them this summer.'

'Isn't it a sad place, Daddy?'

'Well, yes, some very sad things happened there, but also some amazing and lovely things. And it's a beautiful place with people I love in it. You will love them too and they will most definitely adore you.'

Cathy found Cleggan on the map and imagined being able to paddle in the sea. She even began to dream about the sea and riding in a boat. As the time drew nearer for their trip, Cathy began to worry about leaving her Mammy alone to cope with the shop and the pub but Daddy said she shouldn't fret about a thing as he had sorted everything out with Jimmy and Eileen. Mammy would have Rose and Aggie for company after all. Not only that, Mammy's friends, Ellen and Visha, were coming to stay for a few days while they were away, bringing stories of Maisie and Eamonn's new babies.

It was a long train journey to Galway via Dublin but her Daddy used all that time to tell her every detail of his life before he and Mammy had married and to answer her many questions. It was dark when they arrived at the Galway hotel. No sooner had Cathy fallen asleep, it seemed, than her Daddy was shaking her awake the next morning. After a hearty breakfast, Cathy and John were soon swaying in their seats on a little train bound for Clifden.

So many thoughts swirled around Cathy's brain. She had formed vivid pictures of Ruari, Shawna and Aoife in her imagination: the stone cottage by the glittering sea near Cleggan, the little fishing boat with its nets and the windswept graveyard by the beach where Ailsa and poor little Mairé were buried. It scared Cathy to think that death could have so cruelly taken away a sister from her.

They were planning on being away for five whole days. It was such an adventure Cathy could barely concentrate on the book she had brought to read on the train. There was so much to see out of the windows as they travelled through the landscape. Every time there was a glimpse of water, Cathy would ask 'Is that the sea now, Daddy?' only to be told 'Not yet, macushla.' It seemed that Connemara was as much lake as dry land.

Cathy had never seen the sea for real. She had looked at photographs and paintings, she had read lots of books and sung songs about the sea, and she had seen a thin line of blue on the horizon when they had gone to see her grandma in Dalkey. But she had never touched an actual wave. She couldn't wait to dabble her toes in the surf and pick up shells on the shore.

An hour later, Cathy was sitting on the bus as it trundled from Clifden towards Moyard. Cathy thought this must be what it's like to go to a foreign country. The countryside looked nothing like Rowanbridge and the gossip bubbling around her in the bus was in a language she didn't understand. The exhilarating glimpses of blue were finally confirmed as being the real, actual, vast Atlantic Ocean.

When they got off the bus at the turning to Cleggan, a tall dark-haired woman was waiting for them, and some way behind her was a grey-haired man at the reins of a small pony and trap.

'Aoife! My Aoife. It's so good to see you.' John threw his arms around the woman and held her in a way Cathy had never seen him do to anyone except her Mammy, his daughters and that one time to her Grandma in Dalkey. 'And Ruari. You're looking well,' shouted John over to the waiting fisherman. The two men waved to each other.

'John, my dearest John. It's really you. Just the same. Maybe a bit more tired, and a few grey hairs I see. But welcome back, dear man.'

Aoife's accent sounded very strange to Cathy's ears.

'Say hello to Aoife, Cathy.'

Aoife turned to Cathy and kissed her on both cheeks. 'Cathy, hello my dear. Oh heavens, John. It's like I'm seeing a ghost.'

'I know. It's a sort of miracle. Come. Let's go home.'

John loaded their two bags onto the trap and helped up Cathy and Aoife.

'Cathy, come and sit up here beside me. This is where our most important guests go,' said Ruari.

The sound of the sea became more and more inescapable as the journey progressed; they stopped trying to talk over it and just enjoyed the rhythm of the trotting pony until they arrived at the stone cottage where an elderly lady was standing, beaming from the open door.

John was hailed by Shawna like the Prodigal Son that in many ways he was. Cathy was greeted like a visiting princess, presented with a bag of toffees, a knitted scarf and a bracelet made of shells, and made to sit at the table on a specially prepared chair raised up by an enormous stuffed cushion. They talked in English most of the time, but occasionally the three would whisper things to each other in that strange melodious language Cathy had heard on the bus. Shawna smiled and laughed and wiped away a few stray tears as she served up the simple meal. Ruari kept thumping John on the back and filling up his glass with dark beer.

Just as Ruari finished saying a simple grace in Gaelic the cottage door opened and in crept a shadow of a boy, painfully thin and bent, with a tousle of coppery hair.

'This is Liam, John.' explained Aoife.

'Hello, Liam. I'm very pleased to meet you.' John smiled at the boy who nodded back. 'I know all about what you've been through and I'm sorry for that. I used to work at St Joseph's myself.'

Shawna took a dish, filled it with food and handed it over to the boy.

'Here you are, *cuisle mo chroidhe.*'

Liam looked around at everyone, nodded again and walked back out.

'Don't worry. It's not because of you and Cathy being here. We cannot ever make him sit at the table to eat with us. He takes his food away and eats alone, sitting on a log or in the bad weather in father's fishing hut. Like a dog. It's as if he fears it being stolen from him.'

'Would he tell me his story about Letterfrack school, do you think, so that I can write down his testimony and add it to mine? Then I'll take it to the Clifden gardai. Someone has to start telling the world about the evil goings on at St Joseph's.'

'In God's name too, let it be ended.' Ruari crossed himself.

'A few boys have told their story, John, and no-one has ever believed them.' Aoife shook her head.

'Or, more like, no-one has been brave enough to act on their stories. The Christian Brothers have a fearsome hold over this country. So many judges, politicians, military and police were educated by them. But I have nothing at all to lose, and I cannot hold my tongue any longer. I have been trying to get our Sinn Féin candidate in Kilkenny, Thomas Derrig, to do something about what's going on out here. Believe it or not, there's a St Joseph's Industrial School in Kilkenny too and I wouldn't be at all surprised if the same dreadful things were happening there. I'm hopeful that Derrig will at least feel he should look into the one on his doorstep.'

'Please God, let it be stopped, for all those poor boys like our Liam.'

When the meal was over, John stood to leave the table.

'Cathy, you stay here with Aoife. I'm just off for a little walk by myself. Maybe Aoife will take you down to the beach and show you the "mackerel-crowded seas" if you ask nicely.'

John opened the cottage door and closed it gently behind him. Cathy knew where he was going. Tomorrow she would ask to see the graves herself.

Aoife started clearing the table with her mother, but Shawna pushed her and Cathy out of the door. 'You go now, while the sun is out.'

Even though the sky was almost clear of clouds, and the sun was shining cheerfully, the cool wind produced a rash of goose bumps on Cathy's arms as she and Aoife made their way down the pebble path to the shore.

'Can you wait for me a second please, Aoife?' asked Cathy and she turned and raced back to the cottage to pick up her new scarf.

Over the next three days, Cathy couldn't get enough of being by the infinite sea. Like the flames of a fire, it was never still and every second created a new picture to commit to memory. She spent as much time out on the shingle as she was allowed, with her father or Aoife, or both, or sometimes with just Ruari and Liam, watching them sort through their haul of silvery fish. How fierce the waves could be, roaring out on the horizon, but how delicate and fragile they became as their frilly edges shushed onto the pebble beach.

******

Back in Rowanbridge, Hannah was enjoying spending time with her two old school friends, which meant she could offload Rose into the arms of Ellen or Visha whenever Rose was being clingy. Visha proved to be an extremely able child-minder and was full of ways to ways to make Rose giggle or concentrate which amazed Hannah and Ellen.

'Well, aren't you the dark horse with your kiddy-wrangling,' remarked Ellen.

'When you've a waiting room full of tired and sickly children and you need to examine them, you have to learn little tricks like this to get through the day.' Visha was making a coin appear and disappear in her hands to Rose's amazement and delight.

Ellen recounted her visit to Maisie and Eamonn's increasingly crowded home; the recent arrival of a second batch of twins had brought the O'Toole brood to four children under three.

'But Maisie is as happy as larry and just smiles through the chaos. I must say, who would have thought Eamonn was hiding such a ferocious pair of balls in those skinny trousers of his.'

'Ellen!'

'What? I thought doctors were supposed to be unshockable.'

Aggie cooked their meals over the weekend, but Hannah insisted that she at least sit down with them to eat, before she cleared up and made her way home. Ellen pronounced merrily 'isn't it great being all girls together again' but, when Rose was settled in bed, she unpacked her anxieties about Seamus and sought the advice of her friends about their endless engagement. Twelve years now they had been tied to each other.

'I think you should face facts, Ellen. Seamus is clearly avoiding marriage for some reason. Better to make a clean break. And you're not getting any younger.' Visha's no-nonsense approach to life seemed brutal but Ellen had to concede that she was probably right.

'It's not your fault, love. It's that bloody war. But it might be kinder to set him free – and yourself too.' Hannah hated seeing her friend in such low spirits.

'I don't think he'd be avoiding marriage if it were you he was engaged to, Hannah.'

On their second evening in Rowanbridge, Ellen asked to go into the pub next door for a few drinks, just for a laugh. 'There are no men here to disapprove, so why not.'

A hush descended over the assembled customers of McDermott's bar when the three women walked in, but it didn't take long for the buzz of conversation to return to its normal level. 'Gin and tonics all round, please, Jimmy.' Hannah smiled pleasantly at her barman.

'Are these on the house, now? Only, I don't want anyone saying the money is short when the takings are counted.'

'Well, as that will be me, Jimmy, you don't need to worry yourself.' You bloody, insolent bastard, thought Hannah as she led her friends over to the table next to Tricky Byrne and his pint of Guinness. Not a scrap of respect. Hannah introduced her friends to Tricky, but Ellen's attempt to engage him in conversation fizzled out when Tricky just kept turning his face away to gaze at his pint.

Saying goodbye to Ellen and Visha on Monday morning was harder than Hannah had anticipated. The memories of their time at school together in Dalkey had taken her back to such happy times. How simple life had been then, when the biggest challenge on the horizon was what to cook for the monthly student meal.

'Make sure you write to me, you two, as I'm the one stuck out here in the backwoods. Tell me what's going on in the big, wide world.' With promises all round, the three friends parted company.

An hour or so later, Aggie was out in the backyard hanging out laundry when the knock came to the front door, so Hannah came out of the study to answer it. It was Tricky.

'Your man there - Boyle. Fella's robbing you blind. Watched him pocket money again before you came in last night.'

'He's also bloody rude.' And, standing on the doorstep, Hannah and Tricky hatched a plot.

******

On Sunday, Shawna, Ruari and Aoife had taken Cathy and Liam to Mass at Claddaghduff in the trap. Her Daddy seemed less irritated by the de Bhailises' devotion than when she went to church with her Mammy back home in Rowanbridge. After the Mass, Aoife took Cathy and Liam walking, right over the wide blond strand beyond the church, to Omey Island and showed her the graves of her sister Ailsa and niece Mairé. It was so peaceful at their graveside, with no houses or people in sight on the scarcely populated tidal island and the only sounds were the wheeling gulls over the tireless sea.

Aoife knelt by the graves and closed her eyes. Cathy realised she was saying a prayer and thought maybe she should too – Mairé was her sister after all - but she stayed standing next to Liam. After a few minutes' reflection, they began the long walk back across the sand to Claddaghduff and then through the lanes to Cleggan, where they found John helping Ruari mend nets at the harbour.

Cathy loved to pick up the stones and shells on the beach. For a girl who had never been by the sea before it was like Aladdin's cave, so many treasures just waiting to be discovered. She resolved to find twenty identical cockle shells to place on Mairé's grave and she wondered whether polished white pebbles would make acceptable silver bells. As for the 'pretty maids' well, hopefully the daisies growing around the stones would do. Though she could tell, from the way everyone spoke of the little girl, that Mairé had never been 'contrary' in the slightest.

On their third day, Cathy woke to hear the wind blowing hard. There were dark clouds gathering from the west. Cathy hoped that Ruari would be safe out alone in his tiny boat. He was alone because John had finally persuaded young Liam to go with him into Clifden to visit the Gardai and make a statement about St Joseph's Industrial School at Letterfrack and the shameful goings-on there. Liam had not wanted to go at first, shaking his head whenever Ruari said his wrongs should be righted and that he deserved justice. It was only when John had said that, by bearing witness to the police, Liam might be able to end the suffering of other pupils like him that the boy agreed to go.

Over the last three days, Liam had slowly become less shy in front of Cathy. He still said very little but he had taught her how to skim stones through the tops of the waves and, most crucially, how to identify the perfect flat stones to use. Cathy could now make the stone skip two or three times before it sank but she wanted to match Liam's six or seven. Practice, practice, just the same as with her piano scales.

Aoife plaited Cathy's golden hair to save the painful evening task of teasing out the tangles the fierce wind delighted in weaving. As she picked her path over the pebbles, Cathy was pleased that she didn't need to keep pushing her hair out of her eyes to spot the prettiest shells. Their nacreous inner surfaces fascinated her. How could something so exquisite - more beautiful than diamonds - not be worth a fortune? Well, she would collect them and offer up her bounty to Rose when she got home. As she stood up, holding a prize shell, Cathy felt a stone whizz past her right ear and out to sea. Liam and Daddy were back.

That afternoon, Cathy asked Liam to come with her on the long walk to Omey Island as he wasn't out fishing with Ruari. They were just about to step onto the pristine beach, when Cathy took Liam's hand to pull him back.

'Just look at it. It's perfect, isn't it, with all the patterns of sea ripples carved into the sand. It seems a bit of a shame to walk on it and leave our great shoeprints all over it, don't you think? If we take off our shoes, at least we'll make marks that could have been made by monks who first went out to Omey. And the sea will wash away everything tonight, anyway. The sea can wash almost anything clean again.'

Cathy looked back on their trail of barefoot prints when they were halfway over to Omey.

'They could be Robinson Crusoe and Man Friday's footprints, you know.' But Liam had never heard of *Robinson Crusoe*, let alone read it. Cathy offered to send him the book but that forced him to admit that he could barely read at all, though Aoife was now teaching him.

Liam looked on as Cathy arranged the cockle shells and white pebbles as prettily as she could on Mairé's grave.

'Are your mother and father alive, Liam.'

'I never knew my father, but I guess my mother is still alive in Cork. Somewhere.'

'Maybe you could go and live with her.'

'I think she'd just send me back to the Christian Brothers. I'd rather stay here, if I can, helping Ruari.' And Liam looked out to sea as if hoping to see the little fishing boat making its way to harbour.

'Now Liam, when I'm gone home please try and keep the pattern looking like this. And replace any shells that get broken or blown away. Will you do that for me, please?'

'I will. I promise.' Liam nodded seriously.

Cathy was confident he would keep his promise, but for how much longer would he be able to stay in Cleggan? One day, he would surely leave and go back to his hometown of Cork, if he could evade the brothers of St Joseph's at least.

Supper that evening – their last before their journey home the next day - was a fish stew with the added luxury of one of Ruari's precious lobsters caught that morning. Liam, as usual, came in to take his portion away to eat in solitude. As he turned for the door, Cathy got off her chair and took his hand.

'Liam, it would be lovely if you could stay with us for our last meal. So that we can be all together.' Liam paused for a moment and then drew up the three-legged stool to join the others at the table.

Over supper, John recounted how the Clifden Gardai had reacted to his and Liam's story that morning. At first, the duty constable had listened but was disinclined to make any sort of official record of their complaints. But John had insisted and finally demanded to see the sergeant who reluctantly took a form out of the drawer and made notes.

'He kept saying that no-one was likely to believe Liam's word against the word of the Holy Brothers, and that my testimony was all very well, but I was going to be a long way away in County Kilkenny after the next day. What more can I do, do you think? I shall give Thomas Derrig a full account including the negligence of the Gardai when I'm home.'

'Well, maybe I should go too and tell them what my parents and I have seen with our own eyes.' Aoife put her hand on John's. 'As God is my witness, we must tell them about the half-starved wretches we see working on the

Letterfrack School fields. They just need to go and visit the place to open their eyes.'

'People can be very blind when they don't want to see, you know.' Shawna put her arm around Liam's stiff shoulders. 'We shall just have to save these poor souls one at a time.'

An hour later, Cathy lay in the little bed, next to her Daddy's big bed, trying hard to get to sleep. Normally, the crashing of the sea sent her off within minutes but there was too much to think about tonight. This bed must have belonged to Mairé; her head must have rested on this pillow and she would have looked over at that strange picture on the bedroom wall of Christ with his sacred heart on show, looking for all the world like a big, radiant strawberry.

Cathy could hear voices outside; it was her Daddy and Aoife. She must try to be asleep before he came up to the bedroom. Her Daddy seemed very happy here. Sure, he was angry about Letterfrack school, but somehow he still seemed more at peace. Soon, he would be back in Rowanbridge, trying to be a landlord and shopkeeper, and attempting to keep her Mammy satisfied. Cathy was not looking forward to those tussles and tensions one little bit. Maybe if they could all come and live out here by the sea, everything would be fine. Cathy knew that she, at least, would certainly come back one day.

Chapter 13 - December 1930

'Cathy, please take very special care of those plates. They belonged to your Grandmother Evaline, and I cherish them. They can't be replaced for love nor money.'

Aunt Stasia was directing operations with military discipline. Peter had also been roped in to help set up the buffet table; he spent about five minutes taking cutlery and napkins from the kitchen to the dining room, but only Cathy was deemed responsible enough to carry the heirloom china. Peter soon disappeared upstairs to join his brothers and Rose in the nursery as Cathy diligently finished the task. She didn't mind. She was the eldest of all the children after all and her Mammy couldn't do much to help, being six months pregnant. Cathy knew that everything she did instead of Hannah was helping the baby grow and thrive.

Tonight, Stasia was hosting a New Year's Eve supper at the villa for several family friends. After the supper, Hannah, John and Seamus were going to play for everyone. The three had been practising the Mozart Divertimento for the last two days ever since Seamus had arrived from Dublin.

'I reckon my snobby sister thinks she can create a salon here in sleepy Rowanbridge like our Aunt Lily's in Dublin,' Hannah remarked to John. 'She's even more deluded than I thought.' Deluded or not, it was still an opportunity for Hannah to show off her musical skills and so she was taking it seriously and practising hard.

Cathy didn't understand why Seamus seemed so much happier than the first time he had come to Rowanbridge considering Ellen had broken off their engagement soon after she had stayed with her Mammy last July, while she and Daddy had been in Connemara. Grown-ups were confusing, but her Mammy explained that Ellen had 'released' Seamus and that's why he was feeling so much better.

Aggie had been drafted into the preparations too and had set up a production line in the kitchen; she was slicing bread for Bessie to butter and then Maud was making up sandwiches from the ham that Uncle Edmund was carving off the bone.

'Bessie, don't forget to put out the pickles. But leave the trifle in the pantry until the savouries have been cleared away. And Maud, you'd better go up and check on the children. It's far too quiet up there. The little ones need to be packed off to bed as soon as possible.' Stasia was in her element, presiding over the 'staff' which included her son and niece.

At seven o'clock guests started arriving; Louisa and Nicholas Byrne with his mother, Father Stephen, Mrs Magee and various other friends and acquaintances whom Stasia deemed respectable enough, or whom she thought would appreciate some chamber music. Tricky had declined the invitation and was in his usual seat at McDermott's Bar. Shortly afterwards, Hannah and Seamus arrived at the kitchen door, Seamus carrying both their instruments.

'John will come along just as soon as Aggie gets back to take over from him in the pub, Stasia.' Hannah replied to Stasia's anxious enquiry. 'We can't afford to close on New Year's Eve and there's no Jimmy Boyle now. So, don't wait for him before you serve the food.' Hannah took Seamus through to the hall to hang up their coats.

'To be honest, I'm relieved to be going back. It's not exactly my type of music,' Aggie whispered to Bessie. 'They must have played it through twenty times at least since he arrived. But I'll just take a couple of these sandwiches home with me.'

Since the Cleggan trip, John had been forced to become the regular barman at McDermott's pub, because Hannah had taken it upon herself to fire Jimmy Boyle while he was away. She said John would never have got around to the job. Together with Tricky Byrne, Hannah had devised a plan to catch Jimmy taking money from the bar till. Before opening time, Hannah had swapped five single pound notes in the till for five notes on which she had made a small mark with one of Cathy's red crayons. Tricky took up his post in the corner of the bar with his pint and made sure that Jimmy had pocketed at least two of the notes before he tipped the wink to Hannah near to closing time. Hannah waited until Tricky was the only customer left and then she confronted Jimmy, asking him to turn out his pockets with Tricky standing by as both witness and protector. Sure enough, there were the two marked notes in his hand. Caught, literally red-handed, Jimmy stormed off into the night cursing Hannah and saying that the Fitzgeralds were a joke and would never cope without him.

On his return from Connemara, John listened to Hannah's story of the event. He was visibly shocked and appalled that Hannah had not given the man at least one warning and a second chance. 'Second chance? Are you mad John? Exactly how destitute did you want us to become before we gave that idle thieving bastard the heave-ho?'

They debated whether to find a replacement for Jimmy, but Hannah thought they should try and absorb the duties themselves, to save money. Hannah assured John that she would help out more with all the book-keeping and with the shop so that he could devote himself to the pub. But then, in September, when she announced that she was three months pregnant, John had forbidden her to do anything strenuous.

When Eileen resigned back in August, clearly in protest at her husband's sacking and having found herself a job at The Monster House in Kilkenny, everything had fallen on John's shoulders. In the months since, he had surrendered every activity that gave him any pleasure at all: playing the cello, attending political meetings, and even spending time with Cathy and Rose reading or walking.

When he was finished in the pub – usually about half past eleven - he would collapse into bed exhausted and could barely read a poem or two before he fell into a deep sleep. There was no longer time for any music from the gramophone in the mornings. By the time Cathy awoke, her Daddy was already up and sweeping out the bar next door or loading up crates with empty bottles, or away stocking up the shop before Hannah opened up.

So, when Seamus arrived after Christmas, Cathy was thrilled to see her father take his cello out of its case for the first time in months. The deep warmth of its timbre made her spine tingle. Unlike Aggie, she would happily have listened to the three of them practising the Mozart for the entire day; she found that the more she heard it the more she wanted to hear it again. She realised with sadness that this evening's performance would be the last time she would hear it for a while.

'Cathy, could you take this plate of sausage rolls and offer them around to people please. Tell them to watch out as they're very hot.' Aggie handed down a full platter to Cathy. 'You're such a good girl, aren't you? I'm off now, to take over from your Daddy, but you'll help out Bessie here, won't you.' Aggie bent over to kiss Cathy's cheek, brushing a sausage roll off the dish in the process. She picked it off the floor and popped it straight into her bag. 'Waste not, want not.'

Cathy spent the next half hour taking round plate after plate of finger foods and then, conscious of Aunt Stasia's fierce scrutiny, clearing away the precious china plates. After a few initial 'How you've grown, Cathy,' or 'What a helpful girl you are,' comments from guests, she was largely ignored, which she was perfectly happy about.

'Make sure you get something to eat yourself now, girlie,' said Bessie. 'Do you like these little mushroom vol-au-vents or the stuffed eggs maybe?' But Cathy was saving herself for the trifle, her absolutely favourite dessert, which only appeared at Christmas time or on occasions like this. This was one time she was not prepared to stand at the back of the queue. She followed Bessie into the dining room to make sure she was the very first person to be served the creamy, custardy, fruity bowl of heaven.

Cathy took her serving of trifle over to stand in the corner where her mother was sitting, chatting gaily to Seamus. She thought how beautiful her Mammy looked tonight. She hadn't worn that necklace for years.

'That looks delicious, Cathy,' said Seamus, dipping his finger into the cream and then into his mouth. 'I love a spot of trifle meself.'

'Would you like this bowlful? I can get another one.'

'That's very kind, but there's no way I am stealing trifle from a child. I'll get myself some. Can I get you any, Hannah?'

Hannah shook her head, 'No, the nerves are kicking in. Maybe after we've played…'

John arrived at just gone half past eight. He took a glass of punch from Bessie but turned down all offers of food and made a brief tour of the dining room greeting all the guests to finish up in the corner where his wife was watching Seamus scoff down his second bowl of trifle.

'Come on you two. We'd better get ourselves set up in the drawing room. I don't want to start playing any later than nine o'clock. I need to get back to let Aggie have a decent night of New Year's Eve fun.'

'Ah, you don't need to worry about her, John. She'll be enjoying the attention from her many gentlemen admirers.'

At nine o'clock, Stasia clapped her hands for silence and invited the guests to take a seat in the drawing room where the string trio was ready to play.

Cathy and Peter sat cross-legged on the floor, right at the front.

'You'll like this Peter.'

'Mmm. I don't think I will, but it's better than going to bed.'

Cathy thought her father looked very tired as the trio began to play, but the music unfolded and his energy visibly lifted. It was wonderful to see the three players listening so intently to each other, and the two men watching Hannah for the slightest signal for tempo or dynamic.

Cathy had heard the Divertimento many times now but she had never found the second movement quite so moving. She tried not to blink, otherwise the tear sitting in the corner of her eye would roll down her cheek and she didn't want her parents to think she was sad. She was very far from sad; watching her Mammy and Daddy doing something together that they loved made her very happy indeed. Mozart plus trifle; days were rarely as full of treats as that New Year's Eve.

Chapter 14 - March 1931

The weather was wicked all through that winter of 1930 into 1931, but there were worse things for people in Rowanbridge to endure.

Mr O'Rourke hadn't worked since Christmas. Like several other families, the O'Rourkes had become reliant on the alms given out by Father Stephen, donated by the better-off families of the parish.

One way the Fitzgeralds had been able to help the O'Rourkes was by giving a job in the shop to fifteen-year-old Bobby - or Roberta, as Aunt Stasia insisted on calling her. As Hannah grew heavy and weary in late pregnancy, she relied on Bobby to be her legs and hands. By February, Hannah would stay at home most of the day, doing accounts or orders, only popping in once a day to see if Bobby was OK on her own. But the girl was a gem.

Rose's third birthday in February had been a very modest celebration, with a cake and candles for sure but only two presents from her parents and they were a book and a jigsaw that had belonged to Cathy before her. Not that Rose knew or cared. The news that Sam McCarthy's three-year-old brother had died of measles the previous week, because they couldn't afford to call out the doctor, made Rose's hand-me-down presents look like luxuries.

Inevitably, the less money people had, the less they could spend in the shop and the pub. Some nights there were maybe only three or four customers drinking. But Tricky was always there, on his chair behind the door, drinking his three pints of Guinness steadily over three hours. Tricky rarely spoke to anyone, but he always reported to John when another McDermott's regulars had switched their custom to McLoughlin's. Since Jimmy Boyle had started working there, several old boys had made known their preference for

Jimmy's gossip and licentious banter by abandoning John's calm and serious stewardship of McDermott's.

'Piano-playing now. Down the road,' Tricky delivered the latest news about the rival pub as he took the creamy pint from John's hand and tucked himself into his corner.

'Will you be taking your custom back there then, Patrick?' John asked as he polished a glass.

'Nope. Don't like music.' So that was one customer safe, for now at least.

That morning, Cathy woke to hear her father outside, bringing out casks from the cellar for collection. She rose and brought her mother a tray of tea at seven o'clock before getting a scratchy Rose up and dressed. The new baby wasn't due for another two weeks but Hannah looked marooned, huge in the bed there.

'Mammy, you know my brown coat that I haven't worn for a year or so. Can I give it to Bernie please?' Cathy had noticed that Bernie's winter coat was badly torn and frayed at the armhole, beyond repair in truth. Hannah hesitated, worrying perhaps whether they would need to put it to some other use, but seeing the hope on Cathy's face she gave in.

'Whatever you like, Cathy, if you're sure you won't need it. Could you fetch me up my porridge as soon as Aggie arrives please? And thank you for the tea,' she shouted at Cathy's disappearing back.

After breakfast, with a very grumpy Aggie banging around in the kitchen, Hannah fetched the brown coat and stuffed it inside her satchel.

'Where are you going with that coat?'

'Mammy says it's OK to give it to Bernie. Her coat is threadbare and all worn.'

'Well, isn't your mother just the Lady Bountiful now. Maybe she should pay her own staff before dispensing charity to the needy. Go on. I'll take over with Rose. Off you go now.'

Cathy left the house and passed by her father out on the pavement. Her Daddy grabbed her for a big hug. He felt freezing cold to her touch but the hug was the warmest thing she had been given all morning.

'That's a very stuffed satchel you have there, macushla. Are you sneaking Rose into school for the day?'

At break-time, Cathy showed Bernie the overcoat.

'It doesn't fit me any longer so Mammy thought you might like it.'

Bernie looked hard at Cathy. Bernie was a good two inches taller than Cathy but decided not to say anything in case the offer was withdrawn.

'Well, if it's just going begging...'

'It is. It's yours.'

Bernie exchanged her tight, bedraggled blue coat for the soft brown one with the velvet collar.

'This is grand. Bit short on the arms maybe but it'll be perfect for our trip - over to America.'

'You're going to America? When?' Cathy was surprised and impressed.

'After Easter.'

'All of you?'

'Oh sure.'

'When will you be back?'

'Whoops. I wasn't supposed to say anything, because Bobby has to hand her notice in first to your Mammy. We're going to America - all of us - for a better life, my Da says. We're not coming back. Not until we're rich anyway.'

Cathy wanted to cry but instead she smiled and put her arms around Bernie. 'That's exciting. I hope it all works out. And when your Daddy has become a millionaire you can come back and buy up all the Byrnes' land and farms.'

'And the Hughes's and your shop and your pub. And then you can work for the O'Rourkes instead of us always working for you.' This was, clearly, already a topic of conversation in the O'Rourke house.

As the three friends walked home later, Cathy wondered how many more times Bernie, Marion and she would share this journey, shuffling through leaves in the autumn, sliding on frozen puddles in winter, blowing raucous notes through fresh spring grasses, and picking blackberries in summer, all the while making sure to avoid Tricky Byrne. The three walked into the kitchen of the Main Street House hoping for bread and jam, only to hear loud bawling which Aggie was pretending wasn't happening.

'That's a very fine coat you have there, Bernie O'Rourke. I'm just making your mother some beef tea, Cathy, which you can take up to her. Go and see your new baby brother at the same time. I hope he's not going to be quite such a handful for long. Two weeks early, tore his way out and a pair of lungs on him fit to blow the house down. I'm sorry you two, but you'd better be off to your own homes now.'

A brother. Cathy felt nervous as she pushed open the bedroom door to find her father walking up and down, trying to pacify the baby, as her mother smiled radiantly in bed with her arm around Rose who was sitting as if hypnotised by all the screams.

'Cathy, my darling. Come and meet Fergus, your new brother.' Hannah took the cup from Cathy and waved her towards her two men.

John handed the noisy bundle into Cathy's expert arms. 'He's all yours.'

Cathy looked at her brother and saw a stranger. When she had first seen Rose, she had seen herself in the baby, but this one was a totally different beast: a big round head, dark hair beginning to curl as it dried, and sticky out ears.

'He looks just like your Mammy, doesn't he?' said John. 'I think he'll do a grand job looking after his two sisters when he's bigger, but until then you must look after him.'

Cathy looked down at him again. His screams were subsiding and Cathy helped him find his fist which he greedily sucked on. 'I just think he needs to feed, Mammy.' Cathy passed the baby to Hannah.

'Oh, here we go again then.' Hannah unbuttoned her nightdress. 'Not my favourite part of having a baby. Let's get those bottles sorted. But you do realise, don't you, that we are now only one child behind your Auntie Stasia.'

By the time St Patrick's Day arrived, Fergus had settled down nicely, waking just once during the night and then again at about half past five. Cathy often heard him first, grizzling away, and would get up to bring him into her room to stop him waking her mother, while John went downstairs to heat a bottle. Today, her father was already downstairs when she went in to lift Fergus out of his basket, down by her mother's side of the bed. Hannah moaned and stirred but did not wake as Cathy tiptoed over the creaking floor.

As Cathy picked up the baby, he stopped crying and opened his eyes to her. She loved his little determined cleft chin, just like her Mammy's. Cathy crept out of the bedroom taking a clean nappy for him with her.

'I've changed him, Daddy,' said Cathy, when her father appeared at her bedroom door with the warm bottle of milk.

'You are my darling Countess. Here's his bottle. Do you mind feeding him this morning? I would do it but there's so much to do today with it being St Patrick's Day, and your mother has *plans*, God help us.'

John turned and went back downstairs. Cathy looked down at Fergus, guzzling away, practically chewing the bottle. He was going to be a big lad and need a lot of feeding. She was sorry that this baby was not going to get all the time with her Daddy that she and Rose had been lucky enough to enjoy when they were little. Nobody could tell a fairy story or nursery rhyme like him, or sing such a sweet lullaby, but Cathy hoped she would make a good substitute. Bottle emptied and Fergus all full and floppy, Cathy climbed back into her bed with the baby and they both drifted away.

'Cathy! Cathy, wake up.' Rose had been sent upstairs by Aggie. It was now ten minutes past eight and she needed to be out of the door to school at half past.

'Sssh, Rose. Don't wake Fergus up.'

Cathy carried the sleeping baby back to their mother who was dressing.

'Don't leave him here, Cathy. I'm much too busy. Take him down in his basket to Aggie. She can mind him. Happy St Patrick's Day, by the way.'

At eleven o'clock, the whole school trooped off to the church next door, to celebrate St Patrick's Day. Most of the village was there too, including Hannah, Stasia and Edmund, many of them with frilly bunches of shamrock in their buttonholes. Father Stephen climbed the steps up to the pulpit to deliver the sermon. Cathy thought he looked like a kindly giant looking down on them all, and that maybe Jesus might have looked a bit like this dishevelled priest, with his dark hair that needed a cut and his scrubby beard. She wondered what on earth he could find new to say this year about Saint Patrick.

The first year she had come to mass on Saint Patrick's Day, Cathy had been most interested in the stories about the holy man banishing snakes from Ireland and the use of shamrock to illustrate the Trinity. Another year, Father Stephen had chosen the saint's day to talk about the sacred vocation of missionary work and encouraged all the children in the school to consider whether they could offer up their lives to save souls in other countries.

Last year, Father Stephen had used the day to praise tolerance and the acceptance of people different from ourselves. He emphasised the importance of welcoming people from other countries into Irish society – Saint Patrick had come from Roman Britain after all – and how Irish people, trying to build new lives in foreign countries, were benefitting from the kindness of strangers. Cathy thought about Bernie going to a new country soon and wondered how she would be welcomed.

Today, Father Stephen took his sermon from Saint Patrick's early years, living as a slave after he had been captured by pirates. St. Patrick had done the most menial jobs with a good spirit but had ended his life as the most holy and revered man in Ireland. Cathy decided she would never complain to Aggie again about being made to peel spuds or fold sheets.

Cathy ran home as soon as the end of school bell rang without waiting for Bernie and Marion, so she wouldn't be tempted to dawdle. Her parents were going to be busy this evening and she would be needed more than ever.

Outside the pub was the children's blackboard, propped against the wall: 'St Patrick's Day Céili, at McDermott's tonight. Music, dancing and free food.' it said, in green chalk. How exciting. Cathy knew she wouldn't be allowed in to watch, but she would certainly be able to hear the music.

The sound that greeted her as she walked into the kitchen didn't sound like dance music to her at all. It was the mournful cello music that her Daddy used to play back when he had the time to play at all. Aggie was cradling Fergus in her left arm while stirring a pot on the range with her right. Rose was sitting on the floor stroking Honey. The kitchen table was covered in plates of sandwiches and sliced-up pork pies.

'Here, take the boy off me quick. I need to get those plates covered up or the food'll be dry as old bones - if that bloody cat doesn't run off with it all first.'

Cathy happily took Fergus and sat at the table. 'Hi Rosie. Have you had a nice day? Shall we go and see what Daddy's doing?'

'No, Cathy. Don't go in to see your Daddy just yet. He'll come out when he's ready.' Aggie began laying dampened tea towels over the plates of food. 'He has had some very bad news in the post today. Do you remember that young lad out in Connemara? The one who ran away from the Brothers' school? Well, apparently the Gardai arrived and forced him to go back to the school.'

'Liam. Oh no. Poor Liam. How can they make him go back?'

'That's what his mother down in Cork wanted done with him, they said. And until he's fifteen he has no choice.'

'But Daddy went and told the Gardai all about how cruelly he had been treated.'

'That's the thing. Your father is blaming himself. Says if he had left well alone, the lad would still be safe with his in-laws.' There was a knock at the front door which Aggie went to answer. She returned with Ned McCarthy, him carrying a big rectangular case. 'You know Sam's Dad, Ned, don't you, Cathy. He's come to play his accordion for the céili.'

'That's a great pile of food you have there, Aggie.' The man's eyes widened as he lifted up the corner of the towels and he sneaked a piece of pie off the plate and straight into his mouth.

Aggie slapped his hand. 'Get off the food, Ned McCarthy. Now, put that accordion down and help me carry these behind the bar.'

They had been gone no more than two minutes before Hannah walked into the kitchen, carrying her violin case. 'How do I look, Cathy?' Hannah had draped a green scarf around her waist, tied a knot at the front so as to hide her post-pregnancy bump, and put a green ribbon in her hair holding a bunch of shamrock by her ear.'

'Very nice, Mammy. Very … green. Saint Patrick would be jolly pleased.'

'If this doesn't knock the stuffing out of McLoughlin's this evening, nothing will.'

Rose went over to her Mother and held up her arms to be lifted but Hannah took no notice of her or of the sleeping baby. She took her violin out of its case and opened the kitchen door to shout across the yard. 'Hey, Ned. Come on and get your accordion. We need to tune up.'

Cathy could barely believe it. Her Mammy was going to be part of the céili band. It was fun, she supposed, and it was just for one night, but she hoped news of it never reached her Auntie Stasia's ears.

'When your father comes out of his study, Cathy, tell him that we need him to open up in good time. Come on then, Ned, let's get over to the bar.'

Her father's playing stopped; jigs and ballads from the pub next door soon took its place. Cathy waited until twenty past six before tapping gently on John's study door.

'Come in.'

John was sitting at his desk. The lock of golden hair was in his hand and Cathy could tell he had been weeping. He looked ravaged.

'Just letting you know the time is getting on, Daddy.' She paused, then went over to his chair and put her arms around him. 'I'm very, very sorry about Liam. Do you think you can do anything else to get him out of there?'

'Not me, macushla. What can I do? I am useless. I tried to save him but I just made matters worse. I destroy everything I touch. I cannot run a business, I have thrown away all that I was given and I have brought my family to the edge of bankruptcy. And look at your mother. What have I brought her to?' He groaned and sunk his head into his hands. 'There was a time when she could have made a name for herself around the world as a professional violinist but now she's forced to play old tunes for drunken villagers to dance around to, while she's still bleeding from giving birth.'

'You haven't destroyed us Daddy.'

John took Cathy's arm and brought her round to stand in front of him. He put his hands on her shoulders.

'You are my beautiful Countess Cathleen. You were perfect from the moment you were born and even I couldn't do anything to spoil the beauty of your soul. You and Rose are the only things I can be proud of in my life.'

'And Fergus. We all love you very, very much.'

Her father wept. Cathy climbed onto his knees and put her arms around his neck. She offered him her hankie which he used and then put in his breast pocket.

'Thank you, macushla. Here - you take this in exchange and look after it now. It's a lock of your sister Mairé's hair that I have always treasured. You can see how exactly like yours it is. Never forget that you had an older sister once.'

'I won't Daddy. Not ever.'

Chapter 15 - April 1931

'Have you seen John anywhere, Aggie? I've looked high and low.' Hannah was tight-lipped. 'He's not in the pub. Maybe he's in the shop. Do you mind running down to check?'

The family was due to go over to the Hugheses for Easter Monday tea. Aggie returned saying the shop was all shut up.

'Bloody man. He's obviously gone off to Kilkenny to waste more time on politics, forgetting about us going to Stasia's.'

After a rushed tea over at the villa, Hannah and the three children walked back into the Main Street House.

'John? John!' Hannah shouted in the hallway. 'Is he not back, Aggie?'

'No sign, I'm afraid.'

'Well, can you just open up the bar and hang on while I run round the village.' But Hannah's search was fruitless. After walking around the streets looking for her husband, Hannah walked into the pub at just gone seven o'clock and sent Aggie home.

'You go now, Aggie. Cathy is fine with the babbies. Frankly, who needs my feckless husband anyway?' Tricky was sitting in his usual corner, listening.

'No man then?'

'No Tricky. John Fitzgerald has taken it upon himself to go off to Kilkenny for the evening, leaving me to cope with a busy pub all alone.' Hannah's Saint Patrick's Day Céili had made a real difference to the business, and Hannah would now play for half an hour most evenings to the delight of the other customers, if not Tricky himself.

Soon after eight o'clock, Tricky stood and came behind the bar beside Hannah.

'I'll serve. You play.'

'Well, that's very kind, Tricky. Yes, you can certainly help me out just for a little while. Just fifteen minutes or so. Thank you.'

By closing time, there was still no sign of John. He was usually back from his political meetings by nine at the latest. Tricky stayed to help Hannah wash glasses and then wished her goodnight.

'Thanks Tricky. You're a true friend. John's obviously stayed on drinking or something and missed the last bus.'

'It's fine, Hannah McDermott.'

Hannah went to bed alone that Easter Monday.

The next morning, Cathy was woken by a knock on the front door at what must have been just gone seven and heard Aggie answer it and then run upstairs, followed by the noise of two people going back down. A great and dreadful noise followed, like a giant piece of furniture being dragged across the floor or perhaps what the start of an earthquake would sound like, tearing open the ground.

Cathy got out of bed, her heart full of terror. She walked downstairs and into the kitchen. Her mother was on the floor on her knees, rocking back and forth with Aggie standing over her. Her father's body was spread-eagled on the kitchen table and Tricky Byrne was standing over it, with his sly, gloating face. She didn't need to be told that her Daddy was dead.

******

There were still white flowers from Easter Sunday all over the church four days later when John's funeral took place, but everyone in it was wearing black. As she walked up the aisle between her mother and grandmother, following the pall-bearers, Cathy scanned the congregation. She was sure many of these people had never even met her father, but a funeral was a good day out for people with no money for the picture house in Kilkenny.

The three chief mourners slid into the front row and Father Stephen started saying prayers. Then Felix Brennan began to play a piece that Cathy recognised from her mother's practice: the Bach *Chaconne*. As the violin keened, Cathy's thoughts went back and forth over the events since John had been carried home by Tricky. This is how it will be for the rest of my life, she thought: the time before Daddy died and the time after. How strange it was to be sitting here between her grandmother and mother, who had still not spoken a word to each other.

Hannah had stayed up in her bedroom yesterday afternoon when Lily arrived from Dublin bringing Letitia Fitzgerald and Felix Brennan with her, but Cathy was waiting for them all in the dining room, guarding her father's open coffin, as she had done for the last two days.

Cathy now knew what it meant to see someone collapse. Her grandmother had walked into the darkened room, as steely and resolute as Cathy knew her to be, but, on seeing her son in the open coffin, Mrs Fitzgerald's legs seemed to disappear into the carpet, and she was left sobbing on the floor.

Cathy ran to help her up, but she could only rise to her knees at first, clinging onto her grand-daughter moaning, 'John, John,' all the while. Eventually, Cathy managed to get Mrs Fitzgerald seated and went to fetch her a cup of tea. When she returned, her grandmother was standing by John's coffin, stroking his face and holding his hand.

'So cold. So cold. Why didn't I hold his hand more when it was warm and alive, Cathy?'

Cathy didn't think an answer was needed but just encouraged her Granny to sit and drink. The tea at least was good and hot.

'Tell me everything, Cathy. When your Aunt Lily arrived with the news on Tuesday – your Aunt Stasia had just telephoned her – she said that John had died in a field - I presume from a heart attack - and that he had been found there by a Mr Patrick Byrne. Is that right?'

'Yes, that's right, Granny. As far as I know.' No-one had told Cathy any details and even now, as she looked at her father's coffin, she wasn't any clearer about exactly how John had died.

The *Chaconne* ended. And now she heard Father Stephen say her name and she was dragged back to the present moment and the church full of mourners. The priest was talking about John, about the love he had for his family, his great intelligence and kindness, what a talented musician he had been, how much he would be missed by all who knew him. Thankfully, Father Stephen said very few prayers out of respect for John's atheism, but Hannah had insisted John be given some sort of Catholic burial, loudly supported by Stasia when Cathy had nervously questioned it.

'Cathy, of course your father must be buried properly in the sight of God. The more prayers we can all say for him the shorter his time in Purgatory. I think your father was a good enough man not to be sent to hell, despite being a heathen, if that's any comfort.'

Seamus stood and walked to the front of the church and started reading *The White Birds*.

'This was the first Yeats poem your Daddy ever read to me,' Hannah whispered to Cathy, and she took her daughter's hand.

Father Stephen blessed everyone and then the service was over and they all filed out behind the coffin to John's burial place, away from the other graves, in the corner by the hedge. A steady drizzle fell on the shuffling mourners and it was really quite cold. At least, Cathy felt very chilled and she could see her Granny shivering by the side of the open grave. She glanced sideways at her mother. Hannah was standing like a marble statue.

Since first seeing John's dead body, Hannah had been either frozen like this or a writhing, wretched, screaming heap of grief, but only when alone in the house with Aggie and the children. In front of others, of even her sister, she refused to share the pain she was feeling. Rose had become very wary of her mother and had stopped going to her in case she was screamed at, and instead she sought out Cathy or Aggie for anything she needed. Fergus had continued to smile, gurgle and bawl as normal, utterly unaware of the household's devastation.

Aggie was standing at the back of the mourners, sniffling loudly as she had been doing fairly constantly for the last four days. But she had managed to keep the family fed and clothed; Mr Fitzgerald had been such a kind and decent man to her, she kept saying to anyone who would listen.

Cathy had cried many bitter tears for her Daddy, of course. She was her Daddy's darling Countess Cathleen. But she tried to cry only at night-time, for the sake of Rose and Fergus.

The earth had been dug out and piled behind the grave. Some dead leaves had blown in which at least stopped it looking like a bottomless black pit. The pile of earth was sodden and sticky but Cathy could see some primroses and violets sticking out of the edge of the mound, not totally engulfed by the mud.

Chapter 16 - July 9th 1951

Cathy put her case inside the church porch, so that she could take her time looking at the graves. The birds were singing loudly but other than the scrunch of her shoes on the gravel paths there was no other noise.

Here were the graves of her grandfather, whom she had known well and loved so much, and her grandmother whom she knew only through the stories of her mother, Auntie Stasia and her Great-aunt Lily. Next to it was the grave of another James; James Hughes - Auntie Stasia's last baby, born many years after her other boys - had lived for only a few hours. The band of apostles would never be completed.

Cathy walked around all the paths seeing the names that had filled her childhood: Boyle, Magee, Byrne, O'Rourke, McLoughlin, O'Connor. Here were some McCarthys. Cathy remembered when little Kevin McCarthy had died. She wondered what his big, handsome brother Sam was now up to. She had kept a soft spot in her heart for Sam over all these years and that cheese and onion sandwich they had shared.

Finally, Cathy walked to the far side of the graveyard where her father was buried. The grave was well-kept, free of weeds, no moss on the stone and with fresh red roses in the vase. A precious life summed up in the bald inscription: John Fitzgerald 1888-1931.

Cathy stood looking and thinking for some time before placing the honeysuckle she had picked for her mother on her father's grave. She turned back to the church, picked up her case and continued her long walk round to Main Street.

Chapter 17 – April 1931

'Well, at least let us buy the shop from you, Hannah. The village needs a shop that opens.' Stasia was sitting in the Main Street parlour drinking the tea that Cathy had served while Hannah looked stonily out of the window.

'You can't just do nothing. Something needs to be sorted. You need money. You cannot run two businesses alone, with three children and just one servant, however loyal she is.' Stasia handed Cathy her empty cup, to be refilled. 'And you need to talk through what happened if you are ever going to recover. I am always available, with a listening ear, you know. Or Father Stephen of course.'

'I do talk to Stephen.'

It was true. Every day, Father Stephen would arrive after mass in the morning and Cathy would hear her mother wailing for an hour before he left. Hannah would then usually go to evening Benediction and stay to talk further with the priest.

In the intervening times, Hannah had just sat in the parlour, looking out into the street or she would go upstairs and listen to music on the gramophone. Yesterday, she had picked up her violin for the first time and tried to play the Bach *Chaconne* which caught Cathy off guard. It made her burst into tears at the memory of the funeral and that had startled Fergus and made Rose start crying too, without her knowing quite why.

'Anyway, you don't need to worry any longer, Stasia. The shop and pub will be open tomorrow and we will start getting back to normal. The children need that.'

'Who will mind the shop now that Roberta has gone off to America?'

'I shall do it myself, until I can find a good soul to replace her.'

'You can't do that and manage the pub, Hannah. You will wear yourself away.'

'I have help organised. Now, I'll see you on your way, Stasia, as I need to get on and sort out things ready for tomorrow.'

Cathy bid her aunt farewell. There had been too many good-byes in recent days. The day after the funeral, Slattery had come to the Main Street house and driven Cathy to the Kilkenny hotel where the elder Mrs Fitzgerald was staying. Her Grandma had talked a lot about her son John, Cathy's Daddy, when he was a child; how he was a natural teacher and should never have agreed to take on a business, and how, aged only nine, he had insisted on choosing the cello as his instrument even when he was too small for it after he had been taken to hear the Haydn cello concerto.

Cathy loved to hear all these stories but time ran out and she had to get back in the car to return home. Her Grandma embraced her for a long time, stroking her golden hair. As Cathy got into the back seat, her Granny bent and kissed her goodbye once more and said that Cathy was more than welcome to come and stay with her in Dalkey any time and for as long as she liked. Mrs Fitzgerald promised to write to Cathy every week and then waved her grand-daughter farewell as the car drew away. By the next day, the whole Dublin contingent had disappeared.

Saying good-bye to Bernie on the Monday had been hard too, but at least Bernie was excited and looking forward to new and hopefully better things across the Atlantic. Cathy took her some humbugs for the journey and a copy of *Little Women*.

'It's the only American story I had. My granny gave it to me last Christmas. I loved it and so will you, I think.'

'Aww, cheers, Cathy. You are my very best friend and I'll never forget you. You can come and visit us when we know where we're going to live. At least I'll always know where I can find you.' They gave each other a long hug.

'I'm so sorry about your Daddy, but don't worry about him being buried in unconsecrated ground. God won't care about that.'

Despite that unintentional punch to her stomach, Cathy had said nothing in response but hugged Bernie even harder. After school the next day she had knocked on Father Stephen's door and asked to see him. He looked rather nervous when his housekeeper showed Cathy into his study.

'Cathy, my child, come in and have a chair. How can I help you?'

'Father, I just wanted to ask... is my father buried in unconsecrated ground?'

Father Stephen let out a long sigh. 'Yes, he is, Cathy. That's why he is resting over by the hedge.'

'Why does he have to be there?'

Father Stephen paused and rubbed his stubbly chin for a moment. 'Well, it's like this, Cathy. Your father always said that he had no faith and that he wanted no truck with the church. I only agreed for his funeral to take place in church because that's what your mother wanted. Funerals are really for those left behind, I always think.'

'But what does it mean? Will he never get to Heaven now? And will my mother not be buried with him, when she dies?'

'Oh Cathy, you ask questions that I have no certain answers to. None of us understands the extent of God's love and forgiveness – we all need that, heaven only knows. The best you can do is to keep saying prayers of intercession for your father and let us all hope we shall be reunited with him in Heaven one day.'

Father Stephen bid farewell to a partly reassured Cathy at his front door. She went to stand by her father's grave, shaded by the hawthorn and elder but now covered with smooth earth. The primroses and violets were in full bloom and Cathy picked a few to lay on the grave as she asked

God to look kindly on her darling father and to take him up to heaven.

Back at home, Cathy heard the front door close. She began clearing up the tea-cups before her mother walked back into the parlour.

'Sit down Cathy. I want to talk to you.' Cathy took the hard chair by the door and waited as her mother gathered her composure. 'This has been very hard for all of us. It will continue to be painful but we will survive. We must all work as hard as we can, and I know I don't need to say that to you because you have never done anything else. I know I am to blame in some ways for your father's death. He never wanted to come here but he did it because I asked him, but it killed him in the end. I hope you will forgive me. We could sell up and buy a small house somewhere, but I fought to have this business and I intend to keep it.'

'I was a very spoilt girl in my youth. I turned my back on God for a long time and what has followed is, I believe, a punishment for those sins. Your father and I gave you a poor start in life and kept you from the church but now I want to make that up to you. Now that you're eleven, I want you to start at Our Lady's Convent in Kilkenny in September, where Stasia and I went to school.'

'But you hated it, Mammy.'

'I did, but I was a stupid girl who had been allowed to run riot and have anything she wanted. The nuns only had my best interests in mind, but I wasted what would have been a great education. I want you to have what I threw away.'

'If that's what you want, Mammy…'

'I do want it. Unfortunately, Mother Veronica is still in charge, though she must be over seventy. Her memory is excellent and she remembers me only too well, I was such a thorn in her side. She could easily have turned you down, being my daughter, but thankfully Father Stephen has made a personal plea and told her that you are nothing like me.' Hannah laughed ruefully. 'He impressed upon her your dutifulness, your devotion and your discipline. Despite her initial misgivings she has said yes. So, you will start there next term. That's all. Now come and kiss me.'

Cathy approached her mother's chair. This was the first time her mother had embraced her since her father's death. It felt good to be back in someone's arms. 'I'll try not to let you down, Mammy.'

'You could never do that, Cathy. Now off you go. I can hear Fergus crying.'

Chapter 18 – September 1931

The summer months were frantically busy for all of them. Hannah repainted the walls of the shop and pub herself and moved the furniture around. Cathy was always on hand to look after Rose and Fergus when Aggie had to go home in the evenings, but her mother also expected her to clear out the pub in the mornings, washing glasses and sweeping the floor, given she had 'all the time in the world' apparently, as it was the school holidays.

In July, Aggie moved out of her rented room and into one of the spare bedrooms in Main Street.

'You see, it'll save you money, Aggie, and it means I never have to worry about the children,' pronounced Hannah as Aggie muttered something about a pig in a poke as she lugged her battered cases up to the first floor.

In August, Mrs McCarthy, Sam's mother, started working in the shop in the mornings, when Hannah was busy doing accounts, re-stocking and ordering supplies – and going to morning mass. Hannah took over the shop at two o'clock but was back ready to open the pub at six-thirty on the dot.

It seemed there was very little that Hannah couldn't do herself – carrying crates of full and empty bottles, polishing tables, chatting up the delivery men – apart from taking barrels up and down to the cellar. But she had persuaded Tricky Byrne to do that job the once or twice a week necessary, in exchange for a free pint of Guinness every night.

Cathy hated seeing Tricky doing the jobs that her father had always done, but, for the sake of her mother, she buried her loathing of the man. Stasia was appalled at what Hannah was prepared to do, but the more Stasia expressed her horror, the more Hannah delighted in doing it.

Mrs Fitzgerald was true to her word and every week Cathy would receive a letter, and sometimes a little parcel with a book or a piece of music in it, not that Cathy got much time to play the piano, except in the evenings and, even then, she didn't want to wake up Fergus.

But the best thing that happened to Cathy over the summer was her bicycle. It was a surprising gift from her mother, bought for a nominal amount from Mrs Magee who said her son hadn't ridden it for at least ten years. Sam McCarthy helped Cathy learn to balance until she was steady enough to wobble around the green on her own. She was sad when Sam no longer had to put his arms around her to use the gears or to stop her tipping over, but the joy of a new skill was great compensation. She needed to improve fast if she was going to be safe cycling in to Kilkenny every morning for school and then home again.

But when her first day at her new school arrived, she did not cycle; Father Stephen wanted to take her and Marion in his car and he said he would pick them up in the afternoon.

'I was the convent chaplain you know when I was first ordained and before I came to Rowanbridge.' Father Stephen chatted away to the girls as he drove along the lanes towards Kilkenny. 'I was terrified of Mother Veronica myself at first but she has a kind side to her that you'll discover eventually. I promise. To be honest, I was frightened of all the nuns, and even more terrified of the girls. I still sometimes go back in to say Mass when their chaplain is away or sick.'

The first morning passed quickly in a whirl of new people, places and routines. Cathy was pleased that she at least had Marion with her, however annoying she could be at times.

After lunch, one of the nuns came up to Cathy and said that Mother Veronica wished to see her in her office and led her through the polished corridors. 'Just wait there and she will call for you.' Cathy stood and looked up and down the wooden-floored passageway; she wondered just how many nuns' knees and arms had been exhausted over the years to produce such a deep shine.

'Enter.'

So, this was the formidable Mother Veronica, seventy-six years old and all of five foot nothing. Cathy extended her hand but it was not taken. The Mother Superior sat down again but did not offer Cathy a chair.

'I wanted to see you in person, Cathleen, to impress upon you how very much you owe to Father Stephen. Without his extreme praise for you and his assurances about your character, there is no way I would be allowing Hannah McDermott's daughter into this school. I don't know how much your mother has told you about her time here, but she was without doubt the worst girl we have ever had: disruptive, deceitful, lascivious... I won't go on. If that were not enough to condemn you, I hear that your father had no religion at all and was an idle incompetent who brought ruin on his family and then proceeded to commit the ultimate sin of taking his own life. I will give you no second chances, Cathleen. Let us hope you have inherited the virtues of your aunt, Anastasia. Make every day count and ask the Lord for his mercy. You will need all his help to overcome what must be the worst set of parents in all Ireland.'

Mother Veronica took up her pen again and began writing. Cathy was incapable of speech or movement. Had she really just heard that her father had killed himself?

'You may go to your lessons now.'

Cathy managed to leave and close the door behind her but she stood for many minutes outside the door contemplating what she had just learned.

******

It was nearly eleven o'clock that evening when Hannah finally came up to bed. She was just doing up her nightdress when Cathy knocked and walked into the bedroom. Hannah said nothing but got into the double bed and laid back her head wearily. No magic in that ship any more, Cathy thought sadly.

'I'm sorry to disturb you, Mammy, but this can't wait. Mother Veronica asked to see me today - to warn me that I am there on trial, I suppose – and she said lots of unkind nonsense about you. But she also said a terrible thing - that Daddy had killed himself. Is she right? I thought you said he had had a heart attack. I'm sorry, I know this is difficult but I have to know Mammy. You do see that, don't you?'

Hannah lifted her hand and covered her eyes, before letting it fall back onto the sheets. She patted the bed.

'Come and sit here with me, Cathy, my angel.'

Cathy sat nervously on the edge of the bed but Hannah took her arm and brought her closer to her until Cathy was lying alongside her mother.

'I hoped you'd never have to know. But yes, I'm afraid your poor father did take his own life. He must have been out of his mind, of course, otherwise he would never have done such a thing to us all.'

'Why? Did he leave any note for you – or for me?'

'Nothing. I'm sorry. I suppose it might help to know what was going on inside his troubled mind but we can only surmise that the sheer weight of worries tipped him into insanity.'

'Can I ask – how did he kill himself?'

Hannah shut her eyes and tightened her hold on Cathy.

'Do you really want to know? I guess you do. You have every right to know.'

Hannah put her left hand to her forehead and sighed.

'He was found hanging in Cromwell's Tower. Tricky found him there that morning when he went to fetch the cows for milking.' Hannah let out an agonised groan and paused for a minute. 'He cut him down before anyone else could see and I'm grateful for that. I didn't want to see your father like that and I don't want anyone to know about his shame – the state he was in - so I have tried to let as few people as possible know that he died by his own hand; your Aunt Stasia of course, and Aggie laid him out so couldn't fail to see what had happened. Father Stephen had to know. And then Tricky himself. I have no idea how that woman found out. I suppose Stephen told her, thinking she would be compassionate and have more sense than to tell you.'

'So, Granny doesn't know.'

'No. and I have no intention of telling her. If you feel you should, I cannot stop you. But Rose and Fergus must never know. Promise me that.'

Cathy hugged her Mammy close as both wept, eventually falling asleep in each other's arms.

Chapter 19 - March 1932

Over the next months, not a day went by without Cathy thinking about her father at some moment – often many times across the twenty-four hours; when she brushed Rose's golden hair in the morning, so like their father's, or when she polished the brass fittings on the bar each Saturday as John had always done or when she heard her mother practising the Chaconne. She could conjure up an almost complete picture of him in her mind: how he cut his food up, putting down his cutlery as he chewed; the lovely vanilla smell of his skin after he had shaved; the warm balm of his deep voice reading a story or singing a lullaby to Rose.

Not that there was time to lie around day-dreaming. These thoughts squeezed themselves into the tiny chinks of Cathy's consciousness as she was busy doing the multitude of chores she was assigned. Last month, de Valera had won the election. Her Daddy would have been ecstatic, but Cathy could take no pleasure from Fianna Fáil's victory; it had come too late to give her father any joy.

When she started menstruating - later than most of her schoolfriends - she didn't go to her mother for comfort or advice, but to Aggie, who found her towels, took away her bloody knickers to wash and made her some hot cocoa. Cathy never let her mother know when she was suffering from cramps and gritted her teeth through the all the physical work she was given.

Cycling was the nearest Cathy got to leisure time and she enjoyed the six miles to and from Kilkenny each weekday, even when it was raining. She loved the sensation of streaking past the hedgerows, scaring birds and rabbits out of the way. It was the best thinking time she had, immune from the endless demands of Rose and Fergus. She tried to think her way logically to the answers she so desperately sought about exactly why her father had taken his own life. The business had been in a bit of a state - but not the worst state ever. Things were actually getting a little better for them financially.

John had been frustrated about the political scene certainly, but surely that would never make a man despair so much as to commit suicide. There was always hope of change in politics. 'I'm off to vote in De Valera in memory of your Daddy,' her Mammy had said on polling day in February. And here was Ireland now, after the general election, with Fianna Fáil in power in the Dáil. She wished her Daddy could have shared Dev's victory.

It was true that the part John believed he had played in Liam's return to St Joseph's school had weighed heavily on his mind, but hardly so much as to inflict such a shocking blow to his family, thought Cathy. And even though she knew her mother had often been unkind to John and shown her disappointment in him, they had rarely quarrelled openly and they were still capable of being happy in each other's company – from time to time. She was sure her parents had still loved each other.

As the anniversary of her father's death approached, Cathy was no nearer to understanding what had delivered the final straw. The lack of any sort of note, message or even a sign from him inclined her to believe that his suicide was not long planned but a spontaneous act of madness.

Cathy talked to Father Stephen about this on many occasions, each time hoping to find some loophole in Catholic doctrine that would mean John had not committed a mortal sin and did not deserve to be banished to lie in unconsecrated ground in the graveyard. Father Stephen was sympathetic to her anguish and did his best to twist and bend the church's teaching to give her some comfort.

Her mother looked at John's suicide only through the lens of her own punishment from God; one more way to make her do penance for the many years she had spent rejecting the church.

'But a loving God wouldn't do that, Mammy,' Cathy would say to Hannah. But each time she said it, it had no effect on her mother and a growing effect on herself. Would a loving God have let Liam be returned to the Christian Brothers at Letterfrack? Would a loving God have let little Kevin McCarthy die of pneumonia? Nothing in her lessons at the convent helped her answer those ever-present questions. If anything, the more robotically the nuns preached obedience and faith the more they increased Cathy's doubts about religion.

But, despite those doubts, here she was, sitting in church this Easter Sunday, listening to Father Stephen go on and on about Jesus dying for people's sins. Yes, life had been pretty unfair to Jesus too, she thought. And surely, in a way, Jesus had committed suicide. He knew he was going to be crucified by the Romans but he hadn't escaped nor tried to save his own life. Yet he was worshipped, not humiliated and shamed. Cathy thought she would air that theory with Father Stephen next time they had one of their little chats.

Cathy totted up the many hours she had spent in church over Holy Week, some polishing pews and then others sitting in them praying. But it would soon be over and, when they got back home, Uncle Seamus would be arriving in his new car and then they would all go off to Auntie Stasia's for lunch.

Cathy knew why Uncle Seamus was coming. He had last visited at Christmas time and she had heard him and her Mammy talking in the upstairs drawing room as she had gone to put Fergus back to bed one night. Seamus was asking Hannah to marry him and move to Dublin, but Hannah had said that it was 'too late'. Cathy didn't understand that bit. Surely her Mammy meant that it was 'too early'.

Cathy wondered what it would be like if her Mammy did ever decide to remarry. She was sure that her Daddy would want Hannah to be happy again – and it would probably mean Cathy would have to work less hard and get more treats. And Daddy had liked Uncle Seamus very much; they had been friends and played lovely music together. He would surely bless such a marriage. Cathy decided that if she could do anything to encourage her Mammy to accept Seamus's proposal this time she should not miss the opportunity.

At the end of Mass, everyone filed out into the watery sunshine shaking hands with Father Stephen as they went. Cathy put Fergus down outside to run off to play chase with his big boy cousins. Fergus was two years old now and nearly as tall as cousin Paul, who was almost three years older than him. Cathy thought that if she had to put money on it, she would back Fergus in a fight with Paul any day. It made her so sad that he would never know how lovely his daddy had been, but she realised that to Fergus it was as if John had never existed.

There was much giggling as the younger boys ran around the churchyard. Fergus was chasing Paul and decided to try a shortcut straight through Father Stephen's legs.

'Ouf. Watch yourself there, my son.' The priest picked up Fergus and mussed his dark curls before popping him back down so he could continue his determined pursuit.

'A fine lad you have there,' said the priest to Hannah. Hannah nodded and smiled.

Chapter 20 – October 1932

Tricky's smell announced him: a sour, vegetably whiff, with undertones of sweat, cow and tobacco. Not that Tricky smoked, but he wore the same jacket every evening to sit in the pub until closing time. Cathy was busy wiping down shelves in the pub when she became aware of Tricky's distinctive scent behind her.

Cathy had learned to live with the man's presence. She wasn't sure how her mother would cope without him lending a hand a few times a week. But she hadn't learned to like him any better. If anything, seeing him regularly at close quarters - his lumpen silence and habitual scratching and sniffing – confirmed her view that he was an ignorant, crude, dirty eejit.

Tricky was carrying a hank of rope down the cellar stairs. God knows what he was up to down there. Maybe something to do with the pulley system he had rigged up for hoisting barrels up to the pavement. Cathy turned back to the bucket of water and squeezed out the cloth. Then her heart gasped.

Tricky - carrying rope. Tricky - the only witness to her father hanging in the tower. Tricky, who had cut down her father before anyone else could see him there to verify that story. Tricky, here right now, slowly and cleverly insinuating himself into their lives. Tricky becoming indispensable. Why had she not seen this happening before?

After all her chores were completed, Cathy went to her bedroom and attempted her French homework but her mind was elsewhere. She heard her mother say goodbye to Aggie and watched her come out of the front door from her window, Rose and Fergus in tow, presumably on their way to visit Stasia for the afternoon.

Cathy waited five minutes before running downstairs and jumping on her bike. Time to tell Father Stephen what she had just worked out: that her father had been murdered by Tricky Byrne.

Father Stephen listened patiently to Cathy's vivid imagining of the day her father died; her father unable to sleep, taking a walk at dawn down the lane, encountering Tricky on his way to milk the cows, Tricky who would have seen the perfect opportunity to get rid of his rival.

'Why do you think Patrick was your father's rival?'

'He's always hanging around my mother. He's like her mangy old dog. And the Byrnes have always wanted to get their hands on the McDermott's property.'

'I don't think that's enough reason for a God-fearing man like Patrick to take an innocent man's life. Anyway, your father would have fought him off. He was much taller than Patrick.'

'But Tricky is very strong. And he would have come up behind Daddy, out of nowhere, catching him round the neck with a rope – like this - and then strangled him.'

The priest smiled gently and shook his head. "My child, I understand your need to find an explanation. But sometimes we just have to accept that we can never know why some terrible things happen.'

'I knew my Daddy, Father. There is just no way he would have left us all to cope alone. Taken himself from us in such a cruel way. No message for any of us. No, I will never believe that my father killed himself.'

Father Stephen watched Cathy cycle off over the bridge, away from Main Street, and wondered where she was off to. He turned and put on his hat and coat to pay a visit to Mrs Hughes for afternoon tea. There were important things to be discussed.

Cathy cycled along to the Tower and leaned her bike against the gate, expertly tied up with rope by Tricky's murderous hands she thought as she climbed over it, scratching her leg on the bushes behind the wall, and jumped down into the field. She spat on her hand and rubbed away the spots of blood, as scarlet as the hips and haws that had attacked her.

She hesitated in front of the crumbling archway into the ruined tower but willed herself to go inside and find proof of Tricky's guilt. It was cold and dark and wet. The inside walls of the tower were glistening with damp. Moss and small ferns were clinging to the gaps between the stones and the darkening sky was visible through the few first-floor beams still in place.

If he had hanged himself here, her Daddy must have used one of those beams. There was nothing else he could have used. But how could he have got up high enough? There was nothing here - no boulders, no log pile that he could have climbed onto and then jumped from. Nor could Cathy see any vestiges of a noose, nor any shreds of rope on the ground. She was now as certain as it was possible to be that her father had not died by his own hand.

She ran back to her bike and onwards to her home in the fading light.

'Where have you been to?' Aggie was clearing away the children's supper dishes. 'Your mother's looking for you.'

'Isn't she always.'

'Now then. I can tell you're coming up to thirteen, young lady. Here, do you want the remains of this cauliflower cheese? I think Fergus might have sneezed into it, but sure, that's not going to hurt a soul.'

'No thank you very much, Aggie. And I'm sorry I snapped.'

Cathy dragged herself upstairs to Rose and Fergus's bedroom. Her mother was squeezing out a flannel in the china bowl on the washstand before changing them into their nightclothes.

'I thought you were here doing your homework. I could do with some help. Tricky has had to open up the pub for me and I need to get down there. Here, take over from me.'

'*Please!*'

Hannah glared at Cathy's insolence and walked out of the bedroom. Much as Cathy would have liked to throw the flannel at her mother, the sight of Rose and Fergus sitting abnormally peacefully on the floor, waiting for their bedtime stories, watching this tussle take place, brought down Cathy's temper.

After Rose and Fergus had fallen asleep, Cathy spent the rest of the evening on her Latin and brushing up her confirmation teachings. She was due to be confirmed in three weeks' time at the convent, along with several classmates. Her Aunt Stasia had offered to be her sponsor and she had chosen Bernadette as her confirmation name, in memory of her friend Bernie. She missed Bernie so much. Bernie would have believed that Tricky was a murderer.

When she heard her mother lock up and wish Tricky goodnight, Cathy came downstairs to the kitchen. Aggie had made Hannah a cup of tea and a sandwich.

'Do you want a bite, Cathy, my sweet?'

'No, thank you, Aggie. Mammy, I need to speak with you urgently. Alone.'

'Oh, don't mind me. I'm away to my bed, given I have to be up an hour before everyone else, and a girl of my delicate years needs all the beauty sleep she can get. Night, night.'

Hannah waited until Aggie had shut the kitchen door behind her.

'What is it that can't wait until tomorrow, Cathy?'

'I know how Daddy died.' Hannah put the teacup back on the saucer. 'He didn't hang himself. He was murdered – strangled I'd guess – by Tricky.'

Hannah swung her hand and delivered a mighty slap to Cathy's jaw.

'What are you talking about, you silly girl? How dare you accuse Tricky of killing your father? You know absolutely nothing about it.'

'I do know. I'm not stupid. I know that Tricky wants to take Daddy's place…' Another slap. Hannah dragged Cathy by the arm out into the yard. She opened the henhouse and pushed Cathy inside. There was much flapping and clucking and Cathy fell onto the straw.

'You just stay there until you learn some manners. I shall be expecting an apology – on behalf of Tricky.'

Cathy heard the bolt being pushed home before Hannah stormed back inside leaving Cathy in the warm, sweet blackness. Cathy's eyes slowly adjusted to the dark. She could just about make out the shapes of five hens from the chink of light from the kitchen window coming through the ill-fitting henhouse door and reflecting in their eyes. It could be worse. It was quite soft and she would be able to sleep here.

About half an hour passed. The door opened. Aggie was standing there in her dressing gown holding a lit candle. 'Come on, out you come. Your mother has got me out of bed just to come and get you back inside and up to your own bed.'

'Why did she not come herself?'

'You're joking. That would be practically an apology and Hannah Fitzgerald does not do apologies, as you well know. Come on. Shake a leg. It's bloody nippy out here.'

'No. I'm not coming out, Aggie. Not unless *she* comes to get me.'

'Jeezus. There's more of her in you than I thought.' Aggie stood at the door and peered inside. 'There's probably rats in there you know.'

'Thanks for that Aggie. But I'm not coming.'

'Oh, please yourself then.'

Aggie pushed the door to and went back into the kitchen, returning with a bucket. 'If you insist, enjoy your lodgings. Please use this to crap in. Cleaning out chicken shit is one thing but yours is quite another. Now, last chance to come inside to your cosy, clean sheets… no? Right then. Night, night, my stubborn young madam.'

Chapter 21 - May 1933

Quite who she was most trying to spite by not making her confirmation Cathy wasn't sure, but it was satisfying to think that a fair few grown-ups were extremely annoyed, if not downright incensed. Her mother, her aunt Stasia, Mother Veronica and Father Stephen had been very put out when Cathy declared, a week before the due date in March, that she couldn't go through with it.

She wasn't quite brave enough to say that she didn't believe in God anymore - and anyway that wasn't exactly true – but she did tell them all that she felt she 'wasn't ready'. It was true that her questions and doubts about the Church were mounting up every day and none of these people could give her anything like satisfactory answers. When Tricky had found the dismembered body of Honey in the yard last month, half-eaten by a fox in all likelihood, Cathy notched another black mark onto God's score card of random punishment that he had been heaping on her and her family. They had all cried over the death of Honey, though Rose and Fergus seemed to have forgotten the next day; Cathy and Hannah felt the loss for much longer. But for Cathy it was also yet more proof that, if there was a God at all, he was mighty cruel.

Cathy had no-one at home to give her the confidence to defy all the figures of authority who filled her life but her weekly letters to and from her grandmother had helped to embolden her. Mrs Fitzgerald was far too careful and subtle to instruct Cathy to reject Catholicism, but she invoked the spirit of her son and the intelligent scepticism he always displayed. She suggested questions that Cathy might like to put to the priest and the nuns. 'Why does a loving God allow suffering?' 'Why do Christians believe that theirs is the only true God? Other religions think the same. They cannot all be right.'

Cathy had been allowed to go and stay with her grandmother for a week after last Christmas. It had been such an eye-opening experience, going to the theatre and museums, having an elegant dinner with her Aunt Lily where the conversation between these two mature and sophisticated women, ranging from politics to music and literature, made her almost forget to eat. And she could go out of the Academy's front door and walk to the sea any time. Dalkey was nothing like Cleggan but the primal force of the sea could not be tamed by promenades and boardwalks.

It had been a thrilling week but, as she boarded the train back to Kilkenny, Cathy realised how excited she was to be seeing Rose and Fergus later on at home. She had missed their simple, generous affection that manifested itself so many times across a day and made up for the cool relationship that had developed between Cathy and her mother.

Hannah was working so hard that her contact with her children was quite limited and strictly practical. Cathy still did the various daily and weekly chores assigned to her but with an increasingly resentful and defiant attitude which did not escape her mother's notice. Hannah was careful not to ask Cathy to take on any more tasks than she was already allotted and, when extra help was needed, would turn to Tricky.

The day before her thirteenth birthday, Cathy lay on her bed, finally reading the volume of *Jane Eyre* that her grandmother had given her the first time they had met. She got little enough time to herself but when she did she was normally torn between reading and playing the piano. But since she had started this novel, there had been no question which was going to win. She was engrossed. How admirable and brave Jane was, in the orphanage, walking away from Rochester when she knew the truth, walking out all alone.

Cathy could hear lots of banging and excited talk and giggling downstairs and realised that Aggie was letting Rose and Fergus help make her birthday cake for tomorrow. As long as she didn't have to do the clearing up, Cathy was happy to think of her sister and brother making as much mess as they wanted, cracking eggs and weighing out flour.

There was a brief knock at her bedroom door.

'Come in.' This was new, her mother actually waiting to be invited in.

'Cathy, I need to talk to you about something important.'

'OK, Mammy.' Cathy sat up and swung her feet off the bed.

'Now, please let me speak without you interrupting me. Let me get to the end of what I need to say. Then you can make any comments or ask any questions you wish to.' Hannah lowered her head and fixed Cathy with a stare, waiting for a nod of acceptance. 'You have seen how difficult life is without your father, how hard we all have to work. Even you. But we are out of the woods now. The businesses are on an even keel - better than that actually. But I can't keep working at this pace. I shall wear myself out before I reach forty if I don't ease up. I can't expect Aggie to work eighteen hours a day indefinitely, and you won't be around forever. In short, I need to marry again.'

'But that's great Mammy. Uncle Seamus…'

'Stop. Just listen to me. I have decided to marry Tricky – Patrick – for many good reasons. Yes, I am sure Seamus would have happily married me but that's not what I want. A life in Dublin, giving up these businesses that my Daddy built and that I have fought for. No. I want to be here in Rowanbridge. I have grown to rely on Tricky. I can trust him. I think he will make an excellent partner. I know you had some silly theory about poor old Tricky and your father's death, but I hope you now realise it was all nonsense. I never want to hear a thing about those theories again. I hope you will welcome Tricky into our home as your stepfather and stepfather to Rose and Fergus.'

She had been instructed to stay silent, but, in truth, Cathy was too dumbstruck to say anything.

'We want to get married soon and we don't want to make any fuss. Father Stephen will marry us in church tomorrow; just Stasia and Edmund will be there as witnesses. When you come home from school we shall have our first supper together as a family.'

'But … it's my birthday tomorrow.'

Cathy thought she might vomit. This was the cruellest thing her mother had ever done to her.

'Yes, we shall enjoy your birthday cake with you. Thirteen years old. Practically a young woman.'

'Please, please Mammy. Don't do this to us. I can't bear to think of him in this house, living with us, sleeping in Daddy's place. If it's just about getting more help, I don't mind doing more jobs, and soon Rose will be able to help. Even Fergus might do a few simple things. Uncle Seamus might be happy to marry you and live in Dublin in the week, or maybe come and work in Kilkenny. Anything else. Please, please…' Cathy's voice trailed off into sobs.

'You need to get a grip on yourself, Cathy. I don't know how you have managed to create this fantasy that Tricky is some sort of monster. He's a kind and gentle soul, you know. You'll see that when he's living here. He only wants what's best for me.'

'No. It can't happen.'

'Well, it is happening. My mind is quite made up.' Hannah put her hand on Cathy's shoulder and kissed her on the top of her head. 'I do love you, Cathy, you know.' She left the room.

Cathy refused to come downstairs for the rest of the day. When Aggie brought her some supper up that evening she found Hannah cross-legged on her bed surrounded by all her father's books of poetry that she had taken from her mother's bedroom.

'What's all this?'

'I'm not letting Tricky Byrne get his hands on any of my father's things.' Aggie laughed and cleared herself a corner of the bed to sit on.

'I don't think you need to worry too much about Tricky reading poems to your mother, you know.' Aggie stroked Cathy's back. 'I know this has come as a shock to you, but just think of things from your Mammy's point of view. She couldn't have worked any harder and she needs some help. Tricky is a funny old bugger but he means well.'

'I hate him.'

'Well, that's silly. What's he ever done to you?' Cathy was on the verge of telling Aggie her conviction that Tricky had killed her father, but instead just threw her arms around her and wept.

The next day, Cathy cycled home from school as slowly as she could. She knew that her home would never be the same again. Aggie had laid out a birthday tea in the parlour; in the centre was Cathy's birthday cake, complete with wonky icing writing and an excess of sugar strands scattered over the top.

Rose slipped her hand into Cathy's as her sister looked at the spread,

'Do you like your cake? I did the writing and Fergus put on the sprinkles.'

'It's beautiful, darling. Thank you.' Cathy bent down to hug and kiss her sweet sister, but in her nostrils was the unmistakable smell of Tricky's overcoat, now hanging on the hooks behind her in the hall.

Half an hour later at tea-time, Rose and Fergus gobbled up Cathy's birthday cake with lots of giggling. Sitting opposite them were the newly-wed Mr and Mrs Patrick Byrne. Cathy, at the top of the table, glared at Tricky as he stuffed the cake into his ugly mouth. She slowly picked at her own slice of cake until it was in crumbs.

Cathy couldn't wait to go up to bed; this was the most miserable birthday she had ever had, and surely would ever have. She found all her father's books gone; so, her mother had taken them back to their shelf in her own bedroom, the bedroom where she would shortly be sharing a bed with her new husband. Cathy felt sick.

Cathy woke early the next day and heard someone moving about on the landing. She opened her door to see Tricky coming out of the small boxroom. So, that meant that Tricky was not sharing her mother's bedroom. Not yet at least. Cathy imagined that Tricky's room looked much like a prison cell – no carpet, plain walls, a single hard chair - which she felt was only fitting. But she was filled with the new hope that maybe her mother's marriage was entirely one of convenience and that Tricky would not ever take over her father's place in the magic ship.

Chapter 22 - August 1933

With Tricky now part of the household, Cathy was no longer so pivotal to the functioning of the family. Tricky absorbed more and more of the jobs that she had been allotted previously, and he also took over some of Hannah's physical jobs too, so Rose and Fergus were able to see more of their mother, which they clearly thrived on.

Cathy found herself with the luxury of some free time. She used this to read more – to herself and to her sister and brother - and to practice the piano. She eventually managed to master all three movements of *The Moonlight Sonata*, but the realisation that her father would never hear her play them was a bitter regret.

Rose would be starting school soon, and Cathy was gratified that her sister could already read simple words, given she had been given so much less of her parents' time than Cathy had enjoyed at the same age. Cathy took some comfort knowing her father would have been very proud that his Countess Cathleen had done her best to fill the void in her sister's and brother's lives.

When she asked her mother – very tentatively and politely - whether she could go to Dalkey to spend the month of August with her grandmother, Hannah agreed instantly and told Cathy that she was pleased to be able to let her go. She even gave her some money to spend in Dublin.

August turned out to be not just a rewarding month for Cathy; for Mrs Fitzgerald, seeing her grand-daughter every day, for most of every day, not having to put on her act as the headmistress of the Academy, meant she could learn how to become a proper granny at last. Of course, she and Cathy didn't fill their time with too much frivolity; there was piano practice – hearing Cathy play through the *Moonlight Sonata* and being able to add some refining touches was a joy for the old lady - reading Shakespeare and Wordsworth and doing translations from French and Latin texts. But they also went for walks along the seafront most days and read stories to each other out loud, even some quite fun ones – PG Wodehouse or Agatha Christie - and some quite romantic ones from E. M. Forster or F. Scott Fitzgerald.

Cathy and her grandma both enjoyed a book that had been left behind by one of the students: '*A White Bird Flying*' by an American novelist called Bess Streeter Aldrich. The title reminded them both of the Yeats poem read out at John's funeral but of course neither admitted it.

'This woman, Bess Streeter Aldrich, was very admirable you know, a teacher and scholar. But she only turned to writing to support her family after her husband died.'

'Like Mammy.'

'Yes, I suppose so. But writing is rather more respectable than running a public house and shop, don't you think?'

'I think anything honest that means you can feed your family is just fine. I think my mother is amazing really, even though we don't always see eye to eye. Daddy thought so too.'

'You're right of course, my dear. I apologise. And, of course, I have nothing to be proud of when it comes to parents not seeing eye to eye with their children, do I?'

Mrs Fitzgerald allowed Cathy to sleep in John's old bedroom. Just opening drawers or sitting in chairs that he had touched every day made Cathy both happy and sad. Cathy had been in Dalkey for just over a fortnight, when she answered the front door to find Ellen standing there.

'Hello Cathy. What a lovely surprise. I'm here to see Mrs F.'

'Come in, Ellen. Just go into her sitting room and I'll fetch Grandma.'

Ellen grabbed Cathy's arm and whispered, 'I'm here for a job, so I'd better wait here until she tells me where she wants me to go.'

'Righty-ho. That's exciting, isn't it.'

'Not really. But I reckon being a teacher beats being a secretary. And who knows, there might be a handsome new fella teaching science now that Mr Ord-Hume has retired.'

'I'll ask my Granny if we can have tea together when she's finished. There's lots to tell you about Rowanbridge.'

'Oh, I've heard some stuff - from Seamus. We're back to being good friends now there's no question of any romance. He thinks Hannah has gone a bit mad and I'm inclined to agree with him. Not sure what to think about it at all.'

After forty minutes or so, Mrs Fitzgerald came out from her private sitting room with the interviewee and told Cathy that she could go into the drawing room to take tea with Ellen. Her Grandma said she was going for a rest, so Cathy and Ellen would be able to chat about anything they wished, including her. It was the first time Cathy had heard her Granny make something resembling a self-deprecating joke.

Ellen gave Cathy a hug as she walked into the room.

'I'm in. I got the job and I start in September.'

They both cheered and hugged each other.

'I always wondered what on earth the bloody point was in learning Latin and Greek, even though I was good at them. Now I know the point was to be able to teach other people Latin and Greek. But, hey, I'm not complaining.'

Cathy poured out two cups of tea, while Ellen limped over to the window-seat.

'Come and sit over here. Your mother and I often used to sit on this seat together to gossip about everyone here, pupils and teachers. There'll be some teenage girl next year doing the same about me I guess.'

'Did you used talk about Daddy?'

'Oh my goodness, yes. Pretty much all the time. I was a bit soft on him. Not that he had much competition in this place. Seamus wasn't the first man your mother stole from me you know.'

When Cathy looked shocked, Ellen gave her a friendly punch on the shoulder. 'Only joking, Cathy. I don't think your mother could stop people falling in love with her. She was pretty special. Is *still* pretty special.'

'That's why I don't understand why she's married Tricky Byrne, the most disgusting man I've ever seen – and smelt!'

'Maybe she likes the smell.' They laughed.

'Well, I'm not going to be able to chat and joke like this with pupils in September. I'd better start practicing my serious and stern teacher face.'

******

Cathy came back home to Rowanbridge in the last week of August. She wanted to make the best use of her last free week before the new term started when so much of her time would be taken up with homework and chores.

The time in Dalkey had allowed her to immerse herself in many of her father's things, and now she resolved to dive deeply into her father's library, to understand more about what her father had valued and believed. Holding the books he had held, reading the words that had moved him, would be a precious way of spending time with his memory.

Cathy tiptoed into her mother's bedroom after lunch one day and took all John's various volumes of Yeats back across the landing. They had clearly been treasured and fell open easily at his favourite poems; *The Lake Isle of Innisfree, The Countess Cathleen in Paradise, The White Birds* had been read again and again.

Cathy had the whole afternoon ahead of her. She worked her way through the volumes in what she hoped was chronological order. She didn't read everything but tried to read those poems which she believed were crying out to be read because they opened themselves up to her. So much wonderment and mystery, love and pain. These short, tight verses told of a life of immense disappointment. That was unmistakable. They had meant such a lot to her father but she hoped he himself had not been as weighed down by melancholy as Yeats.

There was only an hour left before tea-time when Cathy picked up *The Wild Swans at Coole*. Some of these poems were quite long, though she thought she remembered one of the short ones, *To A Young Girl*, that her Daddy had read out to her when she was very little and the three of them were all sitting in the magic ship of her parents' bed.

Cathy kept turning the pages, reading intermittently as she went. Eventually, she came to a page that had been cut out, very neatly, and then returned to the book folded up. On the outside of the folded page was written 'Hannah' in her father's hand, across the end of the printed poem. Cathy carefully unfolded the yellowing paper. At the top of the page was written: 'I love you too much. I am so sorry for everything. John.' What did that mean? When had her father written this – and why?

Beneath it was the poem called *Broken Dreams*. She started reading:

'There is grey in your hair.
Young men no longer suddenly catch their breath
When you are passing…

Cathy realised that her father had not cut out the page randomly. This poem was about her father's love for her mother and how, despite disappointment and pain over the years, he loved her still.

'Leave unchanged
The hands that I have kissed,
For old sake's sake.
The last stroke of midnight dies.
All day in the one chair
From dream to dream and rhyme to rhyme I have
ranged
In rambling talk with an image of air:
Vague memories, nothing but memories.'

'Cathy, come on down. It's tea-time.' Rose was standing by her bedroom door. 'Aggie's been calling for ages.'

'OK, Rosie. Tell her I'm coming right now.'

Cathy kissed the page before refolding it and slipping it back into its hiding place in the book. She took all the books back to their shelf in her mother's bedroom, grateful that they had never had to witness Tricky exercising his conjugal rights.

Chapter 23 – Christmas 1933

Peter and Cathy helped to clear away the soup plates, under Aunt Stasia's exacting gaze, while Bessie and Aggie carried in the two glistening roast geese and placed them in front of Uncle Edmund. The other five Hughes and Fitzgerald children were eating their Christmas feast in the kitchen with Aggie, Bessie, Maud and the Byrnes' kitchen maid. From the shrieks and giggles coming through the dining room door they were probably having more fun than the ten diners around the long mahogany table.

Peter and Cathy had been told they were grown-up enough to join the more mature guests: Old Mrs Byrne, Nicholas and Louisa, Father Stephen, Hannah and Tricky plus of course the hosts. Aunt Stasia had told the two cousins they should feel honoured but Cathy suspected they had only been invited to make sure all the dining chairs were occupied around the beautifully laid table, bedecked with Waterford crystal and candles, so that Stasia could show it off at its best.

Uncle Edmund took up the carving knife and fork. He was a man of few words but plenty of action. He knew how to make things work perfectly and precisely. He could fix all the various pieces of farm machinery himself and he kept their car in good order, usually attended by cousin Andrew who shared his father's love of the mechanical. Uncle Edmund had even built himself a crystal radio set last year to pick up the new Radio Athlone service. All the children would watch mystified as Uncle Edmund twiddled various knobs and then out of the speakers would come talking or music, without any sort of disc having to be rotated. It was like magic.

In fact, Uncle Edmund was dextrous enough to be an actual conjuror, thought Cathy, as she watched him turn the two great, lumpy, greasy birds into elegantly sliced meat on each plate, though he would definitely reject a top hat and sparkly cape in favour of his trusty brown tweed suit.

'I'll hold the dish, Cathy, and you serve yourself.'

Father Stephen smiled as he held out the enormous dish of roast potatoes; it was rare for her to eat spuds she hadn't peeled herself.

'Thanks Father. Let me hold them now for you. This is just like your sermon, isn't it.'

'I suppose so. I'd like to think that everyone who listens to my sermons comes straight out of church to put them into practice like you, Cathy.'

At mass that morning, Father Stephen had taken the spirit of generosity as his theme. Christmas was a time to look forward to getting gifts, but it was even more pleasurable to give presents than to receive them. Cathy understood this, even though Peter and all the other children were extremely unimpressed and could barely sit through mass knowing that under the tree were lots of little packages waiting to be opened.

Father Stephen's sermon had moved on to the generosity of forgiveness; we are all sinners, he said, but we are all blessed when God forgives us, and also blessed when we forgive others. Christmas Day was a reminder that God had given the world the greatest and most generous gift of all by sending his son to earth to save us from our sins.

These days, Cathy didn't buy that at all. She thought it was a lovely story – who doesn't like babies in stables, and angels calling to shepherds, and wise men following a star – but not much more than that, though she still enjoyed going to church to have some time to sit and think in peace. And she definitely loved going to church at Christmas time, if only to sing the traditional hymns.

On the other side of the table sat her mother and Tricky. Cathy realised that she couldn't smell him at all today. He must have had his weekly bath and be wearing his new suit and a clean shirt. She saw her mother discreetly show Tricky the correct piece of cutlery for each course, and when he started gulping down the wine too fast she gently steadied his arm.

After pudding was finished, Stasia and Louisa helped Mrs Byrne from her seat and led her into the drawing room. Hannah sent Peter to fetch a tray and helped Cathy to clear the table. Nicholas pushed his seat back and took out his cigar case, which he offerred around to Edmund, Father Stephen and Tricky. Only Tricky accepted. Cathy had never seen him smoking anything before but guessed that it had been a Byrne family ritual. Nicholas rose and walked over to light his brother's cigar for him.

'Now, I've been thinking. What would you all think if I stood for the Dáil as a Fine Gael candidate at the next election? I think this new alliance has got a real chance and someone has to defend us landowners from that socialist De Valera, who will ruin us all if he's allowed to have his way.'

Edmund fetched the decanter of port from the sideboard, while expressing a note of caution.

'Maybe, if you can find the time. And if your farm manager is trustworthy enough. I find politics such a waste of time though. Nothing ever seems to change. I'd rather be at home keeping my eye on everyone and everything.'

The other two men said nothing. Father Stephen picked up his glass of port and looked awkwardly out of the window. Tricky puffed away doggedly.

'De Valera is the only hope for Ireland,' pronounced Hannah. She might have been picking up dirty linen napkins but she was game at any time for a debate with her two brothers-in-law. 'How are we going to get Ireland out of this terrible depression without more reforms.'

'But you'll be paying for it. You have businesses that will be hit too.'

'That's nonsense, Nicholas. We'd all be better off if we had customers with jobs and money in their pocket. Anyway,

I'm off to join the women for a cup of tea. Do follow – when you've finished burning money and stinking out the house.'

Cathy followed her mother out, proud that she had voiced her opinion and that it was the very opinion her father would have expressed had he been still alive. Hannah poured herself tea and sat on the sofa next to Louisa while Cathy went to sit on the drawing room floor where Rose, Fergus and all the apostles were playing with Andrew's new train set.

'How quickly time passes,' observed Louisa. 'I can remember when Fergus was born as if it was yesterday. Look at him now, almost bigger than Paul. And where does he get those curls from?'

At the mention of his name, Fergus stood up and came over to Hannah, carrying one of the little railway wagons. He climbed up onto his mother's knee to show it to her properly.'

'Yes, isn't it grand. I'm sure your cousins will let you come over and play with it sometimes.' Cousin Andrew didn't look too sure about that.

Fergus snuggled against his mother's breast and stroked his mother's stomach with his empty left hand. 'Mammy's tummy - too big.' He gave it a little punch.

'All our tummies are too big today, Fergus.' Aunt Stasia was fast to respond. 'Too much Christmas pudding, that's our trouble.' She forced a laugh.

'Are you having a baby, Auntie Hannah?' Paul was curious.

Out of the mouths of babes, thought Cathy. She had noticed her mother's stomach growing and now she realised why. How could she not have realised. Her mother's bump was actually quite pronounced when you looked properly. Maybe she hadn't wanted to acknowledge what was happening to her mother. There was a baby on the way: Tricky's baby.

'Yes, I am, Paul. Aren't you the clever one.'

'Congratulations, Hannah.' The childless Louisa tried to sound delighted. 'I had wondered but didn't like to say anything.'

When the men later joined the women and children, there were more congratulations. 'Well, done, brother.' Nicholas slapped a sheepish Tricky on the back. 'At last, we have the next generation of Byrnes on the way.'

Chapter 24 - July 9th 1951

Cathy stood on the bridge over the Nore, looking down into the lazy river. How many sticks and twigs must have been thrown over the side since she had first done it herself, nearly thirty years ago.

As she approached her Aunt Stasia's villa, she could hear the faint sound of the harvester and, looking out to the horizon on the hill behind the Byrnes's estate, could make out the machine lumbering along, painting ochre stripes in the sloping top field. That would be Andrew driving. The boy who loved his toy trains so much had grown into a man who loved all machines.

The Hugheses' villa looked much more blended into the countryside after thirty years of weathering, and the garden around it had grown up well. The line of trees behind the villa, planted to screen out the Byrnes, was fully mature and it was only just possible to see the roof and chimneys of the Georgian farmhouse. What a big, sad, empty house that must be for just Nicholas and Louisa to live in, thought Cathy.

Cathy clambered down from the bridge to the river path and headed towards Mill Lane. Ahead of her she saw two young men, stripped to the waist and glistening with sweat, digging out a dyke that led down to the river. A friendly brown Labrador ran up to her.

'Hey, Lady! Come back here.' The man whistled the dog who obediently ran back to his side.

'Hi there, you two strangers.'

Peter and Paul turned around again, and, seeing their cousin, threw down their spade and shovel and walked towards her with outstretched arms. 'How are you, lovely girl? I'm sorry - we're a bit smelly and muddy.' Peter tried to give Cathy a hug without his hands touching her.

'I don't mind. It's good to see you, however mucky you look. Is this really Lady?' Cathy bent down to stroke the dog.

'Well, probably not the Lady you knew. Her grand-daughter maybe. But just as soppy.' Paul squatted beside the excited dog and gave her a vigorous rub all over.

'Great to see you home, Cathy, though I wish the circumstances were happier.'

'How is Mammy?'

Peter looked at Paul, before speaking. 'Well, Mother said she looked a bit better yesterday. And Aggie got her to eat something. So, it could be worse, I guess.'

'No, Cathy, it's very bad.' Paul, always the straight talker. 'She won't last the week out, so thank God you're here.'

'If she'll see me, of course.'

'I'm sure she will. Of course she will. She asked Mother whether she had had any word from you, though Ma didn't mention that you were coming down, in case you changed your mind. She certainly wants to make peace before she passes.'

'There's not much that makes Hannah Byrne back down, we all know that.' Paul gave a rueful laugh. 'But facing eternity, that'd do it for anyone.'

'Well, I'd better get over there then.'

'Here, let me carry your case for you.' Peter ran back to the ditch to pick up his shirt. 'Come on, coz. Let's be off.'

'Great. Thanks for leaving me to do all the fecking shovelling, man. Make sure you send him straight back here, Cathy. No cups of tea for him now.'

Peter and Cathy followed the river path until it started to tunnel under Mill Lane, where they climbed up the bank and turned left to head back to the centre of the village. As they walked along the lane, Peter brought Cathy up to date with all the family news.

'Yeah, Mattie managed to escape Rowanbridge by being super clever. There was no way mother could object to him becoming a doctor, now could she, even though she might have preferred for him to be locked in the back-office learning from Dad how to do the books and where she could keep an eye on him. He's not too far away though, in Carlow, and married now with a new baby. The three of us boys left at home are hopeless with women. We could do with you being here to introduce us to some of your friends.'

'Surely Bridie Byrne is the best catch around here. And it's perfectly legal to marry your cousin.'

'No way. Not that she isn't a sweet girl. A real beauty actually. But who'd want Tricky as your father-in-law? Mother would love it though. A chance to get her hands on the whole Byrne estate. So, don't you dare suggest it, now.'

Cathy thought she was prepared for the moment when they would pass Cromwell's Tower, but she found her heart beating faster as it came into view. It looked so much smaller than she remembered it, but still heavy with all sorts of memories. She walked past it at a quickened pace. When they reached Main Street, Cathy took the case from Peter.

'Thanks so much, coz. Best just leave me here now. I need to gather myself together - and Paul'll kill me if I don't send you back.'

She kissed her cousin's cheek and waved as he turned and walked back down Mill Lane. 'Happy digging.'

Chapter 25 - January 1934

Mrs McCarthy squinted and bent down to scrutinise the shop scales.

'Make sure I get the full eight ounces now.'

Mrs McCarthy removed a sliver of butter from the lump on the scales and returned it to the butter tub. She didn't like May O'Connor very much. She deftly folded the greaseproof paper to make a neat package. One day, thought Cathy, as she wiped down tins of fruit at the back of the shop, I'll be able to cut off half a pound of butter in one fell slice as accurately as Mrs McCarthy.

'So, then. I've heard of honeymoon babies but this new one is more like an engagement baby, don't you think? That Tricky Byrne is a sly old dog.'

'She was very early. Very small. Only just over five pounds.'

'You think?'

There was some whispering between the two women which Cathy assumed was to alert May O'Connor to the existence of the new baby's big sister – half-sister at least - behind the curtain, engaged in stock-taking.

'Oh yes, that'll be it. A premature baby. Hannah Byrne hardly looked pregnant at Christmas now, did she?' May O'Connor didn't sound convinced. 'Well, she might be small, but she's going to be a very rich little girl one day. Who else is going to inherit all the Byrnes' land and money? That Louisa Byrne is clearly never going to give Nicholas an heir.'

A few more purchases and May O'Connor left the shop. Mrs McCarthy put her head round the curtain. 'Cathy, you go home now. It's time. You've done plenty and I can finish off.'

Cathy put on her coat, hat and scarf against the January cold.

'Sorry about that terrible May O'Connor.'

'Don't worry, Mrs McCarthy.'

Cathy had got used to people whispering about the early arrival last week of baby Bridget Byrne, nearly two months early, theoretically at least.

Hannah could now afford to employ Mrs McCarthy for the full day on Saturdays, so Cathy got the afternoon off, but she wasn't too keen to go back home and be made to look after the controversial baby, so she started looking at the front pages of the newspapers.

'Sam will be here in a minute to pick up his sandwiches. Why don't you let him walk you back?'

As soon as he had reached fifteen, just before Christmas, Sam had left the Christian Brothers school in Kilkenny. Tricky had immediately given him work, doing all sorts of odd jobs. He was a hard worker, clever and quick. It was nice to have Sam around the place, and Cathy often found an excuse to go out to feed the chickens or collect eggs when Sam was working out there, mucking out the pony's stable or sweeping the yard.

Sure enough, the church bells had just rung one o'clock when the shop doorbell tinkled and Sam walked in.

'Hello Mam. Thanks. What have you made me today?' said Sam as he took the greaseproof package from his mother.

'Cheese and onion, your favourite. And Cathy needs walking home. Off you both go.'

Cathy and Sam were rather more awkward with each other than when he had taught her to ride a bike only a couple of years before or when they used to play tag in the school playground. They arrived at the front door of the McDermott pub.

'Actually, do you fancy going for a walk, Sam. I don't want to go in just yet.'

'Sure. Are you warm enough though? There's a real bite in the air today.'

'We'll just walk faster.'

Without any debate they carried on past the Main Street house and turned down Mill Lane. When they got level with the tower, Sam climbed over the gate and held out his hand to Cathy to help her over too. She hadn't been back to the tower since she had come looking for clues to her father's death. But here was Sam inviting her in.

'Come on. We can get out of the wind inside the tower. And I might even let you have one of my sandwiches.' Sam winked at Cathy.

The tower felt very different from the last time Cathy had walked inside. It was just a pile of stones after all. Sam took off his overcoat and put it down in the most sheltered corner and sat on it. He opened his pack of sandwiches and held it out to Cathy. She took a triangle from him and sat down next to him. It tasted very good.

They talked village trivia: the fate of school-friends they shared, the various building projects around the village, the rivalry between McDermott's and McLoughlin's bars. It was an easy-going sort of conversation - so far.

'This is where my father was found – dead. Did you know?'

'Oh God. I remember now. I'm so sorry for bringing you here, Cathy. Don't know what I was thinking of.'

'Don't worry, Sam. It's good for me to realise that it's just an old ruin. Not the tower's fault that my Daddy died here, though I reckon his wasn't the first … death it has witnessed.' Cathy had nearly said 'murder'.

'And am I right that your Mr Byrne found his body and carried him to the house?' Cathy nodded. 'That must have taken some strength but Mr Byrne is stronger than he looks. He doesn't say much, does he, but he's a fair boss. I've no complaints. And I'm grateful for the work. Truly.'

'It's beneath you, Sam, working for that man.'

'Not at all. Everyone has to start somewhere.' They munched through the sandwiches, casting occasional glances at each other.

Sam screwed up the greaseproof paper and stood up, holding out a hand for Cathy to take. As she leapt up, Sam caught her in his arms and kissed her quickly on the lips.

'Sorry. Couldn't resist.'

'That's OK. I liked it.' And Cathy kissed Sam back, for longer. Cheese and onion, she thought. Nice. That's what I must taste like too.

'Mmm. You're lovely, Cathy. Great kisser.' Sam gently ran a finger over Cathy's lips. I've always been a bit sweet on you. My mother knows too – I bet that's why she made me walk you home. But I'd better get back, Cathy. I only get half an hour's break.'

'Come on then. Catch me if you can.' Cathy ran out of the tower and was over the gate before Sam could pick up his coat from the floor.

******

The baby was yelling in her basket on the kitchen table when Cathy sauntered in through the back door.

'Can you pick her up Cathy, please. I have my hands full here.'

Aggie was trying to serve up lunch to Rose and Fergus at the same time as baking bread.

'And then can you go and call your Mammy and Tricky in. They're doing stuff in the bar I think.'

Cathy looked down at the angry little bundle of cloth. What a hideous baby. She picked up Bridie brusquely, making no attempt to comfort her, and walked out into the yard and in through the pub's back door.

'Your food is ready and your baby is screaming. Here you go.'

Cathy dumped Bridie on one of the pub tables and walked out, as Tricky rushed over and picked up Bridie.

She was walking down the steps into the yard when a huge kick on her backside sent her sprawling, banging her head against the wall.

'Don't you ever speak to us like that again or treat your sister so wickedly. Her just a fortnight old and not strong.' Hannah was standing at the top of the steps with her hands on her hips, her hair flying loose in the January wind, glaring at her eldest daughter

Cathy sat on the ground rubbing her knees.

'Well, frankly, I wouldn't care if she died.'

This statement silenced Hannah. Cathy was even shocked at herself. Did she actually mean that? It wasn't the baby's fault after all that her father had killed Cathy's father. But there was no way she would ever love her, or even like her.

'Go to your room and stay there. No food for you for the rest of the day,' Hannah hissed.

Cathy was on her feet now. 'I don't care. That's great in fact, because you won't be able to make me do any more jobs and I won't have to pick up your ugly baby.'

Cathy marched back inside and on up to her room, flinging herself onto her bed. Her rage had anaesthetised the cut on her forehead but Cathy realised what had happened when blood dripped onto her pillow. She might get a scar but she didn't care. It would be a badge of pride.

Chapter 26 – March 1934

Tricky drove the new car out of the yard to the front door and waited for Cathy to come out. She was off to spend the Easter holiday with her grandmother and she had reluctantly accepted a lift from him to Kilkenny station because her case was heavier than usual and she didn't fancy carrying it to the bus-stop.

Cathy put on her coat and hat and went into the kitchen. Aggie was peeling carrots and Rose and Fergus were sitting at the table playing snap. Bridie was asleep in her cot in the corner.

Cathy gave Rose and Fergus big hugs and lots of kisses and then the same for Aggie.

'What's this in aid of?'

'Just saying bye. Where's Mammy?'

'She's gone over to the church, to do the big pre-Easter clean out.'

'OK. Well, tell her I said good-bye.'

'OK. Have fun up in the big city and be good.'

'It's Dalkey, Aggie, not Dublin. Full of ancient admirals.'

'Now, they're the worst.' Aggie pointed at Cathy with her peeler. 'I could tell you a few tales about old seadogs. Or, as the old joke goes, discharged seamen.' Aggie gave Cathy a nudge.

Cathy looked around at the peaceful domestic scene and went out the front door. Sam was standing by the car, having loaded her case into the boot.'

'Jesus, that's a heavy one. Have you got a body in there or something, Cathy? I know, it's your week's supply of Guinness, isn't it?'

Cathy and Sam smiled at each other. If Tricky hadn't been sitting at the wheel watching them in the mirror, she might have given Sam a kiss goodbye, but there was no way she was going to let Tricky see such an open expression of her feelings.

'Bye then, Sam. Have a happy Easter.'

'You too, Cathy. Come back soon.'

Tricky was a very slow and methodical driver, but they had left plenty of time to cover the six miles. Not a word was said. Cathy spent the whole time trying not to look at Tricky but gazed out of the window at the hedges and fields and then, as they approached Kilkenny, some of the new building sites. She breathed shallowly so as to take in as little of his odour into her lungs as she possibly could.

Tricky drew up outside the station. Cathy moved to open the car door but Tricky took her right hand. She froze.

'Hannah. She's a good woman. You should forgive her.' That was more words in one go than Tricky had ever spoken to her.

'Thanks for the lift.' Cathy pulled her hand away and got out of the car to get her case from the boot.

******

Cathy struggled to carry the case up the two flights of stairs to her father's old bedroom. But she finally made it. She flopped into one of the leather armchairs and looked around. Definitely a nicer room than hers back in Rowanbridge: a proper desk to work at, shelves for her books and a big squashy bed to roll around in. Better get back down to her Grandma though for that cup of funny tea she always made. She'd get used to it.

'Ah, Cathy. Come and sit now, my dear. You must be exhausted. I always find train travel utterly debilitating. Well, any sort of travel these days is a trial for me.'

Mrs Fitzgerald poured the smoking, smoky tea into the china cup, which she handed over to Cathy.

'Now. How is everyone in Rowanbridge? Rose and Fergus? I should dearly love to see my other grandchildren, but I fear I just couldn't cope until they are a little older.

Maybe in a year or so's time, Rose will be old enough to come with you for a holiday.'

'Yes. She's a very good girl and no trouble at all. Fergus is a different kettle of fish. Just a little bit wild at the moment but absolutely adorable. Very loving and cheeky. He makes us all laugh a lot.'

'And the new baby?'

'Well enough. Growing. Out of the woods they all keep saying. So here to stay.'

'That's good to hear.'

Cathy took a couple of sips of tea and then put down her cup. 'Granny, I need to ask you a very big favour. I hope you won't be too shocked.'

'Very little shocks me these days, Cathy. And I would do anything for you. You must know that.'

Cathy took a deep breath. 'I want to leave home. I don't want to go back to Rowanbridge. I'd like to live here with you, if that's OK. But, if it isn't, I shall go and ask my Great-aunt Lily. And if she says no, I shall find myself some work as a maid or something. I'm fourteen now and quite grown-up and I can do any sort of house or shop work. I've done plenty at home and I'm fairly good, I think. And I work hard.' Cathy's outburst came to a temporary pause.

'Slow down, slow down, Cathy. Just take a breath. Now, first of all, you shall always have a home here. There's no way I would let you go and find work. That's absurd. You need to be learning still. But I need to understand what your mother thinks of all this. She dislikes me intensely already without me stealing away her daughter.'

'I don't think it's that she dislikes you. Aunt Stasia says she just can't bear anyone trying to stop her having what she wants and that it comes from being the second child.'

Mrs Fitzgerald smiled. 'There might be something in that. But there are things that I did when your mother and father married that, at the time, I thought were the right thing to do but that I have since come to regret. We may have more in common, your mother and I, than either of us would care to admit. You, though, are very much your father's daughter.'

'I used to think that – and I'd like it to be true - but I'm not so sure. Aggie says there's more of my mother in me than she thought. I'm a bit frightened by that.'

'Whatever mixture you are, you are very dear to me. Let us try to get along and enjoy our Easter break here together. Now, I must telephone Lily and ask her advice. I'm sure she will have an opinion on the best course of action. You go and unpack and I'll see you at dinner-time.'

Cathy finished her tea and wandered back up the two flights to her new bedroom. She opened the mahogany drawers to put away her clothes. She had stuffed as many into her case as she could manage, but she would need to send for more. Cathy didn't think that her mother would be spiteful enough to withhold them.

The drawers smelt of sweet wood but also had other scents - vanilla and grass - that she liked to think were the smells of her father. Yes, this would be a good place to live. Cathy resolved that from this day she would devote her life to her father's memory. She would study hard, practice the piano daily and make the best use of everything her grandmother and Dublin could offer. This had been her wonderful Daddy's home and it would now be hers, whatever objections her mother could throw at her.

Chapter 27 – July 1935

After the initial and inevitable explosion that Cathy's escape provoked when Lily rang Hannah with the news that her daughter had rejected her home - and by association her mother - life in Dalkey settled down into an agreeable routine. Cathy spent her first year living at the Maple Academy being tutored personally by her Grandma, but, when she reached fifteen, Cathy joined the Academy as a proper full-time student.

Cathy enjoyed returning to the disciplined structure of a school day and having class-mates to befriend but some aspects of her life as the proprietor's grand-daughter were not removed. Cathy felt slightly guilty to be the occupant of such a spacious and luxurious bedroom, when the other students were two, three or even four to a room, but they didn't seem to resent her privilege.

And then there was the regular presence of Ellen in the classrooms, reminding Cathy of their shared history with her father but also Ellen's still close friendship with her mother. Cathy tried not to see her as a potential spy and she could tell that Ellen's affection for herself was real and warm.

At the start of the school holidays, Cathy would get on the train to Kilkenny to go and spend time in Rowanbridge. It was wonderful to see Rose and Fergus, who were growing up very fast, and of course Aggie was always generous with hugs, advice, gossip - and the best roast potatoes in the county. But it was always daunting to come home to her mother's cool embrace and what Cathy believed was her disapproving judgement.

Hannah studiously avoided asking after Mrs Fitzgerald but was always eager to know from Cathy all about Ellen's new life at the Academy; was she a good teacher or not, how was her bad leg, was she 'walking out' with any particular gentleman? It was also clear that Ellen was writing regular letters to Hannah so she already knew some of Cathy's news.

'Congratulations on winning at the Feis Ceoil, Cathy. A real triumph to win at such a prestigious music festival. Maybe you'd play for me some time the piece that won you the prize. Did you know that I won the violin class when I was a bit older than you, so that's something we have in common now.'

Coming home also meant living with the lurking presence of Tricky. It hurt to see him sitting at the table in her father's chair but he seemed to be making her mother's life easier.

And then there was Bridie. Cathy loved all babies and looking after them, but Bridie was different. Cathy would look at her half-sister and try to reason with herself. Her dark curls were very much like Fergus's, her nose was like her mother's and she smiled and laughed when someone bounced her on their knee, as Rose and Fergus had done at the same age. But Cathy could only see Tricky looking out at her from the child's eyes.

Cathy never volunteered to look after Bridie, but the day after she arrived back home she found herself left alone with the toddler up in the drawing room while her mother, sister and brother were off at Mass. Bridie was napping on the sofa while Cathy read *Howards End*.

Bridie was not quite walking independently yet but she could stand up and support herself on the furniture, clinging onto chairs and tables as she staggered around a room. When she came to a chasm between her various stage posts she would hold out a chubby hand for help and someone would guide her to the next prop.

Bridie seemed to be safely asleep so Cathy went to the piano and started to play quietly. Suddenly there was a protesting 'Da' behind her. Bridie had woken up, slid off the sofa and was now at one end of it, looking for a hand to take her over to the side table and the pair of armchairs. 'Da,' said Bridie, with her free hand making the little twisting motion that indicated help was required.

Cathy spun round on the piano stool and stared at Bridie. 'Da'.

Bridie was sounding more irritable but Cathy stayed put. Eventually Bridie collapsed onto her bottom and shuffled over to the armchair, and then pulled herself back up to a standing position. Cathy turned back and started playing again. Two minutes later and Bridie was stuck again. More shouts of 'Da' were ignored as Cathy continued with her Mozart sonata.

The ear-piercing scream did finally make Cathy stop. Bridie had managed to get herself over to the fireplace and had clearly tried to use the fire screen to navigate over to the piano, but this had toppled over on top of her, leaving a cut on her temple from which a little thread of blood trickled. Not much blood at all really but loads of crying - the loudest crying and screaming Cathy had ever heard. And it was getting louder. Cathy sat and looked at Bridie with her bawling mouth, red face and gushing tears, thinking that she would have to get up and sort out the cut soon when the drawing room door opened and in ran Tricky.

Tricky scooped up Bridie and cradled her, shushing her screams and dabbing the blood and tears with his dirty shirt sleeve.

'There, there, there.'

Bridie cleaved to Tricky, saying 'Da, Da, Da,' between yelps and massive intakes of breath. Slowly the screams became sobs and the sobs turned to sniffles. 'There, there. There you go, little birdie.'

When Bridie had calmed completely, she stuck her thumb in her mouth and closed her eyes, snuggling into Tricky's shoulder. Tricky stood and carried the clingy baby out of the room and downstairs. Not a word was spoken between him and Cathy, who turned back to the piano when they had left and finished the sonata.

******

'Poor little birdie. Did silly old Daddy let you fall over in the yard?'

Bridie was sitting on Tricky's knee at the Sunday lunch table as Hannah fed her mashed-up food from her own plate. Bridie opened her mouth dutifully for the loaded spoon, all the while staring accusingly at Cathy. Whatever explanation Tricky had given to Hannah, Cathy had no intention of correcting it but she felt that Bridie knew exactly who to blame for the plaster on her forehead.

Cathy needed to get away from that stare. As soon as the plates were cleared, she excused herself and went out into the yard. The hens ran up to her, expecting a scattering of grain but that was now one of Rose and Fergus's duties – and pleasures. Cathy opened the various shed doors along each side of the yard until she found what she was searching for. There it was: her lovely blue bike. And riding it was as easy as when she had had to do it every day, to and from Kilkenny. She came out onto Main Street and set off pedalling at a leisurely pace, past the Post Office and their shop, turning left at the crossroads towards the church and school, over the bridge, past her Aunt Stasia's and then left again to come back up Mill Lane.

Cathy knew exactly who it was coming towards her before she drew close enough to see their faces. Who else walked with that loping gait, with his dirty blond hair - and who waved his arms around so much around as he talked? Sam McCarthy was holding hands with Marion Magee, walking past Cromwell's tower, with Rowanbridge behind them. They stopped for some serious smooching. When they pulled themselves apart, Cathy was just drawing up alongside them. Sam dropped Marion's hand the instant he saw who it was on the bike.

'Hi there, Cathy. I didn't know you'd be home today. How is life up in the big city?' Awkward despite the bluff chat.

'Hello Sam. And hello Marion. Lovely to see you both. I got back yesterday.' Everyone waited for someone else to say the next thing. Cathy could only think of one thing to say. 'So… are you two sweethearts now?'

Marion giggled and took Sam's spare hand. 'I guess we are.' She looked up to Sam for reassurance but he said and gestured nothing. 'We like coming for a Sunday walk together, don't we Sam?'

'Well, don't mind me. I have to get back. My mother needs me to do something for her this afternoon. But I'll see you around. I'm going to be here for a few weeks.'

'Okay then Cathy. Mind how you go on that bike.' Sam sounded mightily relieved. 'You were always a bit wobbly.'

Everyone forced out a laugh as Cathy remounted and started to pedal furiously, pleased that the rushing air was drying the tiny tears springing into her eyes.

Chapter 28 – July 9th 1951

Cathy stood at the front door on Main Street wondering what would be an appropriate manner for entering her own childhood home, not seen these last twelve years. Should she knock and wait to be allowed in, like a visitor? Should she go through the yard to the kitchen door, which was always open, like a member of the family? Instead of either, she thought that maybe it would be a good idea to go in via the pub, which was about to open to the public. She could hear noises within.

Sam was on his knees in front of the bar, banging nails into a floorboard.

'Cathy!' He stood up, hammer in hand, looking confused. 'Welcome home. I'm sorry you're here in these sad times.'

'Thanks, Sam. I should have come before. But … you know…'

'Yeah. I know your Mammy can be difficult. But Rose always gives me your news, you know. I was very sorry to hear about your husband, and so near the end of the war. What a bloody tragedy.'

'Yes. It was very hard.'

'And you with a little boy, and all.'

'Yes - Johnny. He's seven now. You'd never know he was born in England and had an English daddy. He sounds as Irish as you and me.'

'Well, that's grand then.'

Cathy and Sam looked at each other and smiled.

'Here let me carry your case up to your bedroom. I'll just lock the pub door again for two minutes. The punters can wait.'

'Thanks, Sam.' Cathy walked through the side door into the main house. The parlour looked much as it had done the last time she had been here, just with twelve years' worth of wear and tear.

No-one seemed to be around downstairs but she could hear floorboards creaking upstairs. She wasn't ready yet to face her mother so she walked down the hall to the kitchen. Aggie was busy at the sink and didn't see Cathy until she had her arms around her.

The two women said nothing at first. They hugged each other hard. Aggie looked much the same, just more faded and worn. Aggie let go eventually, sniffed and wiped her eyes with her pinny.

'Now. Sit yourself down and I'll put on the kettle.'

'No Aggie. Let me make it. You must be exhausted. That's what I can do now I'm here – give you a break.'

'Well, Rose is very good and even Bridie does an evening stint in between the two of us while we all have our suppers. She tries to do her homework up there but the light is not good.' The Main Street house had had electric lights fitted in 1937 but only downstairs. Upstairs, the oil lamps were still being used. 'She's coming up to her last year at school. She's a very, very clever girl and wants to be a lawyer. Can you believe it?'

'Well, it does stretch credibility that a child of Tricky Byrne's should turn out to be a genius.'

'Don't Cathy. Don't start all that. He's a funny old stick but he's a good man and he adores your mother.'

'How is she today?'

'I think a little better than yesterday but we never know what to expect. Some days she just lies with her eyes closed and takes only the odd sip of water, the next she can be quite chatty and finish a little food. But you'll be very shocked to see her. There's nothing to her – light as a feather – and her hair is streaked with white, even though she's only fifty-one. Look at me. Sixty-two and not a grey hair in sight.'

'No bottle involved in that then?'

'Maybe, maybe. What's so wrong with a girl trying to keep her good looks? I need all the help I can get if I want my old gentlemen to keep buying me the odd drink. I'll be dying of thirst soon enough.'

'So… who's up there with Mammy?'

'Father Stephen. He comes twice a day, bless the man. Says Mass and brings her communion when she can manage. Heaven knows what he'll do when she goes. Rose is sitting with her, and your Aunt Stasia went up about half an hour ago. She comes most days too, would you believe.'

'Where's Tricky?'

'He's out with Fergus harvesting in the top fields.'

'So he uses Fergus to work on the Byrnes' farm.' Cathy's anger was fast to rise.

'The Byrnes' farm? Yes, I suppose so. But it will be Fergus's farm one day you know, along with Bridie. Nicholas and Tricky agreed that it should pass to the pair of them when they are gone. They've written a will and everything. Bridie has no intention of being a farmer so she will get money. Rose will inherit the shop and the pub - and this house of course. All three of them will be very well looked after.'

'Nothing for me of course.'

'Stop it, Cathy. Your mother agonised about it but she talked to Stasia and Father Stephen about it and they all agreed that because your Granny left the Academy to just you it was only right that the other three children should share out the rest. Anyway, your Grandpa James would be very amused to see the whole village divvied up amongst his children and grandchildren. And Stasia is having to get used to her sister's children owning more of Rowanbridge than her own.'

'So, Mammy won in the end. Marrying Tricky Byrne was one hell of a pact with the devil.'

'Now that's proper bitchy, Cathy. What would your father make of his darling treasure if he could hear you now, eh?'

Fortified with tea and cake, Cathy climbed the staircase to her mother's bedroom. A single hardback chair was standing guard outside the door. The door was closed but

Cathy could hear her Aunt Stasia's voice. Cathy knocked gently and walked in.

Father Stephen was sitting by her mother's bed. Stasia was sitting on the window seat, looking out into the yard, and Rose was sitting cross-legged at her feet, with a book. At first, Cathy could hardly make out her mother. Hannah's greying hair and pale skin camouflaged her against the pillows and her skeletal body was swallowed up entirely by the bedclothes.

'Oh Mammy.' Cathy ran to the bedside taking her mother's hand from the priest.

'Is it you, Cathy? My darling angel. Come and kiss me.'

'I'm so sorry I haven't been before. Please forgive me.'

'Don't be silly. I stopped you coming. I'm the one who needs forgiveness. Stephen knows that better than anyone. He keeps trying to absolve me of my sins but they go too deep.'

'God forgives all repentant sinners, Hannah.'

'So you say.' Hannah shook her head.

Cathy turned and walked into a fierce and tearful hug from Rose. Her aunt then kissed her.

'We've all missed you very much, Cathy. With your nursing skills, you could really have helped your mother.' Oh Auntie Stasia, thought Cathy. Could she not resist adding that little barb of blame in her welcome?

'I haven't nursed for seven years, Auntie. But, like riding a bike, I guess you never lose it. That's what I'm here to do. That's what I want to do. You all need a rest.'

'Cathy, Cathy.' Hannah called her eldest daughter back to her bedside. 'I need to tell you things. Show you my will. Explain what I've done.'

'Don't worry Mammy. Plenty of time for all that.'

'No, there isn't plenty of time. I've been waiting for you.'

Cathy looked at her mother's emaciated hand. The cancer had spread from her breast throughout her body and it was clear that there was very little time left.

'Go now, Stasia, Stephen. Rose too. I'm sorry to send you away but I need time alone with Cathy.'

The three sickroom visitors picked up their belongings, Rose and Stasia kissed Hannah and the three walked out of the room, Father Stephen looking back to give a final salutation. Cathy followed them to the door, closed it behind them and turned back to face her mother.

Chapter 29 - December 1936

Slattery arrived at six-thirty pm precisely to transport Cathy, her grandmother and Ellen from Dalkey over to Pembroke Street for Lily Murphy's intimate Christmas soirée. As the car rumbled through the suburbs, Mrs Fitzgerald and Ellen took the opportunity to discuss various issues to do with the Academy and its students. Occasionally they would dip their voices so that Cathy, sitting up front next to Slattery, couldn't pick up anything too confidential.

Soon to be seventy, Mrs Fitzgerald was becoming increasingly reliant on Ellen as her right-hand woman. She had formally made her the deputy headmistress for the new school year, putting Miss Murray's nose rather out of joint.

'Patricia Murray has been with me for twenty-two years and is an exemplary teacher, but she has no business sense whatsoever,' she explained to Cathy. 'Ellen is a very smart young woman as well as an excellent teacher. And I trust her to do the right thing for you and for me.'

Mrs Fitzgerald had even converted one of the Maple Academy's outhouses into a small home for Ellen to move into so that she could be always on hand. She was increasingly treated like part of the family. Cathy was always welcome to pop in for tea to Ellen's little stable apartment at the weekend. They would talk about the Academy, about what they were reading, a little politics sometimes and Ellen would eagerly swap news from Hannah and Rowanbridge with Cathy. Ellen often joined grandmother and granddaughter for Sunday tea in the crimson sitting room. Ellen was so stitched into the family that Lily had included her in the invitation for that night.

Mrs Fitzgerald tapped Slattery on the shoulder. 'Mr Slattery, excuse me for asking, but can you speak any Irish?'

'Only the Our Father and the Hail Mary, Ma'am, that my mother taught me when I was little. I can still say them today but I have not another word of Irish in me.'

'You see. I think these politicians are going against the progress of history, trying to make everyone speak Irish.'

'Either way, I think we are going to have to introduce it at the Academy,' reasoned Ellen. 'There are more and more jobs open only to people with some competence in Irish.'

'Ridiculous. And where are all these teachers of Irish supposed to spring from, I wonder?'

'I know someone – and so do you grandma.' Cathy turned to the back seat. 'I don't think she would want to come to Dublin mind, but do you remember Aoife out in Connemara, Daddy's sister-in-law. She's a fluent Gaelic speaker and a teacher.'

'Yes. Your father brought her to the Academy once – along with her sister, just before John married Ailsa.'

The car drew up outside Lily Murphy's imposing Georgian town house and Slattery came around to help Mrs Fitzgerald out of the car and up the steps to the front door.

Everything was always so beautifully arranged at Great-aunt Lily's. The holly swags in the hallway had exactly the right number of berries and the glossy scarlet ribbons holding them onto the picture rails sported perfect bows. The champagne glasses shone and the canapés were lined up immaculately on the silver platters.

'Letitia, welcome. I haven't seen you in an age. You are looking so well. And Cathy my dear, come and kiss me. And Ellen is here too. How lovely.' Lily swept down the hall to greet her guests. 'It's just a small group of ten of us this evening. Dinner and then a little music. Come into the drawing room. I think you'll know almost everyone here, Letitia.'

Cathy followed her grandmother and Ellen into the elegant room to see six men of varying ages, heights and shapes standing talking and drinking. She recognised some of them. Uncle Seamus, of course. She hadn't seen him for a couple of years but he still looked very much the giant, but a happier giant than the last time she had seen him down in Rowanbridge. And the skinny, elderly man with the pointy beard; wasn't he the man who had played the violin at her Daddy's funeral? Mr Brennan, that was his name. Her Mammy's old violin teacher.

Mrs Fitzgerald shook hands with everyone in turn and exchanged a couple of words in a very regal manner, while Ellen limped after her around the room. As soon as Seamus had greeted Ellen, with an affectionate kiss, he dashed over to give Cathy a hug.

'It's very lovely to see you on a happy day, Cathy. I hope you are well. And how is your mother – and the rest of the family of course?' Her mother was always top of Seamus's mind.

They soon filed into the dining room where Lily had seated Seamus in between Cathy and Ellen while she and Mrs Fitzgerald took charge of the older gentlemen: Felix Brennan, a history professor from Trinity, a theatre director from the Abbey with a disturbingly loud voice, and the ancient cellist from the Gaiety whom Felix had brought along to take part in the quartet planned for after dinner.

The remaining guest was seated next to Ellen and was clearly a mate of Seamus.

'Ellen and Cathy, meet my friend, Colm O'Brian. He's a new solicitor in my firm and he has pretensions to being a violinist. We have taken pity on him tonight and let him come and play with the grown-ups.'

Colm O'Brian was a shortish, roundish younger man with a brush of carrot-coloured hair on the top of his head and on his chin. He blushed deeply at Seamus's introduction and meekly shook Ellen and Cathy's hands.

'Very pleased to meet you ladies, I'm sure. Seamus has told me all about you both, and about your mother, Cathy.

Apparently, I shall never ever come close to the brilliance of her playing. I know my place.'

Seamus and Ellen did most of the chatting over dinner while Cathy and Colm listened in, laughed at their jokes and quaffed the wine a little faster than the other guests. At the other end of the table Lily was kept busy replenishing Felix's plate, his appetite undiminished over the years.

'So, when will you be going home for Christmas, Cathy?' asked Seamus.

'Actually, I've decided not to go home this year. It's so busy at home, so many children; they won't miss me. And I don't want to leave my grandma alone with just Lizzy. I saw Mammy in the summer and I'll go at Easter. And I do write to her regularly and sometimes I telephone her when I know she'll be at Aunt Stasia's. They haven't installed a telephone yet in Main Street.'

'I've been playing some of the duets I used to play with Hannah with Colm. He's not a patch on your mother but it's better than nothing.' Seamus turned to Colm. 'I said, you'll never match the wonderful Hannah McDernott but you're better than nothing.' Colm laughed off the insult and immediately flushed scarlet again.

'Have you any ideas about what you're going to do when you finish at the Academy, Cathy? Are you going to try and get into a university, stay in Dublin or go back home?'

'I definitely won't be going back home to live. I can't imagine living in Rowanbridge now. It's so small. And I don't think I'm clever enough to do a degree – well at least, I'm not as clever as many of my fellow students at the Academy. My grandma would like me to stay and help her run the place. But I'd like to travel a little maybe and do something to help other people. I don't know what that might be though.'

'I never understood how Hannah could have been happy to go back to a village life when she was so talented and could have done so much. It's not as though your father was encouraging it either. The reverse, I'd guess. But you have plenty of time to decide, Cathy.'

'Well, I'll be seventeen soon.'

Seamus laughed. 'Oh heavens, that is such an *enormous* age. The thing is, you'll be a completely different person by the time you're twenty – I certainly was - so don't go making any decisions that you can't change. But you don't want to hear that right now. I understand.'

After dinner, Lily led the small party into the drawing room to take coffee and then the four string players set up their stands and chairs ready to play for their small and select audience.

When the players were settled and tuned up, Felix stood to address the six onlookers.

'Ladies and gentlemen – though mainly ladies – the last time Seamus and I played this quartet in this room Ireland was still ruled by England, the Great War was raging, we were surrounded by dozens of glamorous people - and we had practised adequately. Today, thankfully, the war is long behind us, we are a proud, practically independent nation and, although the audience is smaller, it is no less glamorous and a very precious one to us, particularly because we know you will be forgiving of our lack of practice.' Felix acknowledged the ripple of amusement. 'That night I was reduced to playing second violin because we had an amazing young talent here to lead us: young Cathy's mother, Hannah McDermott. Sadly, she gave up playing, in public at least, though I suppose it meant that people like me still kept our jobs. Anyway, please enjoy Beethoven's *Harp Quartet*.'

The slow introduction sucked Cathy in. The music was deeply familiar to her but for reasons she couldn't quite remember. It was joyful and, as the first movement developed, she let herself be carried into its heart. She couldn't believe that her mother had been able to match Felix's virtuosity when she was only about the age Cathy was herself today. How could she have given up all of this? What had been worth losing all this for? Not for love, Cathy was certain of that. Her father would never have asked her mother to give up the violin for his sake. Hannah could have had love *and* music if she had wanted. Something else had driven her back to Rowanbridge. Whatever it was, it wouldn't be the same for Cathy.

Chapter 30 - July 9th 1951

'Come and sit here by me.' Hannah dropped her rosary onto the counterpane and held out her bony hand towards Cathy. 'Now tell me all about my little grandson, Johnny. I would so love to see him before I pass but it's not going to happen now, is it.'

'Well, he's not so little for a start. He's seven. He's a great reader and his great-grandma insisted he learn the piano and gave him lessons in the early days. I started him on the cello six months ago too.'

'You must take back your father's cello for him then. It's in the lumber room I think.'

'I have some new photographs in my bag downstairs. He still looks very like Daddy. The same golden hair and sweet smile. I know I mustn't try to turn him into Daddy though. He's his own person. Uncle Seamus has been teaching him to ride a bike and fish…'

'Dear old Seamus.' Hannah touched Cathy's face gently. 'How wicked I was to send you away. I know I don't deserve you coming back to me now, but you must believe me, Cathy, when I tell you that I love you as fiercely as I do your sisters and brother. And I always have done.'

'Why did you send me away then, Mammy?' Cathy suppressed the sobs that were rising in her chest.

Hannah closed her eyes and sighed. She was silent for several minutes. Cathy wasn't sure whether she had fallen asleep. Was she still breathing? Just about. She stroked her mother's greying hair and Hannah opened her eyes.

'Why did I send you away? It's very complicated.'

'You said it was because I had married a heathen against your will. But you had done exactly the same when you married Daddy.'

'Yes, that's what I said. But it was an excuse. I think it was more … that I was mortally ashamed and I didn't want you to find out my secrets.' Hannah entwined her fingers around her rosary again.

'Your secrets? What secrets would they be now?' But Hannah had closed her eyes again and seemed to be properly asleep now. Cathy sat, gazing at her mother, incredulous that this tiny frame had given birth to four children, had made grown men cry with her exquisite playing, had turned an ailing business around - and had so tormented her eldest daughter.

After some minutes examining her mother's sleeping face, Cathy looked around the bedroom for something to occupy her. On her mother's bedside table she saw her father's volume of Yeats' *The Rose*. She flicked through it. The book fell open at a much-thumbed page. Cathy read the poem there: *The White Birds*. She knew it well but now it took on a special significance. God or no god, she hoped that her mother and father would soon be together again, free to soar to the skies. Somehow.

The sound of steps running quickly up the stairs returned Cathy to the here and now. The bedroom door opened and a beautiful young girl with a head of dark curls walked in.

'Hello Cathy. Remember me? I'm your sister Bridie. Aggie says I was only five years old the last time you saw me.'

'Hello Bridie. I'm sorry it's been so long.' And Cathy stood up to kiss Tricky's daughter on the cheek. Now that wasn't so hard, was it. Cathy caught sight of a small scar on the side of Bridie's forehead and realised guiltily that she was responsible for it, from the day that she had neglected toddler Bridie and let her fall into a fireguard.

'You two sisters will have such a lot to talk about.' Hannah had woken and was struggling to sit up.

'Here you go, Mammy.' Bridie was expert at arranging the pillows behind her mother's back and positioning her comfortably. 'Cathy and I can talk later but Aggie says she must go downstairs for her supper now while I stay with you a while.'

'Yes, off you go, Cathy. Bridie will sit with me and tell me all about her day at the convent. You won't believe it, Cathy, but that monster Mother Veronica is still alive.'

'Barely alive, Mammy. She must be over ninety and she's bed-ridden, but everyone still does exactly what she commands.'

'Over ninety! That's what a life devoted to God gets you I suppose. The fact that I'm dying at fifty-one proves just what a sinner I've been.' Hannah chuckled weakly at the horrified look on the faces of her two daughters. 'I'm only joking.'

Cathy walked into the kitchen to see Aggie serving up boiled ham and cabbage to Father Stephen, Tricky, Rose and a curly-headed Adonis, who immediately stood up and ran towards her, smiling broadly. It was Fergus. He picked her up and spun her round before setting her down again on a chair.

'You used to do that to me, do you remember? So, I'm just returning the favour. I bet you couldn't lift me up these days.'

How had that cheeky eight-year-old lad back in 1939 turned into this mountain of muscles and smiles?

'Fergus. Darling Fergus. I've missed you so much.' Cathy stood up again and gave her brother a proper hug. Rose came around the table and joined in the tight embrace.

'Stop that you soppy lot. Sit down and eat your food.' Aggie's stern reprimand was accompanied by a sniffle and the wiping of her eyes with the edge of her pinny.

'Welcome home, Cathy.' Tricky, seated at the bottom of the table, was already tucking in but lifted his head from his plate to greet her.

'Hello Patrick. Is it OK to call you Patrick? I'm sorry, I can't call you Father.'

'Tricky. Tricky's just fine.'

'Now then, fair Aggie, would there be any tea left in that pot on the draining board?' Father Stephen, sitting at the head of the kitchen table, held up his cup and saucer.

The conversation slowly eased into something comfortable and familiar: how the harvest was going, the price of grain, what colour they should paint the farm-cart, cousin Matthew's new baby. Rose and Fergus had plenty of questions for Cathy about their nephew Johnny, the Academy and Great-Aunt Lily. No-one mentioned their mother or the state of her health until all the plates were cleared away.

'Right then.' Father Stephen rose and stretched, rubbing his stomach in appreciation. 'Thank you to the talented chef, Miss Agnes Carroll, for a most delicious repast. A hundred times nicer than the scrambled eggs on toast I would have made for myself. I shall just pop back upstairs to give your mother a blessing before I leave, and I'll send Bridie back down.'

Father Stephen ruffled Fergus's head of curls as he walked behind him to the door. Two minutes later, Bridie appeared and plonked herself at the head of the table, next to Fergus, and poured herself a cup of tea. The sight of them together made Cathy breathe in sharply. Bridie and Fergus looking like two peas in a pod. Practically twins. No mistaking it. Good god. Well, that was one of her mother's secrets solved at least. Anyone who saw Bridie and Fergus together could only reach one conclusion: Tricky was Fergus's father too. Not much of a secret really. Just a secret from Cathy - until today.

Chapter 31 - May 21st 1939

'Damn and blast!' Diana, Cathy's room-mate, peeled off her left stocking and threw it onto her bed. 'That's my last good pair I've just stuck my nail through. Caught my others on that bloody jagged bed-frame this morning when sister made me redo my envelope corners. Thanks a lot, Demon Denton.'

'Here. Have these. I've got another pair.' Cathy took an unopened packet of stockings from her top drawer.

'No, you wear the new pair and I'll wear your old ones. It is your birthday celebration after all.'

Tomorrow it would be Cathy's nineteenth birthday, so tonight she and her fellow student nurse friends – the ones off-duty at least - were going to the big dance in Colchester Town Hall. But Cathy already felt totally grown-up. Just weeks after Ireland had voted in 1937 for a new constitution which distanced it even further from Britain, naming itself Eire for the first time, she had perversely left Dublin for England. Both she and her homeland were happily embracing self-reliance.

Cathy's arrival at Colchester Infirmary to start her nursing training had introduced her to some prime examples of repressed English spinsterhood, of whom Sister Denton was a fine specimen.

'Of course, Demon Denton would never ask you, her star pupil, to redo your beds.'

'That's because I get them right first-time. It's just easier that way. I grew up with a very demanding mother so Denton presents no challenge at all for me.'

'And I suppose when you had no electricity, boiled cabbage at every meal and earth toilets, the deprived life of a student nurse must seem like luxury.'

'Not quite, but I don't mind it. Here, can you fasten my necklace please?' It was the first time since coming to

England that Cathy had deemed the occasion worthy of wearing the pearl necklace her granny had given her.

Mrs Fitzgerald had not wanted Cathy to leave the Academy to go and train in England, but she had accepted her grand-daughter's wish with good grace. She had stumped up the considerable fees for the three years of training, and the evening before Cathy was to leave on the ferry crossing she presented Cathy with a modest pearl necklace.

'Here, take these with you. I haven't worn them in an age. Your grandfather gave them to me on our wedding day. They suit a very slim, young neck and I haven't had one of those for thirty years.'

Cathy, Diana and four of their pals tumbled off the bus in the centre of Colchester; they could hear the band as they approached the fine Victorian town hall. Diana started to run towards the entrance. 'Come on you lot. We need to bag a table.'

Once a table and chairs had been secured, the six girls bought themselves gin and Its or Dubonnets and lemonade and started to survey the smoky scene. The band was playing '*Jeepers Creepers*' and the dance floor was packed with couples attempting enthusiastic but mostly clumsy versions of the quick-step. Amongst their number were about a dozen soldiers from the royal artillery regiments stationed at Colchester Garrison, but on the opposite side of the hall was a bigger group of squaddies laughing at the antics of their mates while knocking back pints of bitter.

'Plenty of talent for us tonight, girls.' said Diana. 'Bagsy the one on the end with the moustache and the muscles.' Diana drained her drink and stood up, dragging Cathy up with her. 'Come on, Cath. If we start dancing together they'll come over and rescue us.'

'Oh Jesus, no. Not me. You know I can't dance for toffee.' Cathy sat down again and Diana grabbed Suki instead. 'Please yourself.'

The band started to play '*The Lambeth Walk*'; everyone seemed to know the steps. There was a rush of bodies making up couples. A pair of soldiers sprinted over to the girls' table and gallantly whisked a couple of them onto the dance floor. Diana and Suki were split up almost instantly by a couple of lads, though the soldier Diana had fancied ended up with Suki.

'You don't mind us leaving you here, do you Cath?' Brenda and Maggie decided to wait no longer for a man and seemed more than happy to dance with each other. Before Cathy could reply, Brenda and Maggie were parading round the hall with everyone else, slapping their thighs and shouting 'Oi'.

'It's not exactly Fred and Ginger, is it?' Cathy looked up. A tall soldier was standing by her table.

'Would you mind if I joined you? I can see you haven't the appetite for dancing to this and, frankly, neither have I.'

'Oh, yes. Please do.'

'Thank you. Let me introduce myself. My name is Joe - Joe Ashfield - and I'm a sergeant in the 27th Royal Artillery over at the garrison.'

'How do you do. My name is Cathy Fitzgerald. I'm a student nurse down at the infirmary. But originally I'm from Ireland – but you can probably tell that from my accent.' They smiled at each other as they shook hands and Joe sat down next to her.

'To be honest, it's not just the *Lambeth Walk* I can't stand. I don't dance at all.'

Joe looked at Cathy quizzically. 'Really? Well then, neither shall I. Let me get you another drink. What was it?'

Over the next couple of hours, Cathy and Joe exchanged their life stories while around them people became louder and more reckless in their dancing and dating. Joe was from a mining family in Ollerton up in the Midlands; he had joined the Army in 1936 to get away from following his father down the pit.

'Mining killed my Dad when he was only thirty-four so there was no way I was going underground to lead that hellish life.'

'I didn't want to do any of things my family wanted me to do either – to run a shop or be a teacher,' confided Cathy. 'Not quite sure why I chose nursing other than it was a way to get quite a long way away from them.'

'The army was an escape for me too. I'm quite happy messing about with tanks, polishing boots and parading about, but God help me if I ever have to go and fight anyone.'

As they shared their histories, their various companions came and went, drank and chattered, danced and canoodled, but Cathy and Joe were oblivious to them all.

The band started playing *The Nearness of You*. 'Oh, I love this song, don't you? I heard it in a film Diana and I went to see recently.'

'I do. It's beautiful.' Joe took Cathy's hand. 'Shall we give it a try out then? It's very slow. We just need to shuffle around a bit. But that way I get to put my arm around you.'

Cathy hoped that Joe couldn't see her scarlet cheeks in the dim lighting, but she allowed herself to be led gently onto the dance floor where Joe expertly enveloped her and helped her to sway to the music. Cathy felt the warmth from his body and the strength in his arms and rested her head on his chest. He smelt of coal tar soap. Was dancing really this simple?

The song ended but the next one followed straight on. Cathy made a move to return to her seat but Joe held on and they started dancing again. 'Did you hear Fred Astaire sing this in *Shall we Dance?* last year.'

'No. I was still in Dublin - and listening to Handel mainly.' Cathy laughed.

'Nothing wrong with Handel – my Mam sings *The Messiah* every year - but Gershwin is more my sort of thing.' The song was only halfway through when Cathy was aware of a hand on her shoulder, pulling her away from Joe's hold.

'Sorry mister. Come on, Cath. We need to run or we'll miss the last bus and get shut out. It's gone nine-thirty already.'

Diana turned to go with her hand pulling at Cathy's neck. Suddenly there was a burst of beads; the necklace had snapped. Pearls were popping and bouncing amidst the dancers' shoes. Diana, Cathy, Joe and a few of the girls scrabbled on the floor to pick them all up, avoiding dancing feet as best they could.

'Oh, bloody hell, Cath. I'm sorry. I hope it wasn't an expensive necklace.'

Handfuls of pearls were emptied directly into Cathy's purse. Hasty goodbyes were said before the girls ran out and the cool evening air hit them.

'Come on, Cath. Shake a leg.'

Forty minutes later, Diana and Cathy were in their nighties, drinking cocoa.

'You did alright for yourself tonight, didn't you. Tall, dark and handsome soldier, showing you his best moves. His mates said he's the best dancer in the regiment.'

'Really? He said he didn't want to dance.'

'That's just 'cos he was chatting you up, you ninny.'

Cathy emptied all the loose pearls from her purse onto a plate. Now that she could see them, it was obvious that many were missing but she said nothing for fear of adding to Diana's guilt. She just hoped her Grandma would forgive her. Never mind. It was only a necklace and she had had a wonderful time. Cathy took an envelope from her writing box, poured in the pearls and sealed it, humming *You Can't Take that Away From Me*, remembering her last dance.

Chapter 32 – July 9th 1951

'**R**ight, I'll be off back up to the field. Can't afford to waste a beaut of an evening like this.' Fergus rose from the tea table and lifted his shirt to scratch his hairy and muscled stomach. Bridie took the opportunity to tickle him. Even though death was in the house it couldn't smother the vigorous life-force of her brother and sister - half-brother and half-sister really - who clearly loved to laugh and have fun together.

'And I'd better get on with my Latin.' Bridie got up to go to her room and was showered by a handful of water thrown by Fergus.

'Gotcha' And Fergus ran out of the back door, jumping over Aggie who was sitting on the step smoking. He grabbed the familiar old blue bike leaning against the hen-house.

Cathy started to clear the table but Rose stopped her.

'No, Cathy. I can do that. You should go up to Mammy. You haven't seen her for twelve long years and you should make the most of the time. She hasn't got long.' The sisters looked hard into each other's eyes; Cathy nodded.

Cathy opened her mother's door gently. Father Stephen was sitting by Hannah's side holding her hand while she moaned in pain.

'This is always a bad time, Cathy, just before Dr O'Connor comes for the evening injection at about nine o'clock. The morphine has nearly worn off, you see. I try and stay until he comes – saying the rosary together takes her mind off the pain sometimes. I don't want the children to see her like this. And Aggie does the same in the morning and keeps them away.'

'Don't worry Father. I can stay with her now. I'm a nurse. I've held the hands of many dying people.'

'It's no bother to me at all. But I'll go and let you be alone with her.' The priest laid Hannah's hand gently on the sheet and stroked her forehead, before making a small sign of the cross there. Then he kissed his fingers and put them to her lips.

Cathy felt awkward. This was a strangely intimate exhibition from a man of the cloth.

'Good night now, Cathy. God bless you.'

Cathy lit the oil lamp as the sun sank outside. She sat down by her mother and took her hand. 'It's me Mammy. Cathy. I'm back now. You seem in a lot of pain. Is there anything I can do? Here, drink some water.'

Hannah didn't answer or open her eyes but squeezed Cathy's hand to let her know she understood.

After about half an hour there was a knock at the door and Dr O'Connor walked in. 'Hello Miss Cathleen. I'm sorry, I don't know your married name.'

'It's Ashfield. But please, 'Cathy' is fine.'

'Well, I did bring you into the world you know. I'll never forget it. It was your Aunt Stasia's wedding day and she was none too pleased about you making your appearance.'

'I don't think my aunt has ever forgiven my mother, though she has never held it against me personally.'

'Oh, I think they will have forgiven each other for everything by now, you know. Now then. Your mother seems in a terrible lot of pain this evening. Let me just give her this. Then we can talk.'

The elderly doctor opened his bag to find the syringe and a phial of morphine.

'You're a nurse, aren't you? Your mother was very proud of how brave you were going off to the front line to nurse the wounded.'

'Really? She always told me I was a traitor to Ireland joining the British Army.'

'No, no, no. That must have been her little joke.'

Cathy pushed up her mother's sleeve to expose her arm, to find a cluster of bruises from previous injections. Dr O'Connor's skill with a syringe was obviously rusty.

'Would it be OK for me to give her this? It's been a few years but I was very used to giving morphine injections.'

'It's a bit out of the ordinary… but I don't see why not.'

'And if you could leave me some spare morphine I could always administer it if her pain gets too bad. Without having to get you out of bed in the middle of the night, you know.'

'Yes, yes. That would be very helpful.' The doctor considered his options. 'Here. I'll leave you just one more dose. But I'll be back in the morning.'

As the needle sank into her mother's arm, relief flooded Hannah's face. Cathy's relief was almost as great. She was still a good nurse then.

'Well, your mother screamed a lot more when you were born, you know, but that sort of pain is a very different kettle of fish. A happy outcome after it all. No happy outcome here I'm afraid, as your mother knows only too well.'

'I've seen many wounded soldiers who would have said that death was a happy outcome after the pain they were suffering.'

'Yes. God's mercy always comes eventually to take them up to heaven.'

'God's mercy? I'm sorry, Doctor. I find the idea that any sort of loving God would let people suffer like this quite offensive.'

'Oh, dearie me. I can't start discussing the finer points of theology with you now, Cathy. I have to get to my bed. Talk to Father Stephen about it tomorrow.' And, after quickly packing up his bag, Dr O'Connor scuttled away.

'Cathy. Come here my angel.' How long had it been since anyone had called her that? Her mother looked much more comfortable floating on a cloud of morphine and was trying to sit up.

'I want to talk to you, but that stuff makes me very sleepy. So, we need to be quick. Go and look in my top drawer. There's a little key on the left side under my gloves. That will open the marquetry box at the bottom of my wardrobe. Bring it to me please.'

Cathy found the dusty box and carried it to her mother.

'Open it. There's your father's volume of Yeats's middle poems inside.'

So, there it was. Cathy had looked for that volume of Yeats so many times, the book she had found as a child with the two cut out pages; the later page with the poem *Broken Dreams*, on which her father had written that enigmatic message and then returned it to the book, but with the earlier cut-out page totally missing.

Cathy opened the book from the back and found the folded-up page of *Broken Dreams* at the place in the book from where it had been removed. There was the message again: *'I love you too much. I am so sorry for everything. John.'* It was so obvious now. Her father really had committed suicide; Tricky hadn't murdered him, though he was in part to blame because no doubt her father knew that Tricky was Fergus's father and this had added to his anguish.

'The other missing page is there too somewhere. Keep looking. It's near the start. It's for you.' Hannah stretched out a frail hand to Cathy. 'I'm sorry. I've hidden it from you for all these years.'

Cathy took her mother's hand and kissed it. 'Don't worry, Mammy. It's all a long time ago now.'

Cathy leafed through the book. Amid the early pages she found the missing page, folded and inserted at the spot where it had been removed. The poem was called *'A Prayer for my Daughter'* but she had no interest in reading that, only the unmistakeable writing of her father which filled all the unprinted space to the right of the poem and the margins.

Cathy stood and walked over to read it in the light of the oil lamp. *'My dearest macushla, I can barely write this through my tears, knowing that I will soon be leaving you all.'* Cathy lowered the page and stared at the lamp for a moment, trying to control the bitter emotions that were rising inside her. *'Please forgive me, Cathy. I am going because I know your lives will get better without me here. I have chosen this poem for you. You have brought me nothing but joy; you are beautiful, kind and learned and I hope you find a bridegroom one day who will cherish you. But don't think you have to 'root yourself in one perpetual place'; Yeats and I don't see eye to eye there. Please don't judge your mother. Whatever has happened is entirely my fault. Look after your sister and brother, and remember your other sister, who was born with the sound of the Atlantic in her ears. I love you so much, my darling Countess Cathleen. Goodbye, macushla, my beloved daughter. Your adoring Daddy.'*

Cathy didn't know how long she had spent reading the message over and over, wiping her eyes, when there was a faint knock at the bedroom door and Aggie walked in with a cup of tea.

'Oh, right then. I see she has given you the message from your Daddy. You'll be needing this cup of tea, I reckon.'

As Cathy gratefully sipped the tea, Aggie woke Hannah gently and lifted her onto a chamber pot. 'There you go. Now you can sleep sound, Hannah. Nighty night.' The servant wrapped up the featherlight body of her mistress in the soft bedclothes before giving her a kiss on the cheek.

'Now Cathy. Off you go to bed too. Tricky will watch her until about three o'clock when I take over and then Rose comes in at seven. '

'No, I'll stay. I want to stay. And she might need the extra morphine that Dr O'Connor left for her.'

'Don't be a crazy woman. You must be exhausted from all your travelling. We can come and wake you if we think she needs an injection. Anyway, Tricky is already at his station and on-duty. He never comes into the bedroom. You'll see. He has a chair outside and he looks in from time to time. Like a lady's maid - or maybe even a prison warder. We've been managing OK without you all this time, you know.'

Aggie opened the bedroom door and gestured for Cathy to exit in front of her. There was Tricky, sitting on his hard chair, with folded arms.

'She's sleeping now, Tricky.'

'Right.'

'Goodnight then.' Aggie turned for the stairs.

'Night.'

'Goodnight Tricky.' Cathy took a deep breath. 'Thank you for looking over Mammy.'

Tricky shook his head and looked down at the floor. 'Night.'

Chapter 33 – August 1939

Cathy and Joe stood outside the jeweller's in Museum Street, holding hands, looking at all the rings for about ten minutes before taking the plunge and walking inside. The bell above the door tinkled and the shopkeeper emerged from the back of the shop. He was doing a good trade in cheap wedding rings since another war had begun to look inevitable.

Cathy had known that she wanted to marry Joe when he had turned up at the nurses' residence the day after the Town Hall dance – her nineteenth birthday - with eleven missing pearls in his jacket pocket. He had waited until the dregs of the dance had been swept out by the Town Hall's caretaker and then Joe had slipped him a ten bob note so that he could check over the floor with the lights full on.

Several of the pearls had been jived into the gaps between the floorboards; others had rolled away into dark corners. Up in Cathy and Diana's room, Joe took off his jacket to fish each little bead from the tweedy corners of his pocket and tip them into a saucer, while Cathy admired the back of his sunburnt neck, his muscled fore-arms and deft fingers.

It was no more than a week after that first dance that Cathy and Joe had become an 'item', as Diana called them. They saw each other at every possible free moment over those blissful few summer months in Colchester, as nations manoeuvred overseas and the prospect of Britain being dragged into a war with Germany drew closer. But walks in the park, bus trips to the coast, hand-holding in the back row of the cinema and gentle goodnight kissing when Joe delivered Cathy back to the nurses' residence couldn't completely obliterate a sense of foreboding.

At the end of July, as they sat on the beach at Frinton, Joe asked Cathy to marry him. He didn't go down on one knee but he did take a ring box from his pocket containing a modest diamond engagement band. Cathy said yes instantly as Joe slipped the ring onto her finger.

'Diana helped me choose it, and she said your hands were about the same size. But we can change it if you don't like it or if it doesn't fit. Whatever you want, duck.'

'Don't be daft. It's lovely.' And Cathy kissed him briefly.

They celebrated with an ice cream before getting on the bus back to Colchester. As the bus rumbled through the Essex lanes, Joe broke the news to Cathy that his regiment was being prepared for a likely war.

'So... I want us to get wed as soon as we can and I hope you want that too. We can go home to Ollerton and my Mam will do the wedding breakfast and maybe some of your people can come over from Ireland. We've got plenty of neighbours who'll give them a bed.'

'Well, the first thing is to go and ask my mother's permission to get married at all. I'm only nineteen you know and without her agreement there's nothing we can do.'

'Best get over there quick then, duck. I reckon this war's coming soon and then it'll be dodgy getting over to Ireland.'

During the crossing over the Irish Sea, Cathy wasn't sure whether her queasiness was caused by the rolling of the ferry boat or the anticipation of confronting her mother with the news that she was already engaged to an English, working class atheist.

The exchange, when Cathy finally launched into it after a day home in Rowanbridge, was even worse than she had imagined.

'Are you out of your mind, Cathy? You're only nineteen.'

'You were younger than me when you married Daddy.'

'And what a disaster that turned out to be.'

'Why would you say that? You loved each other very much. You had the three of us. Joe and I love each other very much.'

'Love is not enough.'

'Love must be enough.'

'Nonsense. Quite apart from your age, why in heaven's name would I agree to you marrying an English soldier and a heathen to boot? I learned the hard way what happens when you turn your back on God.'

'That's ridiculous, Mammy. You're telling me God killed all your babies because you didn't worship him? If such a God exists I want nothing to do with him.'

'I cannot make you have faith. Time will do that to you, I'm sure. But I can stop you marrying this man.'

'You just can't bear the thought of me being happy can you.'

And so, Cathy had returned to Joe in Colchester with the frustrating news that they would not be able to marry until she was twenty-one, nearly two years away.

'But we will be married in our hearts, Joe.'

Joe replied, 'Of course, love' and he said that he would wait as long as it took, but why shouldn't they go and buy the wedding ring anyway. Then Cathy could wear it as if she was legally Mrs Ashfield. So here they were, looking at gold wedding rings in Colchester, fending off prying questions from the diminutive jeweller whose aspirations for a juicy sale this Tuesday afternoon were fading fast.

With the cheap gold band in Joe's breast pocket, he and Cathy went to the off-licence on the corner and bought a bottle of champagne before walking back to the nurses' residence. Cathy had drunk it before at her Great-aunt Lily's but neither of them had ever bought it before and they were both appalled at the price but hid their shock from each other.

When they got up to Cathy's bedroom Diana was in there, washing her smalls. They showed her the wedding ring and she congratulated them heartily, advising them to leave the warm bottle that Joe was clasping in a basin of cold water for a while before opening it. Diana was a woman of the world. She was also good at taking a hint. She quickly finished her chores and gathered up her coat and bag and announced she was going out 'with the girls' and wouldn't be back until locking up time at ten o'clock.

Cathy and Joe had nearly five hours ahead of them. They had never before lain on a bed together to do their kissing. This was more like it.

Joe got tired of waiting for the champagne to cool down and decided to open it anyway. The exploding cork and spurt of foam took them by surprise but made them laugh like drains. Cathy mopped up the spill with her towel and rinsed out the tooth-mugs for Joe to pour the champagne into. They stood by the window and clinked their mugs as a toast.

'I love you, Mrs Ashfield.'

'I love you too, Mr Ashfield. Come home safe to me.'

And they exchanged effervescent kisses as the summer breeze wafted the prematurely closed curtains.

Cathy had never had sex before, but she had had a few boyfriends during her time as a student nurse and had got dangerously close to it a few times. And she was a nurse and understood exactly how men's bodies worked – in theory at least; she knew about condoms and she thought that there was nothing Joe could do that would surprise her. But she hadn't expected the shuddering orgasm that Joe's tender and accomplished lovemaking delivered. Cathy's 'wedding night' with her lovely, kind soldier was as joyful as Cathy had dreamt it would be, albeit one that had to end at ten o'clock when Joe was bundled out of the residence before Diana returned and the front door of the nurses' residence was locked tight.

Chapter 34 – March 1946

The three Ashfield women took it in turns to take the ration books and queue up at the Ollerton shops. It was Cathy's turn to queue at the butcher's and it was starting to rain. The paint around the shop window was covered in the obstinate black dust that came from the pit, so oily that even the rain couldn't shift it.

There were about seven other women ahead of her in the queue; Cathy calculated that it would take at least twenty minutes to get to the head of it and inside the shop. She turned up the collar of her coat and folded her arms against the relentless wind and wet.

None of her fellow queuers looked well; they were either painfully thin or bent from exhaustion, their grey faces frozen in resignation. This was what victory looked like.

Cathy thought back to the early days of the war when hopes of victory had been so intoxicating.

Two weeks after their pretend wedding in August 1939 – and five more stolen love-making sessions courtesy of Diana's discretion - Joe had left Colchester for somewhere secret to be taught how to direct a tank regiment while helping train up new recruits. He wrote to Cathy twice every week. Early the following January, Cathy could tell from the new writing paper and its smell that he had moved somewhere else and from Joe's hints she thought he must now be in France.

She kept on plastering the broken arms and stitching the cuts of the good people of Colchester, keeping Sister Denton happy with her exemplary bed-making. But, after the disaster at Dunkirk and Joe's shocking reports of the wounded and dying in France, Cathy resolved to get herself nearer to the fighting. Nearer to Joe. She was now a fully trained nurse and the Queen Alexandra's Imperial Army Nursing Corps was only too happy to accept her.

Cathy wrote to tell her mother and grandmother that she would be leaving Colchester to go and work near the front line. Her grandma wrote back praising her bravery, offering advice about living abroad – boil all drinking water, always wear a hat, don't eat too much greasy food - and sending money and very much love. Cathy received not a word from her mother.

Cathy's twenty-first birthday, in May 1941, was spent in a field hospital in Athens, picking shrapnel out of the legs of four British soldiers and holding the hand of another mangled soldier who died later in the night. Cathy thought about how it would feel to be his wife when she received the news of his death. Being married to a serving soldier was not going to be easy, but she desired it above all else and was now free to marry Joe without her mother's consent.

Easier said than done. She and Joe were still writing faithfully to each other twice a week but arranging to be in the same place at the same time to get hitched was quite another matter. It was Christmas 1941 before they managed to get any leave home at the same time, with a special dispensation from Cathy's matron. Their sparse wedding, in Mansfield's mercilessly cold Register Office in the January, was a speedy and functional ceremony, attended only by Joe's mother, his sister Shirley and a few family friends. Cathy's grandma, Mrs Fitzgerald, sent money for a new outfit for her and Mrs Ashfield had saved up her rations of sugar and butter to make a cake, so there was some sense of occasion to the day.

But all Cathy wanted was to be in Joe's bed, in his arms and in his heart. Their first twelve blissful days of married life flew by and then they were both back on ships, off to serve Britain wherever in the world it needed them. As Cathy read Joe's letters, lying on her thin bed in Athens, she thought how much warmer she had felt in grey and grimy Ollerton, cuddled up in bed with Joe, than here in the Greek sunshine.

After a brief trip 'home' to Ollerton with Joe for Easter in 1944, only the third leave home they had shared since their marriage, Cathy returned to the field hospital. Six weeks later, when she had to run from the operating theatre to vomit, she regretted not following her grandma's advice about eating too much greasy food, but it only took a couple more days of sickness to realise that she had fallen pregnant.

Joe was thrilled to hear the news and wanted her to leave nursing instantly and go to Ollerton to be cossetted by his mother. But Cathy wanted to stay in Greece for as long as she could hide her condition from matron. There were a lot of soldiers who needed her. But eventually, towards the end of November 1944, Cathy arrived in Ollerton with her two cases, to await the arrival of her baby. Johnny's birth in January was joyful of course. Mrs Ashfield's common sense and kindness was very welcome. Cathy had held her mother-in-law's hand tightly as she screamed through her contractions and was grateful for the all the wise baby advice Mrs Ashfield – 'Mam' - gently offered. How different from her own mother.

Joe was granted three days' special leave from his regiment to come home to see his new-born son. Cathy took photographs of Joe holding Johnny every time the baby woke up. But she yearned for the war to be over so that Joe could come home and they could start to be a proper family.

'We've got them on the run, duck. Just look after yourself and this little chap for me and I'll be back before you know it.'

Joe came home for a week in May. He couldn't believe how much his son had grown, now sitting up and laughing and eating mashed potatoes and gravy.

'You're a proper belter, my lad. The girls are going to be queuing up when you're a bit older.' He stroked John's baby blonde hair and kissed his hot teething cheeks. Every afternoon of that precious week, Cathy and Joe pushed

Johnny around the local park so they could have some time alone and they took it in turns to photograph each other holding the wriggling baby.

After Joe returned to the front, photos of baby Johnny and Cathy tucked into his wallet, Cathy chose a few of the tiny, square black-and-white photographs to send to her grandma in Dalkey. Then she selected the two very best pictures, one of each of them holding Johnny, and sent them to her mother in Rowanbridge, including a little news and her current address. She didn't know what to expect but she knew what she hoped for.

And then the news arrived that Joe was dead, killed by an abandoned German sniper in a French town Joe's regiment had just liberated, just two months before peace was declared. Cathy did the calculation; she and Joe had been married for three-and-a-half years but had spent fewer than fifty nights in the same bed.

She cried plenty, but not as much as Mrs Ashfield who seemed to weep around the clock. How could one woman of only four feet, eleven produce so many tears? Cathy needed to look after Joe's son and to do that she knew she must stay as cheerful as possible.

A strange life evolved for Cathy and the baby after the peace arrived. There was little to do but take Johnny for walks, sometimes to the park and sometimes to the cemetery where Joe's father lay. Joe himself was buried in France near where he had fallen. Other times, like today, Cathy would leave Johnny with his granny so she could queue up alone with their ration books for the scant groceries. When Johnny had been put to bed, the three women would play endless hands of tedious card games, or sometimes Cathy would help Shirley, a dressmaker by trade, by sewing buttons and poppers onto the blouses and dresses she was making for her customers as they listened to the crackle of the radio.

Cathy couldn't wait to escape to her bedroom each evening. By the faint light of her bedside lamp, she would try and lose herself in the elegance of Jane Austen or the romance of Emily Brontë, worlds as far from Ollerton as she could imagine. Before she switched out the light, she would gaze at some photos of Joe while their son snuffled in the cot beside her. Without those photos, Cathy wasn't sure she would be able to recall Joe's face.

Ten months ground past. When Johnny started to crawl, Cathy was happier for him to be out in the muddy park than in the cramped semi, with scarcely enough room to walk between the solid items of furniture and with Shirley's carelessly abandoned pins and needles lying hidden in the rugs waiting to ambush the baby. She thought about her own childhood in Rowanbridge and that of her sister and cousins and how lucky they had all been to have food, space and freedom.

'Move up, duck,' said the woman behind her in the queue, not unkindly. Cathy, startled, closed up the gap in front of her. Only three women ahead of her now, all huddled against the wind, exchanging scraps of gossip. They all looked pinched and worn. Most of them were the wives of miners. Their husbands had returned from the war to what? To a life spent in the pitch black, breathing in coal dust. Was this the life her son - now more than a year old - could expect?

She eventually reached the front of the queue and bought some best end of lamb neck. She hurried home with it. Mrs Ashfield would make something tasty.

As she sat drying her stockinged feet in front of the range, a cup of tea in hand, reading a book to Johnny nestled on her knee while Mrs Ashfield started cooking out in the kitchen, Cathy made the decision: she would take them both back to Ireland to live at the Academy with her grandmother. She would never queue up at that butcher's again.

Chapter 35 – July 10th 1951

Despite the many tormenting thoughts and questions that had followed the discovery of her father's parting note to her and the secret of Fergus's paternity, Cathy had fallen asleep almost instantly in her old bed the previous evening. She was woken by Aggie, shaking her shoulder and holding a cup of tea. There was a jug of steaming water on the washstand.

'I'm sorry to wake you, Cathy love, but I thought you'd want to be up and about.'

'What's the time?' Cathy sat up and rubbed her eyes.

'It's gone half eight. Dr O'Connor will be here at nine to give your mother her injection.'

'Oh God, Aggie. You should have woken me earlier. How is Mammy?'

'Well, she's still breathing - just about. She has some fight in her. Always was a stubborn one, that Hannah McDermott. I'm off to my bed for a few hours now. Rose will make you some breakfast.'

Once washed and dressed, Cathy crossed the landing to her mother's bedroom. Tricky's chair was empty. She wondered how long he had kept guard.

'Hi there, my darling sister,' whispered Rose as she rose to greet Cathy and hug her hard. 'Mammy has just gone off to sleep but she's been groaning since I came in at seven. She needs more pain-killer, you know.'

'Don't worry, Rose. I'll tell Dr O'Connor. He trusts me with extra doses. I could go and get the one he gave me last night but it seems silly to wake her now she's gone off - and anyway he'll be here in ten minutes.'

'Can I leave you then and go and get some breakfast? I'll bring you up some toast in a bit.'

Cathy settled herself into the bedside chair and examined her mother's sleeping form. Was she still breathing? Cathy leant over and felt a thin thread of air from Hannah's nostrils. She took her mother's wrist; she could just make out a pulse. Surely, her mother had little time left.

Cathy looked around. There, on the bedside table, was her father's volume of Yeats where she had left it last night. She opened it up, located the first loose page and re-read his farewell message to her, this time without any tears. She started then to read, for the first time, the two sides of poetry the message was written on. It was called *A Prayer for my Daughter*, clearly not a randomly chosen page.

Once more the storm is howling, and half hid
Under this cradle-hood and coverlid
My child sleeps on. There is no obstacle
But Gregory's wood and one bare hill
Whereby the haystack- and roof-levelling wind,
Bred on the Atlantic, can be stayed;
And for an hour I have walked and prayed
Because of the great gloom that is in my mind.

I have walked and prayed for this young child an hour
And heard the sea-wind scream upon the tower,
And under the arches of the bridge, and scream
In the elms above the flooded stream;
Imagining in excited reverie
That the future years had come,
Dancing to a frenzied drum,
Out of the murderous innocence of the sea...

It was a long poem with many verses that Cathy read through carefully several times. She smiled as she imagined her Daddy watching over baby Mairé and making wishes for her future while a storm raged outside the cottage in Cleggan. She didn't understand it all, but she got a good sense that her father had wanted his daughters to grow up to be modest, kind, educated, open-minded - and happily married to some good man. She didn't think that the council house in Ollerton Joe had brought her to was quite as 'ceremonious' as her father would have wished, but she loved the idea of metamorphosing into a green laurel. She also wondered whether the *'great Queen'* – Venus maybe - choosing *'a bandy-leggèd smith'* was some bitter reference to Hannah and Tricky. How wounded her Daddy must have been to be usurped by someone as unattractive and just plain weird as Patrick Byrne. What had her mother been thinking? But the poem was insistent on a rejection of hatred. She wondered whether her father would be proud of how she and Rose had turned out and had enough self-knowledge to conclude that he would. She folded the page and returned it to its home.

There was a knock at the front door downstairs. That would be Dr O'Connor. Cathy heard Rose speak to someone followed by purposeful footsteps mounting the stairs. 'Come on in, Doctor,' Cathy entreated the knock at the bedroom door. Not Dr O'Connor but Father Stephen, looking flushed and a little out of breath after his speedy ascent.

'Morning, Cathy. How is she? I can never start the day until I see how the land lies with her.' The priest walked over to the bed, took Hannah's hand from Cathy and kissed it. He stroked Hannah's face until she opened her eyes weakly.

'How are you, my love?'

Cathy blushed; this surely was not how a priest should behave.

'It's you. I know you.' Hannah raised her thin hand to Father Stephen's face. 'I am worn out, Stephen. I want to go. Is that wicked, my darling?'

'Not long left, my love. We'll all be here with you. Nothing to be scared of.'

'But the pain! It tears me apart.'

'The doctor is due any second, Hannah. Hold on.'

Cathy walked up to the bedside. 'Yes, Mammy. And I'm going to ask Dr O'Connor for some extra morphine so that we don't have to let the pain come back at all.'

'Cathy my love, you're here.' Hannah sounded surprised as if her daughter's arrival yesterday had been completely forgotten. 'Thank you, my angel.'

At that very moment, Rose showed Dr O'Connor into the bedroom. She was also carrying a plate of toast and marmalade and a cup of tea for Cathy.

'Morning all,' said the doctor and set about preparing the morphine injection.

'Cathy, take yourself off to the drawing room to eat your breakfast.' Hannah waved weakly at the door. Stephen will mind me for a while when the doctor has gone.'

'If that's what you want, Mammy. Doctor, could you leave me another spare dose of morphine, please?'

'Did you use the extra one last night then?'

Cathy hesitated for a moment. 'Yes. Mammy really needed it at about three o'clock this morning.' She blushed at her lie, especially in front of the priest. It felt like she was back preparing for her first holy communion.

Five minutes later, Cathy was sitting on the piano stool in the drawing room, sipping from her teacup, when her Aunt Stasia walked in, carrying a small tray with her own cup of tea, a jug of fresh water for Hannah and a small vase of sweet peas.

'Good morning, Cathy, my dear. It's wonderful to see you home after so long. It's not the same talking on the telephone, is it. Not that it's a very happy reason for coming home. Give me a kiss now.' They embraced and both sat down.

'I've come to take my turn watching over your mother which I do most days. Rose says she had a bad night.'

'Yes. The pain is really ramping up and she needs more regular morphine. Dr O'Connor has left me some extra doses so I can try and make sure she never gets too uncomfortable.'

'What a blessing that you're a nurse. God provides in unexpected ways.'

Cathy's fingers tightened around the cup but she said nothing. Stasia stood up and picked up the tray. 'Well, I'll leave you to finish your toast. '

'Father Stephen's in there with her at the moment, Aunt Stasia.'

'Ah, that's fine then. I'll just wait here until he's gone.' Stasia resumed her seat on the sofa.

This wasn't at all like her aunt, thought Cathy. She would normally want to be right at the heart of action, and particularly if it involved the priest.

'Just smell these, Cathy. Aren't they divine. I picked them for her this morning. Your mother has always loved sweet peas...'

'Auntie Stasia, what's going on? Why does Father Stephen behave so ... intimately with Mammy. He kisses her and calls her "my love" and she calls him "darling". You must have noticed. I thought I was imagining it at first, but it really is happening and it can't be right.'

Stasia drank some tea and then returned the cup to the saucer, avoiding Cathy's stare. Then she looked up.

'Do you really want to know, Cathy? Are you ready to hear this?'

'Of course. I need to know.'

'Well then.' Stasia's voice dropped to a whisper. 'I cannot believe that a secret we have managed to keep hidden for nigh on twenty years is now being put in peril by a priest who seems to care nothing for his own and your mother's reputation now that she is on her death bed. He is throwing all caution to the winds.'

'Only with me in the room though.'

'You say that. Frankly, anyone with half a brain and one eye, seeing Fergus and Bridie in the company of Father

Stephen, would have to wonder why they all look so alike. But there's a big difference between having suspicions and having those suspicions confirmed.'

'No!' Cathy's brain raced to take in what her aunt was implying. 'I realised only yesterday that Fergus and Bridie must have the same father but I assumed it must be Tricky. Are you saying that... that it is Father Stephen?'

Stasia nodded and gave Cathy several moments to absorb the news before continuing.

'It could have been a terrible scandal. We managed to convince everyone that Tricky fathered Bridie after he and Hannah married. That worked for quite a while. But it was really very unhelpful that Bridie and Fergus grew to look so alike. I think Bridie was about nine when Edmund made some comment to me that 'anyone would think Tricky was Fergus's father too'. At that point I told him the truth. But for all these years it has just been the five of us keeping the secret. Oh, and Aggie of course. Aggie knows everything. She's always known everything.'

'So, you've always known that Father Stephen and my mother were lovers.'

'No, not always. I, of course, believed that your mother's frequent visits to church were entirely devotional. I assumed that Fergus was your father's son. Why wouldn't I? It was only when Hannah crawled around to the villa a couple of years after your father died, crying and begging for help because she was unmarried and pregnant - by Stephen – that she had to confess. She wanted money for an abortion in Dublin, but I wasn't prepared to do that. She told me then that Fergus was also Stephen's child.'

'So, did my father know about Father Stephen?'

'I'm sure he did – at least by the time he took his own life. That's probably what pushed him over the edge. Money troubles are one thing but... infidelity...' Stasia's voice trailed off and she shook her head.

'Did you ever know that I was convinced that Tricky had murdered my father? I used to go and talk to Father Stephen about it. Oh God, what an idiot I was.'

'Tricky, a murderer? How could you have thought that? No, more like your mother's saviour. It was my idea that she marry Tricky. I knew he adored her and would do anything for her and that man can keep a secret like no-one else. It solved so many problems and he was very happy to do it. Honoured even. I think part of him loved to torment childless Nicholas by – apparently at least - producing an heir to the Byrne estate.'

'Do you think Nicholas suspects the truth?'

'Possibly. But he's not going to make the family look ridiculous by airing his doubts, is he? And the land and money have to go to someone. Why not Bridie and Fergus?'

The drawing-room door opened and Father Stephen popped his head round the door. 'Ah, you're here, Stasia. Hannah has dropped off. I'm must be away now. Ten o'clock mass won't say itself. But I'll be back later.' The priest's head disappeared and the door was about to shut, when Stasia called out.

'Stephen, come back.' The priest came back into the room.

'Shut the door. Stephen, I've told Cathy everything. I had to. She could see what was going on with the pair of you.'

Father Stephen leant against the door, sighed and dropped his head. 'Fair enough. You needed to know some time, Cathy. Your mother wants to tell you before she goes, so she'll be relieved you already know. What must you think of me? My only defence is that I love your mother so very much. I loved her for years before she loved me back. Now then, even though I am clearly unworthy, I must go to take mass, but we can talk as much as you like later. Goodbye for now … and God bless you.' And with a nod of his head, he left.

Chapter 36 – April 1946

Silky red maple leaves were just unfurling either side of the green front door of the Academy when Cathy and toddler Johnny arrived back in Dalkey in the spring of 1946. Ellen was waiting at the front door to welcome them both like her own long-lost family and Mrs Fitzgerald was waiting in the drawing room with a pot of Indian tea – Cathy had plucked up the courage before she had left for England to tell her granny that she really didn't like Lapsang Souchong – and a big chocolate cake, made by Lizzy with young Johnny in mind.

Mrs Fitzgerald was naturally thrilled to have her grand-daughter home and to meet her great-grandson, though his likeness to her own John clearly caused her both joy and heartache.

'What a beautiful child, you have, Cathy. Treasure him always, whatever he might do in the future.'

'Don't worry, Grandma. I'm going to tie him to me with chains of steel. Even if he robs the Bank of Ireland and shoots de Valera, I shall forgive him.'

The three women had a heap of questions to ask each other and news to relay as they sipped their tea. Johnny was glued to his mother's knee for the first half hour, clutching the tiny teddy that Auntie Shirley had sewed for him from leftover pieces of a fake fur collar on a discarded coat. After a while he slid off Cathy's lap and walked tentatively around the drawing room, looking at the pictures far up above him. He made his way to the piano. What a strange machine. He had never seen such a thing before. He looked over to his mother as he stretched up to press down a key.

'No you don't, you little monkey. Not until you've washed your hands.' And Cathy dashed over to scoop him up before he could discover that the key would make a noise if pressed.

'I look forward to teaching him to play – but not until he's at least five. I taught his grandfather, of course, whom he so resembles.' Mrs Fitzgerald smiled fondly at the little boy, but she was haunted by bittersweet memories.

Eventually, Johnny was persuaded to sit on Ellen's knee and he giggled as she held Tiny Ted and made him talk to Johnny in a silly voice. She was a natural with children. The slightly nerve-wracking tea-time came to an end when Ellen decided that Mrs F. looked a bit tired and needed to be left in peace to continue reading her volume of Ovid – in the original Latin, naturally.

Cathy carried out the tray of china, Ellen took the partially demolished cake while Johnny trotted dutifully behind them to the kitchen where old Lizzy was sitting peeling carrots for supper.

'Lizzy, how are you?' Cathy put her arms around her as Lizzy dried her hands on her apron. 'No, just stay there. No need to get up.'

'Oh, Miss Cathy. How lovely to have you home. Your Granny has missed you so much.'

Is this really my home, thought Cathy. Yes, one of them, she supposed, and it would certainly be her home for the foreseeable future. Ellen bellowed up the stairs, summoning a couple of the students to come down and carry all of Cathy's luggage up to the second-floor bedroom that she had previously occupied, her father's old room. Cathy helped Johnny to climb up the two flights of stairs and it took quite a while. They walked into the room, where a small bed had been made up for the little boy next to the wardrobe, and an extra chest of drawers and a bookshelf installed.

After thanking the two lads, Cathy walked around the room, stroking the familiar and well-loved furniture, marvelling at how much space there was compared to the cramped bedroom in Ollerton.

'This is your new bed, darling.' Cathy sat on the low mattress and lifted Johnny to sit beside her. 'You and Tiny

Ted will be so comfy in it.' She gave her son a big squeeze. 'It's a lovely bedroom isn't it? It used to be my father's bedroom when he lived here, your grandfather. You're called Johnny after him.' Cathy could see that the concept of a grandfather meant nothing to the boy; it was hard enough to get him to understand that he had had a daddy once upon a time. 'We can get your books out on the shelves and your crayons and bricks.' Johnny had few toys but the ones he had he loved very much.

Cathy went over to the small bag that contained Johnny's possessions; the boy ran over to pick out his two favourite toy trains which were immediately set down onto the imaginary track of the floorboards. Cathy also took out two framed photographs, one of her and Joe outside Mansfield Register office and one of Joe holding his baby son which she placed on her bedside cabinet. She would do her very best to keep Joe's memory alive, and not just for Johnny.

Over the following weeks and months, life took on a congenial routine that seemed to suit everyone living at the Academy. Mrs Fitzgerald's health had begun to fail towards the end of the war so she stayed mostly in her bedroom and little crimson sitting room. Some days she didn't even get out of bed. Cathy was mostly occupied with Johnny during the first year, giving him the benefit of the sort of home tuition that she had had from her own father. But after a year and half back at the Academy, there was enough time left in the day to start taking on the administration and finances, tasks that had previously been the responsibility of her grandmother.

There were always plenty of people volunteering to mind Johnny for an hour or so, from Lizzy, who would let him roll out pastry or bread sticks, to some of the teenage students, who would take him for walks to the beach, to even Mrs F herself, who would read to Johnny or play the piano for him. He would sit mesmerised by his Great-grandma's playing. Eventually, when Johnny reached five years old, Mrs Fitzgerald started to teach her grandson the piano.

Ellen had become an inspiring educator and an excellent leader over the last eight years, so much so that, just before the end of the war, Mrs Fitzgerald took the difficult decision and promoted Ellen to the position of head-mistress of the Academy over the heads of some longer-serving teachers.

'I've said it before, Patricia Murray is one in a million and she has been with me for the last thirty-five years, but she could no more run a school than fly to the moon.' Miss Murray and the other experienced teachers actually seemed perfectly happy to accept Ellen as the head, so she inherited some fine and dedicated teachers along with a few younger and livelier ones.

But Ellen wasn't so self-important not to be thrilled to have Cathy back in Dalkey as an equal partner, taking on all the administrative and pastoral duties of running the school and watching over Mrs F.

'I know my leg doesn't help, but I really don't know how Mrs F. had the stamina to do it all – all the teaching plus all the business stuff – back in the day when your mother and I were pupils here. We should have had more respect for her.'

There were other people in Dublin whom Cathy loved to spend time with. She took Johnny to see his great-great-aunt Lily, still a vigorous and handsome woman, a couple of weeks after returning to the Academy. She hid it well but Lily was not much interested in the little boy but she relished Cathy's company and wanted to know every detail of her time nursing at the front, of her romance with Joe and her brief marriage – and how relations were with her mother. Cathy knew better than ever to criticise Lily's adored niece, Hannah, so she didn't share how very painful it was to feel that her mother didn't care too much for her eldest daughter. In return, Lily regaled Cathy with all the theatrical, political and cultural news of the city. After a few months, Cathy started to leave Johnny with Ellen so she could go to see her Great-aunt Lily alone and devote all her attention to the glamorous and lively nearly seventy-year old. Sometimes she would stay overnight so that she could accompany Lily to a concert or a play.

Then there was Uncle Seamus, who was anxious to see Hannah's daughter as often as possible and to do whatever he could for her. The occasional evenings he had spent at the Academy while Cathy was in England, visiting Mrs F and Ellen, turned into weekly social evenings of bridge now that Cathy could make up a fourth player. And, every so often, he and his old headmistress would treat Ellen and Cathy – and sometimes an enthralled Johnny - to a few viola and piano duets.

Over the next couple of years, Johnny grew to love his Uncle Seamus who spoiled the boy rotten. Seamus bought Johnny a tricycle and would take him onto Killiney beach to build sandcastles. Seamus would always arrive at the Academy with chocolate for the lad, which Cathy objected to and took it off him to mete out in modest daily rations, but she was secretly glad that Johnny had some sort of solid male presence in his life; it couldn't be good to be surrounded by too many adoring women. They were grandfather and grandson in all but name.

But the one woman she wished would adore Johnny, her own mother, never replied to any of Cathy's letters and cards. It broke her heart to think that Hannah had so little love for her own daughter and grandson. Cathy stopped talking to Johnny about the grandmother in Rowanbridge and concentrated instead on telling him about his English grandmother in Ollerton. Ma Ashfield was only too thrilled to receive regular news and photos of Johnny and her carefully written birthday cards and monthly letters for the boy arrived punctually. Sometimes his Auntie Shirley Ashfield would send a hand-made shirt or pyjamas for her nephew.

'Your Auntie Shirley was the person who made Tiny Ted for you, you know.' Although the two Ashfield women were further away geographically, they were a lot more real to Johnny than the relatives living not that many miles away in Rowanbridge.

Across 1946 and 1947, Ellen and Cathy started to change a few things at the Academy. With financial and legal advice from Seamus, they decided to convert the entire stable block behind the main house to create extra classrooms. More bathrooms were installed in the main house and the kitchen updated.

When 'young John', as his great-grandma insisted on calling him, started proper school in Dalkey after his fifth birthday, Cathy was even able to take on some teaching duties, mainly music and literature. As she stood in the main classroom, reading out Wordsworth or Donne to the dozen innocent and thirsty minds in front of her, she imagined her father's voice doing the same nearly thirty years before her.

Chapter 37 – August 1948

It was a very humid August day in Dalkey. Cathy and Ellen were awaiting the arrival of a new teacher, and a very important and long sought-after one too: Aoife de Bhailis. Cathy opened all the windows in the downstairs rooms; she hoped to get some sea-breezes into the Academy to make it feel fresh for their imminent visitor but it made little difference to the heavy air.

It had taken two years of Cathy's and Ellen's persuasion before Aoife had agreed to leave Cleggan to cross over to the other coast of Ireland and teach the Irish language to the privileged band of Academy pupils. She said she could only bear to leave Cleggan because Dalkey was by the sea, and that as far as she was concerned it was the same sea as the one at home, despite having a different name. All the oceans and seas of the world were really one interconnected entity, in her opinion, and the different names were false distinctions, human-made obstacles, just like the arbitrary borders of countries or religious doctrines.

Aoife had told them to expect her at about five o'clock after a day's travelling from Clifden. Ellen, Cathy and Mrs Fitzgerald were gathered in the drawing room when they heard a taxi draw up on the gravel soon after a quarter past the hour. Cathy ran out to welcome Aoife and help her in with her battered cases.

'Oh, just let me see you for a moment, Cathy. It's been far too long. It must be nearly twenty years, I reckon. You were just a little girl but you have grown into a very beautiful woman. But I see your wonderful Daddy looking back at me.'

They embraced each other warmly.

'You look exactly as I remember you, Aoife. You don't even have any grey hair to speak of. Maybe the odd little line around your eyes – laughter lines of course. Come on

210

in. There's tea waiting for you and you must meet Johnny and Ellen of course.'

Ellen came out to the hall; she shook Aoife's hand and showed her into the drawing room where Mrs F was sitting by the open window reading to her grandson. Johnny ran to his mother.

'Johnny, say hello to your Auntie Aoife.' Johnny clung to his mother's leg, peeking out at the stranger from behind his mother's skirts.

'Dia duit, mo stoirín. I'm sorry, Johnny; that means 'hello, my little love' in Irish. I promise not to confuse you again.'

'Now, you see that just proves what a contrary language Irish is. I know how to spell that phrase and it looks nothing like it sounds. Such a waste of time teaching it to children; they'd be better off learning Russian.' Ellen's views on the government's Irish language policy were very much like Mrs Fitzgerald's. Aoife looked aghast.

'Oops, I beg your pardon, Aoife. Me and my big mouth. Just because I think teaching Irish is silly it doesn't mean that you aren't completely and utterly welcome; we are so grateful to have you here.'

Aoife smiled at Ellen. 'Don't you worry now, Ellen. I'll have you speaking Irish along with the students, just you wait.' Aoife put her hand on Cathy's shoulder. 'You too, Cathy. It's what brought your father out to Cleggan in the first place after all.'

'Well, given Ellen teaches Latin and Ancient Greek, which absolutely no-one speaks, she's clearly talking rubbish – which she does quite a lot, you'll soon find out. I'm looking forward to learning some Irish.'

'Of course, you two have already met.' Ellen took Aoife's elbow and took her over to where Mrs Fitzgerald was sitting. The old lady extended her hand but stayed in her chair.

'Forgive me, Aoife, for not standing up to welcome you. I am a worn-out old woman these days. So much has happened since we first met all those years ago.'

'Hello again, Mrs Fitzgerald. Yes, indeed. Two terrible wars and the loss of so many people we both loved.'

Mrs Fitzgerald nodded, bowed her head and held onto Aoife's hand with both of hers. Ellen took Aoife's hand from Mrs F. and showed her over to the sofa.

'Now, come on you two, no time to be sad today. We've got too many exciting plans to hatch – but let me say right away, we will not be doing it in Irish!'

Aoife gestured for Cathy to come and sit next to her. 'You can't imagine what it feels like, Cathy, seeing you and Johnny. It's like your father and Mairé are back here with us.'

Over tea, Cathy and Ellen plied Aoife with endless questions which she answered with her customary calm kindness in her soft lilting Connemara accent. 'So, now that your mother and father have passed and you've moved here, are you going to sell the cottage?' asked Cathy fearfully.

'I would never do that.'

'Thank heavens. I can remember everything about that trip to Cleggan with Daddy when I was just ten, and I swore I would go back one day. Before too long, I intend the keep the promise I made to myself.'

'Maybe we can all go back together in the holidays. I will certainly go back as often as I can. The cottage has a lodger looking after it for me - Liam, the boy from Letterfrack school. Do you remember him?'

'Liam. Of course, I remember him. He taught me to skim stones. My Daddy talked about Liam a lot, not just to me but to our local Fianna Fáil man, trying to get something done about that evil school. Liam's fate preyed on his mind a lot and it broke his heart when Liam was sent back to the Brothers. He blamed himself, you see.'

'How like John. He had nothing to blame himself for. Well, Liam came to us finally just after his fifteenth birthday, not so long after your father died. And you can comfort yourself, Cathy, that John will have seen what has become of Liam from up in heaven. Any anguish will not have lasted long. He'll be looking down on us all right now with his beautiful smile, delighted that we are all taking tea together.'

Cathy didn't have the heart to tell Aoife that her father's anguish was indeed over, but not because he was up in a heaven she had no belief in.

'Well, if he *can* see us all - which I very much doubt - he won't be at all happy that de Valera is out of office now and we have that rogue Costello in charge - though I think your Grandmother is delighted.' Ellen nodded towards Mrs F.

'Well, I think at the very least that it was time to give someone else a turn. We were turning into a one-party state.'

'How on earth did you manage to get Liam away?' Cathy asked Aoife.

'I wrote a letter for my father to take to the school, offering Liam a job as a fisherman's boy, paying him a proper wage. The brothers wouldn't release boys unless they had a job to go to, you see.'

In 1934, Ruari de Bhailis had knocked on the door of St Joseph's school in Letterfrack holding the letter, now carrying his carefully written signature. An hour later, after being questioned by a surly Brother, Ruari and Liam trotted back to Cleggan together in the trap, the fisherman's rope-roughened hand resting gently around Liam's shoulders, as Shawna and Aoife waited anxiously in the cottage.

Aoife recounted how young Liam had become an expert fisherman under Ruari's tutelage and, as the old man started to lose his powers, Liam's growing strength and confidence more than compensated. Liam was lucky enough to spend five years alongside his mentor and saviour before Ruari died suddenly in his sleep.

Life at the Cleggan cottage had continued much as before, while the war raged over in Europe, with Ruari's fishing duties amply fulfilled by Liam - though the young man never sat in the old man's chair or sang his songs. And Shawna never recovered from the loss of her beloved husband. She visibly shrank, quickly losing her memory, her hearing and eventually all speech. But she never stopped her knitting and would sit in silence by the cottage window all day, clicking away, waiting for Aoife to return from the school and Liam from the harbour.

'When I got the first of your letters, Cathy, offering me a job here, I was very tempted. It would bring me close to two precious people, to John's daughter and his grandson. I adore Liam – I see him almost as my own son - but I thought maybe I should give him the space to find himself a wife. He has grown into a very handsome young man, you know, but he's still very quiet and shy. Every letter of yours that came I would consider the possibility of leaving, but there was no way I could uproot my mother. But then, last summer, she started to drift away fast and she was gone by the autumn, God rest her soul.' Aoife crossed herself. 'This spring, I started to imagine life away from Cleggan. I don't suppose anyone thought it improper for a middle-aged spinster teacher to be living alone with a good-looking, single young man - but maybe better not to risk it,' she laughed.

'Well, I hope you won't regret it. I think we have a wonderful school here and you are exactly the teacher we need, however ridiculous Irish is.' said Ellen generously. 'I am buying my own little house – just a street away – so you can soon move into my rooms in the stable block. Then *you* can get woken up at dawn by Johnny instead of me.'

It didn't take long for Aoife to settle into the Academy and, before Halloween, she was able to move into her own couple of rooms once Ellen vacated them. Aoife would rise early to take a long walk along the Dalkey beach before breakfast whatever the weather threw at her, and sometimes Johnny was by her side. They became best friends; as soon as he woke up he would run across the backyard to the stables to listen to a fairy-tale read by Aoife while he ate Aoife's porridge. And Aoife adored Johnny in return, seeing in him so much that she had loved in his grandfather.

It didn't take long for Aoife to get used to teaching older students than she had been used to back in Cleggan, but it took the students longer to get used to learning Irish; unlike the children back in Connemara, none had grown up hearing the language spoken all around them. But Aoife was a dedicated and patient teacher so most of the Academy students were soon able to hold simple conversations in their historic tongue. Beyond her classroom duties, Aoife was a warm and calming presence to everyone at the Academy, students and staff alike, and Mrs F. increasingly relied on her for various intimate tasks.

Aoife was true to her word and, at the end of her first term, took herself back to Cleggan over the Christmas holidays. While she was away, the Republic of Ireland Act was signed. Eire was now a real thing. When Aoife returned in January, the four women invited Seamus over for a celebratory dinner and they toasted the start of Ireland's fully independent existence.

'Your father would have been so happy to see this day arrive, Cathy.' Seamus put a warm hand on Cathy's shoulder.

'I suppose so. Mostly anyway. He would have been happy to have no more English kings and queens ruling over us, but he wouldn't have been happy to think this was the end of the road. Not until Ireland is independent and totally united again. He would have kept fighting for what was right. But he would have been tickled by how annoyed my Auntie Stasia must be to be finally separated from Britain.'

Another term passed by. At Easter, Ellen decided to accompany Aoife out to Cleggan, leaving Cathy at home to look after her now totally bedridden grandmother. The two middle-aged teachers had become firm friends. Cathy felt their absence keenly, both emotionally and practically. Despite her nursing skills, Cathy despaired to see Mrs Fitzgerald's health deteriorate so rapidly and there was nothing she could do to slow it down. When the summer holidays came around, Ellen again accompanied Aoife out to Connemara and this time for a whole month, so neither of them were on hand when Mrs F. took a dramatic turn for the worse and had to be hospitalised.

Cathy felt terribly alone. She tried to visit her grandmother once a day, in the afternoon or evening depending on whom she could find to look after Johnny. Mrs Fitzgerald's sight was almost totally gone, so Cathy would read aloud a book that her grandma would suggest. She realised that the novels had probably been chosen with her in mind: E.M. Forster, George Eliot or Elizabeth Gaskell. Her Great-aunt Lily came to visit her dear friend a couple of times but Lily was not at her best around sickbeds; she salved her conscience by sending flowers every week.

'I'll be off home now, Grandma.' Cathy closed up *Mansfield Park* and put it on the bedside cabinet. The nurses were bustling around, beginning to prepare the patients for the night. Cathy put on her coat and bent to kiss her grandmother on the cheek. Mrs Fitzgerald took Cathy's hand and held it tight.

'Cathy, I think this might be my last night.' Cathy protested. 'Ssshh, now. It doesn't matter; it will be one night soon anyway. I welcome it. I'm very tired, you know. I must tell you that I've left the Academy to you alone, but I've left a modest sum of money to my other two grandchildren, even though I've never met them. Seamus knows everything. He drew up the will. I just want you to know that you and young John have brought so much joy into my life and I hope that by looking after you I have made some small amends to your beloved father. I was very wrong to cast him out. How could a loving mother have done that? I don't know - but I do know that I always loved him – deeply - even when I was so angry with him. But we must be judged by our actions not our feelings, and on that score I am guilty, so I ask your forgiveness. Now then, I don't want any fuss at my funeral. Promise me that there'll be no priest. Just a few friends and maybe a little music. Very simple. Look after the Academy, Cathy, and look after Ellen. She's a treasure and cares for you very much. And look after yourself and young John. You are so precious.'

Cathy struggled to find something to say. She knew her grandmother could not be appeased with a glib phrase. 'I will look after everything that you care about, Grandma. Always. I've nothing to forgive you for and my Daddy certainly forgave you. But you must forgive yourself most of all. I love you and I'll see you tomorrow.'

Cathy walked away, turning back to wave when she reached the double doors of the ward, but her grandmother's eyes were already closed. They never opened again.

Mrs Fitzgerald's funeral was put on hold until Ellen and Aoife got back to Dalkey. Cathy dug out the pearl necklace her grandmother had given her when she had left for England. It was tucked away at the back of a drawer in an envelope along with all the loose beads that Joe had rescued for her after the dance that special night in 1939. Cathy got the necklace restrung and put it round her grandmother's neck before the coffin was closed. Just Cathy, Ellen and old Lizzy accompanied the coffin to the burial ground but, a few days afterwards, Cathy hosted a small reception at the Academy for Mrs Fitzgerald's friends and several existing and previous Academy students, Maisie and Eamonn among them. Lily gave a eulogy, Ellen read out Prospero's Act IV speech and Cathy played the first movement of the *Moonlight Sonata*. She was comforted by the knowledge that her grandmother would have thoroughly approved of how they marked her passing.

Chapter 38 – August 1950

The summer of 1950 saw the four of them - Cathy, Johnny, Ellen and Aoife - board an early bus from Galway out to Clifden. The train service had closed before the war - a great loss.

'Is that the sea, Mama?' Johnny asked every time they passed a glittering lake, and Cathy remembered doing exactly the same when her Daddy had brought her to Connemara twenty years before. Clifden looked very familiar. Even the local bus they climbed onto looked identical to the one Cathy and her father had taken along those winding lanes so many years ago.

But the tanned, copper-haired man waiting at the bus-stop was quite unrecognisable. Liam was as slender as he'd been twenty years ago but was now tall, straight and broad-shouldered with a ready smile flashing out from his rusty, scruffy beard. He lifted Aoife down from the bus, hugged her, and then climbed on board to take off the party's luggage.

'Here, let me help you down, Ellen.' Liam had learned over the last two years how best to help her, offering his shoulder and lifting her off the bottom step. 'Thank you very much, Liam. You're a dear.'

Cathy was the last off the bus. 'Is it really you, Liam. I would never have recognised you – you look so, well… grown-up - and strong. Though, now I see you close-up, your eyes are just the same.'

'I'd know you anywhere, Cathy. You haven't changed at all.'

Johnny ran ahead of them down the road towards Cleggan as Liam loaded the cases into the trap. They couldn't persuade Johnny to ride with them so Cathy walked the couple of miles to Cleggan holding his hand, while the pony clopped behind them.

Johnny ran ahead, then stopped and pointed. 'Is that the sea now, Mama?' and he squealed with delight when his mother nodded yes.

Cathy was amazed at how tidy the cottage was and how well Liam had prepared for their arrival. The sheets weren't ironed but smelled fresh and the beds were made tidily enough. The floors were swept and the larder well-stocked. On the kitchen table was a jug with cornflowers and campions in it.

'How do you find the time, Liam, to look after yourself and the cottage, as well as all the fishing and the boat-fixing and net-mending?'

'When you've worked for the Brothers at Letterfrack, this is child's play, I promise.'

Aoife stood and put her arm through Liam's. He put his hand on hers. 'Do you remember, Cathy, what a scrawny little runt he was, eating his dinner out the back like a mongrel? All he needed was decent food and sleep and people to care about him. Look at how he's turned out now. The Brothers had taught him nothing you know – he could barely write his name – but he took to books like a fish to water. I so loved teaching you, Liam. My favourite ever pupil. Mammy and Daddy were very proud of you, *cuisle mo chroidhe*, and so am I.'

Liam lifted Aoife's hand to kiss it. He turned to Cathy. 'Now then Cathy Ashfield, can you still skim a stone?

Not all of Cathy's stone-skimming skills had deserted her. She managed to squeeze one or two skips before the pebbles sank into the waves. But Johnny learned quickly under Liam's patient tuition. Cathy went to sit on the grassy dune, watching her son scour the beach for the perfect stone and then run up to Liam for instruction. The feeling of the salty breeze ruffling her hair felt so cleansing and liberating and memories of her first time on this beach burst through from the back of her brain.

Eventually Liam left Johnny to perfect his new-found skill and he came and threw himself down onto the grass next to Cathy.

'He's a grand lad. Looks very like you and your father.'

'I know. I just hope he has a happier life than my Daddy.'

'Why wouldn't he, with so many women around to spoil him? I used to dream of a soft woman's hands when the only people touching me at Letterfrack were cruel men.'

'Did you not know your own mother, Liam.'

'Yes. But I never dreamed of her. You know she sent me away to that school when I was just six, and then she sent me back to those monsters when I thought I'd found sanctuary here with the de Bhailises.'

'Is she still alive?'

'I have no idea, and, frankly, I don't care to find out.'

'I wish I didn't care. I haven't seen my mother for ten years – she's never seen Johnny – but I think about her every day. I just don't understand how mothers can turn their backs on their children. Your mother, my mother – even my father's mother. It's so cruel. Children need their mothers whatever age they are.'

'Why don't you go back to Rowanbridge to see her then?'

'She won't let me. She has forbidden me to come home. We fell out before I went to train in England. I hated her new husband you see. I think I might have even called her a whore.' Cathy winced but then laughed along with Liam. 'And then I made it much worse by defying her and marrying a non-believer. That was when she banished me from Rowanbridge. I just thought I'd show her and refused to say sorry. I was waiting for her to apologise first. No chance of that. I came to my senses eventually, but, even though I've written her dozens of letters and sent photographs and said sorry endless times, she won't budge.'

'She must have a fearsome determination not to want to see you or her grandson.'

'She certainly has that, an iron will. But I just can't fathom why.'

Life seemed so simple in the Cleggan cottage. By the time Cathy and Johnny woke the next morning, Liam had already gone out in the boat, and Aoife was stirring porridge. Daily tasks followed, filling the morning: sweeping out the peat ash, making beds, picking beans that Liam had grown on the sunny side of the cottage, filling the pony's water trough in the field. Ellen and Aoife played with Johnny and read to him while Cathy enjoyed some time to read for her own enjoyment for a change.

Liam made only a short trip out, returning just after midday, bringing home a smaller catch than usual which he then sold at the harbour, leaving just enough fish for their supper later.

'How about coming for a ride in the boat this afternoon, Johnny – with your Mama of course.' Johnny squealed his acceptance and ran to his mother jumping up and down in anticipation.

'Are you sure you can afford the time, Liam.' asked Cathy anxiously, secretly excited at the prospect. She had been on many large ships and ferries throughout the war but had never been out to sea in such a small boat.

'I don't have visitors very often, do I? And I can always make up the fishing time when you've gone back to the city.'

An hour later, Aoife and Ellen stood at the harbour wall, the glinting reflected sunshine dancing drunkenly over their faces, holding Johnny's hands between them until Liam had helped Cathy into the bobbing boat and settled her onto the wooden seat. She was doing her best not to show how alarmed she was at how the boat wobbled at her slightest move. Liam then lifted Johnny into the boat and instructed him to stay within his mother's arms for the duration of the ride. The little engine soon took them out of the harbour.

'Look how tiny your Auntie Aoife and Ellen are now, Johnny.' The two women were still waving at the receding boat from the stone harbour. Then Liam turned the boat into the next bay and they disappeared from view.

'I thought we could stop at this beach and swim a little.'

'You're joking. We can't swim. Not me and not Johnny.'

'Oh God, I had no idea. You live by the sea, don't you? I should never have brought you out on a boat then. There are some life jackets somewhere in the shed, I think. Sorry Cathy, I'm a complete dunce. I should have asked.'

'Don't worry, Liam.' Cathy was getting used to the bounce of the boat over the waves. 'I should have said. We'll be OK.'

Liam cut the engine as they drew close to the sandy cove. He jumped into the shallow water, pulled the boat ashore and lifted his passengers clean onto the beach, first Johnny and then Cathy.

'Right then, young fella, I reckon there's no better time than right now to start learning to swim. It's a beautiful day, the sea is behaving nicely and I'm here to teach you. We'll ask your mother to avert her eyes while we take off our trousers.'

After fifteen minutes or so in the water, with Liam first holding Johnny in the sea by his whole body and then just by his hands, Liam lifted the lad onto his shoulders and strode out onto the sand. Cathy tried not to stare at Liam's sinewy torso, not a morsel of spare flesh on him.

'Ah well. Your mother has seen us in our underpants now. There's no going back.' Johnny giggled and wriggled free from Liam's back to go running manically up and down the edge of the water.

Liam sat down beside Cathy. 'He'll dry off soon enough on the outside, though he has a fair bit of the ocean inside him too now.'

The two sat in silence for a while, Cathy turning a stone over and over in her hands, and Liam letting handfuls of sand sift through his fingers. Cathy gazed as drops of water fell from Liam's hair, trickled down his strong back and slowly evaporated.

'He's a grand lad; he must miss his Daddy terribly.'

'Not really. He never knew him at all.'

'Well, you must miss him at least.'

Cathy paused before replying, 'Yes, of course I do. Or at least I think I do. I miss the idea of him. Joe was a lovely, lovely man. But the terrible thing is sometimes I realise I haven't thought about him at all for days. I take off my wedding ring when I'm baking and then I forget to put it back on. And I have to look at photos to remember what he looked like.'

'I suppose you weren't together for long in the end. Maybe you'll marry again. Your boy could do with a Dad.'

'He has at least three mothers though, you know.' Cathy and Liam laughed.

'You must be lonely out here on your own, Liam. Do you not want to find yourself a wife?'

'Maybe.' Liam sat up and brushed damp sand from his hands. 'I'm too busy to be honest.'

'But a wife could help you.'

'I'm not sure I'd ever make a good husband. I've never… never actually been with a woman, you see. That side of life – it's a bit messed up to be honest, thanks to those bastard Brothers.'

'Oh my God. I'm so sorry. When you said only those evil men had ever touched you I didn't realise you meant touched in that way…'

'Aye, well. Nothing to be done about it. At least I'm alive. Some boys have died in there and more yet to die, I fear. Everyone round here knows about it – they must do - but no-one wants to do anything about it, it seems. Or maybe they are struck by blindness as soon as they come through the front door of St Joseph's.'

'I think the news that you had been sent back to that school was one of the final straws that sent my father over the edge. Did you know he had killed himself?'

'Only since Ellen told Aoife, and then she wrote to me about it. Your father was a very good man – I'd call him a saint. Such a waste. We all mourned when we heard.' Liam looked round. 'I'm so sorry. I didn't mean to make you cry.'

They sat together for a while, in reflective silence, until Johnny ran to them with his hands full of shells.

'Look, Mama. I've found all these lovely shells. These ones have got jewels inside them.'

'That's called mother of pearl, sweetheart, and I think it's even more beautiful than jewels. Like rainbows.'

Cathy jumped up and brushed the sand off her skirt. 'Come on. I know where we can take your shells. You know too, Liam.'

After the bumpy ride to Omey Island, Liam tied up the boat and the three walked up towards to the exposed graveyard by the sea.

'We're going to see the graves of a girl called Mairé and her Mammy. Mairé was my half-sister, so your Auntie in fact, though I never met her, and her Mammy was married to my Daddy, your Grandad, before he married my Mammy. She was called Ailsa and she was Auntie Aoife's sister.'

Johnny nodded solemnly, though it was a lot of detail to remember. But he had heard about Mairé before. 'Is she the girl whose hair you have in your drawer?'

'That's right. Well-remembered, sweetheart.'

The graveyard came into view. Cathy thought she could recall where the graves were but Liam led them instantly to the right spot. Both graves were spotless, free of the moss and grass that covered most of the other graves and the marble was washed clean. On Mairé's small grave were arranged two rows of cockle shells and some polished white pebbles.

'Oh, how wonderful. Did you do this, Liam.' He nodded. 'Do you keep them like this?'

'Yes, of course. Always. You asked me to.'

Chapter 39 – August 12th 1950

When Cathy, Johnny and Liam walked back into the cottage, Ellen and Aoife exclaimed at the state of their damp and sandy clothes. Aoife looked Liam and Cathy up and down. 'Gracious me, you look like you've been living in the Sahara for months.'

'Bloody hell, Johnny, you'll be able to build a sandcastle on the rug at this rate.' Ellen ruffled Johnny's hair and a cascade of silver fell to the floor. 'Off you all go now, back outside again and brush yourselves down properly and take off your shoes.'

'But look at my lovely shells.' Johnny held out a handful of iridescent shells for inspection and approval. He had left his own tribute of shells on Maíré's grave but he had kept a few with the most lustrous inners to present to Ellen and Aoife, which they accepted with lavish thanks. They were much more handsome than any he could find on Dalkey beach; he saved his favourite three shells to take home.

The beachcombers were made to go upstairs to wash and change before eating. The two older women had assembled a simple supper - fish stew and freshly baked brown soda bread. The five of them sat around the scrubbed table. Aoife bent her head to say a personal silent grace while the others waited for her to serve. It was, after all, her home still.

Even though it was August, the summer evening merited a small peat fire in the grate and they sat around it telling stories of the people they had loved and lost. Then Liam rose to go and sort out the boat for the next morning while Aoife told Johnny the story of Finn McCool and taught him a few new words of Gaelic - bád, iasc, cuan - and Cathy and Ellen washed the supper dishes.

'Bedtime for you now, Johnny Ashfield. You've had a full and exciting day,' said Cathy as she returned the last cup to its hook.

'Can I take my shells up to bed?'

'As long as you wash them thoroughly. You don't want sand in your sheets, do you.'

'We'll put Johnny to bed, Cathy my dear,' said Ellen. 'We love to do it. Why don't you go and take a stroll along the water. The light is beautiful out there still. I think it's nearly a full moon tonight.'

Liam was out on the beach side of the cottage, sorting nets, washed in silver light.

'It's a hard life, isn't it Liam, pulling fish from the sea?'

'I'm used to it. But did you know I have sheep too these days, and in winter-time I'm glad not to have to depend on the fish. Though, to be honest, walking over the hills in the middle of the night, in winter, trying to locate a noisy ewe with a tricky birth is just as life-threatening. I sprained my foot last spring, slipping off a rock. And by the time I found the ewe she'd managed to get the lamb out just fine. I virtually crawled home.'

'That's why you need someone waiting at home to look after you.'

'That's what Aoife says too,' laughed Liam. 'You women.'

By the time Cathy slipped into her sheets, Johnny was fast asleep, clutching Tiny Ted, on the little bed beside hers, the very bed she had slept in on her first visit and the one Mairé had slept in too. All was quiet in the bedroom next door where Ellen and Aoife were sleeping. Seeing them here together in the Cleggan Cottage, so comfortably domestic and sharing a bed, made Cathy wonder whether they had become more than just friends. She hoped so. Certainly there couldn't be two more wonderful women who deserved to find love at last in someone's arms.

Cathy heard Liam come up the stairs and the latch close on his door. She lay awake for nearly an hour, trying to put in order all the chaotic thoughts that the day had provoked. She could heal men's bodies well enough but how did one set about healing a man's mind? Cathy also had to admit to herself that her compassionate instincts towards Liam were somewhat compromised by other feelings. She threw back the sheets and sat on the edge of the bed in the dark.

Eventually she stood and left the bedroom, closing the door behind her as silently as she could, and walked the two steps across the landing to Liam's door. She stood with her hand on the cold iron latch for several minutes but then took a deep breath and squeezed it open.

Liam was fast asleep, his face turned away from the door and with his strong naked back on show. The curtains were undrawn allowing moonlight to cast a spectral shimmer over the room. The smell of the sea pervaded everything. Cathy stood watching Liam for at least ten minutes, not sure whether she wanted him to wake or not. She sat gingerly on the edge of the bed, her heart beating fast.

Liam awoke suddenly and sat bolt upright. 'Cathy! God. I was just dreaming about you. Or maybe it wasn't a dream at all. Is everything all right?'

Cathy put her hand on Liam's shoulder. 'Ssshh. Everything's fine. I was thinking about you too. I was thinking ... how much I wish you'd kiss me.'

Cathy leant forwards, put her hand on Liam's cheek and brushed his lips with hers. Liam pulled himself away slowly and searched her face hard, before putting his arms around her and kissing her chastely on the lips.

'That was nice, Liam.'

'Mmm. I have been thinking about kissing you too. All day long.'

Cathy began to kiss Liam more seriously, her mouth softly open and searching.

'Stop. No. I'm sorry. I can't let you kiss me like that.' Liam pulled Cathy's hands from around him. 'Do you realise the filth that has been in my mouth. No-one should have to kiss that.'

'Liam, don't say that. I don't care in the slightest.'

227

'But I do. I can't forget, hard as I try. Those bastards poisoned me, and I can never, ever be right again. I'm ruined. I'm sorry, Cathy.'

'Liam, you've got nothing to apologise for. You're blameless.'

'That's the thing, Cathy. I'm not. You see…it got so that I started to be grateful for it because it meant I wouldn't be beaten. And… my body sometimes… responded to it. You know what I mean.'

'I understand. But that still doesn't make it your fault in any way. Our bodies have a will of their own and they can betray us.' Cathy took Liam's hand. 'Will you let me just hold you for a little while?'

Liam shuffled over to the edge of his bed to make room for Cathy, though stayed under his covers. He held out his arm and she lay down next to him, her head on his shoulder and her arm stretched over his chest.

Liam began to stroke her hair and then his hand moved to her shoulder. He slipped his hand down onto her back underneath her nightie. Though his palms were coarsened from his rough work, his touch was as light and delicate as a bird's. They stayed in each other's arms for over an hour, exchanging gentle caresses and kind words.

'Cathy, I'm sorry but you must go back to your room. There's no way I'll get a wink of sleep like this and neither will you. But just to know that you care for me makes me so, so happy. Bless you.' Liam sat up and took Cathy in his arms; he squeezed her hard before kissing the top of her head.

'Off you go now, macushla.'

Chapter 40 – August 13th 1949

J ust like the day before, Liam had already gone off in the boat by the time Cathy came downstairs for breakfast.

'He was gone even before I saw him this morning,' said Aoife, sitting cradling a cup of tea. 'He works so hard. He just drives himself and he doesn't need to. He has only himself to feed. That's just the way he is. He's looking for something… some meaning to his life.'

'Well, I think he works like a demon so that he *doesn't* have to stop and find a meaning to his life.'

'Maybe.' Aoife nodded. 'Is Johnny still asleep?'

'Yes. All that swimming and running has properly exhausted him, but in a good way.'

'Well, Ellen doesn't have that excuse, but she's still snoring her head off!'

Before Liam got back, Aoife took Cathy and Johnny to check on the sheep, leaving Ellen to mind the bread baking in the side-oven.

'It's one job we can save Liam. Sheep are such silly animals, they have to be checked every day. Now Johnny, we need to count them and there should be twenty-seven.'

Johnny was an enthusiastic helper but more trouble than he was worth as he kept running towards the flock, scattering them to the corners of the field, making them impossible to count.

'I shall come on my own tomorrow, said Aoife to Cathy out of Johnny's earshot, 'Though he can come and run with the pony all he likes.'

At supper, Cathy sat next to Liam. She brushed her hand against his whenever she passed him a dish. He gave her a tiny smile each time. Cathy waited until she was sure Johnny was sound asleep before going to Liam's room. This time he was awake and sitting up in bed.

'I hoped you'd come.' Liam threw back the bed clothes and held out his hand. He was bare-chested but wearing his underpants.

They still just held each other, but it was love-making of a sort. Cathy's bare legs were up against Liam.s, and she slowly insinuated her knee over his thigh; it was impossible not to be aware of his erection though she didn't know what to do about it. Liam stroked Cathy's hair and shoulders and arms. He kissed her hands and she kissed his chest. But when she tried to kiss his mouth he turned his head away.

'I'm sorry, lovely girl. I can't.'

'Don't say sorry. Just being held by you is enough.'

'Is it? I don't think so.'

They fell asleep sculpted together, Cathy's back to Liam's chest, his knees tucked up behind hers. Cathy was woken by Liam kissing her hand. It was barely dawn but he was already up and dressed.

'Good morning, macushla. Sorry to wake you, but I think you need to get back to your own bed before young Johnny wakes up and thinks you've run away to join the circus.'

Over the next week, Liam and Cathy gently and painfully did their best to heal the wounds from Letterfrack. Every night they broke through some barrier to reach a new level of intimacy. On Monday, Liam touched Cathy's breasts through her nightdress and squeezed her nipples; the following night she removed her nightdress and Liam kissed, licked and sucked her breasts like a starving man, before falling asleep on her, one hand cupped around her left breast.

By Thursday, Cathy asked Liam's permission to remove his underpants and touch his erection; he cried out when she did and Cathy was not at all sure that it was not causing him actual physical pain. But he urged her on until he ejaculated over her hand.

'Oh, I'm sorry, macushla, I couldn't help myself. Let me clean you up.'

'It's not dirty, Liam. It's lovely …it's life.' And she rubbed herself between her thighs with his semen. 'Here. You rub it into me yourself.' And she took his hand to her sticky vulva. She found his rough skin surprisingly arousing. Then she guided his fingers into her vagina.

'See, that's where you can enter me.'

Liam moaned. 'Oh, God. So soft. So warm.' They said no more as Liam blindly and gently explored Cathy under the sheet; she came close to a climax.

'Now sleep, lovely girl.'

The following morning, Cathy returned to her room, leaving Liam asleep, but Johnny was not in his bed. She ran downstairs. There he was, happily playing snap with Aoife at the table, both still in their nightclothes.

'Morning, Cathy. Johnny came in to find us so I brought him down to stop him waking Ellen.'

Cathy could feel her face flush scarlet but Aoife said nothing more and Cathy chose not to offer an explanation.

'Hello sweetie.' Cathy kissed Johnny. Who's winning?'

'I am. See.' Johnny showed his mother his fat pile of cards.

'Liam's not up himself yet, which is odd, but I think he mentioned he was going to take the day off to go into Clifden, which is probably why he's let himself sleep on.' Aoife busied herself putting water on to boil. By nine o'clock everyone was up, washed, dressed and breakfasted – even Ellen.

'Now, it's a beautiful day so we mustn't waste it sitting indoors.' Ellen loved to organise everyone. 'I think we should take a picnic down to the beach and maybe do some sketching or painting. What do you all think?'

'I have to go into Clifden to bank all the money, but I should be back by midday if I go now.' Liam started gathering up his papers and leather bag where he kept each day's takings. 'I'm giving myself a day off, as you can see.' Liam flashed a smile at his bevy of women, who clapped and cheered.

'Can I come with you for the ride, Liam. I have never really explored Clifden and I can do that while you're in the bank.' Cathy put her hand on Liam's.

'By all means. It would be grand to have a bit of company.'

'Great. Johnny, would you like to come with mama or stay and go to the beach with Auntie Ellen and Auntie Aoife?'

There was no contest, so Liam and Cathy found themselves alone, trotting into Clifden in the pony and trap. A few cars overtook them and even a bus.

'Maybe we should have taken the bus. It would have been a lot quicker.'

'But not nearly as lovely as this,' said Cathy slipping her arm through Liam's. 'Although, I am determined to learn to drive myself. Seamus is teaching me whenever we can find time. It'd be a lot easier to learn out here in the empty roads of Connemara rather than in Dalkey And it's terrifying driving his Jaguar. I need to buy myself a smaller car to learn in really. And once I'm safe on the road, I'll teach you. We can teach each other; you get me swimming and I'll help get you driving.'

While Liam went off to the bank, Cathy slipped into Clifden's pharmacy and bought one or two things but could see no sign of the one thing she needed urgently; a pack of condoms. Not that she'd ever bought them herself in England but she knew they were freely available. Fat chance here. Oh, Ireland, she thought. She plucked up courage and discreetly asked the pharmacist who gave her back an incredulous look as if she had just asked to purchase a bomb.

When they got back to the cottage, they went together to take the pony back to his field. Liam slipped the bridle off and it galloped away joyously, shaking its mane.

'Look at him go. What it must be to have not a care in the world.' Liam put his arm around Cathy and kissed her cheek.

'Come and sit down here a minute with me.' Cathy knelt on the grass and held up her hand, inviting Liam to join her. The grass was long and ticklish at first but it soon flattened as they rolled across it, laughing as they curled themselves around each other.

'I'm so happy here, Liam. You should be too. It's heaven.'

'Not in the middle of winter, macushla, when the freezing wind would blow up your skirts. Though of course I would always be on hand to warm up that shapely arse of yours.'

'Ha! I'm prepared to give it a try.'

'Well, no need to wait for an invitation.'

'Liam, I will come back, of course. You have to teach me to swim for one thing. But listen.' Cathy sat up. 'I want you to find yourself a proper girlfriend. Get yourself down to the Clifden dance hall. Or the church? Someone you can see every week, maybe every day, in time. I have to go back to Dalkey at the end of the week. You know your way round a woman's body now; the rest will come naturally, I promise, when you love someone.'

'You reckon?'

'Come on, we must get to the beach. They'll be wondering what's happened to us.' Cathy stood up and dragged Liam to his feet.

'Not yet. First, let me thank you, macushla. You can be a quite strict and demanding teacher, but you have a kind and generous soul; you just might have saved mine. Secondly...' Liam traced the line of Cathy's lips with his roughened finger, then pressed his mouth to Cathy's and kissed her, open-mouthed and deeply. When they eventually separated their mouths, each was stretched in a wide smile.

'I'd say you're thoroughly saved, Liam.'

That night in bed together they were very conscious of time running out. Their kisses were urgent and passionate. Liam let Cathy take his erection in her mouth for the first time; it took little time for him to reach a climax.

'Oh, God. I'm so sorry. I just couldn't help it.'

'If you dare say sorry one more time I shall bite your balls off. Anyway, you see... my mouth is now as filthy as yours.'

And she kissed him with his own salty secretions flavouring her tongue.

The first time Liam penetrated Cathy, he managed to last a little longer, but as the last shards of moonlight were chased away by the dappled dawn, Liam lay back on the bed and let Cathy straddle him, with her managing the rhythm so that they both reached orgasm.

'Well, I think we can say that you've now fully graduated from the Ashfield School of love-making, Liam. In fact, I think last night you earned several gold stars.'

'Ah, macushla. I shall miss your lovely body and your lovely lips, but most of all I shall miss your tidy mind.'

After saying goodbye to his visitors at Clifden bus station the next Monday, Liam came home and looked around the empty cottage. It was full of memories of the people he loved most in the world; some of Johnny's shells were on the shelf, three soda loaves baked for him by Aoife were on the table and next to them a pot of hand cream from Cathy, with a note saying, 'Now you've got it, make sure you use it!'

Chapter 41 - July 10th 1951

Rose was sitting on Hannah's bed with a teaspoon of boiled egg suspended in front of her mother's tightly shut mouth when Cathy walked into the bedroom, carrying the vase of sweet peas that Stasia had left behind.

'Just one mouthful, Mammy. Go on. It's an egg from the little brown hen.' Hannah shook her head resolutely. 'If you don't eat Mammy, you'll lose your strength.'

'Huh!' Hannah gave a hollow laugh.

'Don't worry, Rose.' Cathy laid her hand on her sister's shoulder. 'There's no point if Mammy really doesn't want to eat.'

'Why would I want to keep my strength up? I want to die as soon as possible, you stupid girl.'

'Mammy, Rose is just trying to look after you.'

Rose stood up and put the egg cup back on the tray. She was fighting back tears. 'Will you help me give Mammy a bed bath, Cathy? I usually wait until Aggie gets up at about eleven, but it'd be nice to save her one job.' Rose took the tray downstairs and Cathy settled herself on the bed next to her mother.

'That wasn't kind, Mammy.'

Hannah huffed, closed her eyes and slipped down under the sheets. Rose returned carrying a jug of piping hot water and towels. She poured the steaming water into the china bowl on the stand and mixed in cold water from the matching pitcher.

The two girls began the laborious process of washing their mother's fragile body; first, each hand, arm, leg and foot was rubbed with a soapy flannel and then rinsed and dried. Cathy opened her mother's nightdress; there was the livid scar where her cancerous left breast had been crudely sliced off; by its side, her other breast, now pitifully wasted. Every inch of Hannah's upper body was gently washed and dried. Then, Rose supported Hannah on her side as Cathy pulled up the nightdress to soap her mother's vulva and finally her bottom. There were bedsores on both buttocks.

'We put cream on those sores, Cathy. It's there on the washstand.'

When they had finished, they put a clean nightdress on their mother and changed the bottom sheet rolling Hannah from side to side to manoeuvre the clean linen into place.

'There you go, Mammy. All nice and clean.'

'What's the point? Just kill me now, for God's sake.'

Rose folded the towels over her arm and picked up the bowl of scummy water to take downstairs. 'Can I leave you for a while, Cathy? Sam needs a hand in the bar and then I need to sort out some orders for the shop.'

Cathy kissed her sister on the cheek. 'Off you go, Rosie, my darling. I'm fine here.'

Hannah fell into sleep. Cathy sat and studied the foetal shape under the sheets: a woman she loved and hated so strongly, a woman she still couldn't understand. There were the arms that had played a violin so magnificently, the hips that had carried four babies to term and several lost ones, the legs that had run, danced and stood for hours behind bar and counter until they ached, and, above all, the still beautiful face that had won the hearts of so many men – and women.

Cathy picked up the volume of Yeats from the bedside table. Next to it was another spare dose of morphine, presumably left there by Dr O'Connor. She popped it into her pocket and settled herself on the window-seat and immersed herself in the poetry that her father had so loved.

'What are you reading, my angel?' Hannah had woken up after a half-hour of mostly peaceful sleep broken by the occasional low groan or sharp cry of pain.

'Just some of Daddy's favourite poems.'

'Ah yes. He loved Yeats.'

'Mammy, now don't be upset,' Cathy spoke very gently, '...but I know everything now. There's no need to worry. I know about you and Father Stephen. And why you married Tricky. And I know about Fergus and Bridie. And it's all fine.'

Her mother wailed. 'Oh, my God. What a terrible, terrible woman I am. God will never forgive me, no matter how many prayers I say. But will you forgive me, Cathy? I had to send you away because I knew you, more than anyone, would see through our wicked deceit. You would know that the only person who killed your father was me. My vanity and infidelity and cruelty killed him.'

'I do forgive you, Mammy, of course, I do. I don't quite understand why you felt you had to do it, but I love you all the same. I won't pretend I'm not shocked, particularly at Father Stephen. And I feel a bit silly. All those sessions in his study, telling him that I knew Tricky had murdered Daddy.'

'He's not a bad man, is Stephen. He just should never have been made a priest, but it's the fate of many third sons. In fact, I don't think he even believes in God, not really, not like I do. I wish I didn't because then I wouldn't know I am heading for hell. But even hell-fire could be no worse than this bastard pain.'

There was a knock on the bedroom door. In walked Fergus, who went straight over to his mother and wrapped her up in his arms. 'How are you today Mammy? Rose says you wouldn't touch your egg.'

'Don't worry about me. How's the harvest going?' Cathy marvelled at how her mother could disguise her excruciating pain and be momentarily overtaken by an interest in her son's life. 'Fergus my love, will you do me a favour before you go back out? Can you find the old wind-up gramophone? Ask Aggie - I think it might be in the cupboard under the stairs –and bring it up here to my bedroom with all the discs that belong to it. I just have a fancy to listen to something.'

'Sure thing, Mammy. We can all come in and have a dance maybe later on. That'll take your mind off things.' And the cheerful lad stomped off down the stairs. Ten minutes later he walked in triumphantly, bearing the ancient gramophone, like a sacrifice to be laid at the feet of a reclining queen.

'I've never even seen this before, Mammy. But Aggie knew where it was.'

'I couldn't bear to use it – or even see it – after your father died, but Cathy will remember it well.'

Cathy was looking through the pile of discs on the top. 'I certainly do. It was my alarm clock. When I was little, I always knew it was time to get up when I heard the gramophone start playing.'

'How does it work then?' Cathy showed Fergus how to wind up the old oak contraption and then she passed him the record of Scott Joplin rags. 'Do you remember this one, Mammy?

The crackles didn't make the music one scrap less intoxicating. Fergus grabbed Cathy and spun her round. 'This is grand. I love it. Why have we not listened to this before?' he asked. Hannah smiled at her two children. The bedroom door opened.

'What the hell is going on? Sounds like a herd of elephants has invaded. Just as well I was already up and about.'

'Come on in Aggie. You remember this, don't you? We all used to dance to it, even you … back in the day when I was a little girl and Daddy was still alive - and you got all the men.'

Fergus and Cathy pulled Aggie into hold and the three of them jigged around the room in front of Hannah. She was laughing and crying at their antics. 'Stop.' Hannah held up her hand. 'Take it off.' The dancing stopped and Fergus bent to lift the needle.

'I'm sorry. I don't want to end your fun. But I wasn't quite prepared for that.'

'Don't you worry, Hannah.' Aggie walked over to the bed, sat on it and took Hannah's hand. 'I'm feeling mighty overwhelmed myself, not to mention out of breath. Happy times though, eh?'

'Happy enough, Aggie. Happy enough. I just wish I'd appreciated that at the time.'

Chapter 42 - July 8th 1951

Cathy closed the ledger, stretched her back and sighed. Sunday afternoons were for catching up on paperwork. She vividly remembered her mother sitting at a similar desk with pots of black and red ink doing the accounts for the pub and the shop, her hands similarly stained when she had finished.

She looked at the crimson walls and resolved to get them painted a brighter colour before the winter sucked the light away. She had already changed several aspects of the Academy that her grandmother had presided over to make it both easier to maintain and more fashionable.

Low mumbles and frequent laughs from the drawing room reassured Cathy that the students were enjoying their free time. Lying on the floor next to her desk, Johnny was reading *Dr Dolittle*, currently his favourite book. He was resting on his elbows, his legs going up and down alternately, his feet thumping noisily on the carpet. Cathy thought she should maybe get him a proper bicycle for Christmas this year. Seamus would take him out on it, no problem.

Cathy undid the ribbon around a stack of opened envelopes at the back of her desk, chose the top one and slid out the folded sheets of paper. She often reread Liam's weekly letters when she got bored of adding up numbers. She could escape for a few minutes from her enclosed, domestic life to walk in the memory of the waves at Cleggan.

Over the last year, Liam had documented his determined quest for a girlfriend – his 'homework'. Last autumn, he had asked the girl in the Clifden bank to a dance and they had walked out together for several weeks, before it abruptly ended when Liam tried to kiss her and she had slapped him so hard she made him cry in the street. In the spring, he had made himself go to the pub in Moyard a few nights a week and eventually had been treated to a tumble in the wet grass behind the pub with one of the barmaids. But when he got home, he discovered her substantial knickers hanging out of his hastily buttoned trousers. Liam wrote to Cathy of his dilemma: should he return them as they were when he next went to the pub? or wash them and then return them? or just throw them on the peat fire, no questions asked? Cathy often roared with laughter at his stories and was impressed at his persistence. But no girlfriend had lasted. Cathy was sorry that Liam was not having more success but also shocked by how happy she felt when Liam recounted the disasters.

After reading Liam's latest news for five minutes, Cathy packed away the letters and retied the ribbon. She was expecting guests shortly. Normally, she would be looking forward to seeing Seamus that evening for their weekly bridge session with Ellen and Aoife, but today she anticipated his arrival with dread.

Other than the two male teachers at the Academy, Seamus was the only grown-up man Cathy encountered regularly and the only one she ever talked to about matters outside school life.

'Who needs men, anyway?' Ellen would say, when Cathy bemoaned her lack of male company. Ellen certainly didn't seem to. Before the war, Seamus's red-whiskered solicitor friend, Colm O'Brian, had attempted to woo Ellen for a couple of years, egged on by Seamus, but had eventually taken the hint and disappeared from the scene. About a year ago, Aoife had vacated her rooms in the stables and moved in with Ellen. Nothing very remarkable about two middle-aged spinster teachers sharing a home, but Cathy was certain that they were more to each other than friends. She knew her instincts were right and she was thrilled for them. Having been a nurse, she had known a few lesbian couples and seen how happily they had made lives together.

Like Ellen, Seamus didn't seem anxious to marry anyone. As the erstwhile fiancés had made their way through their forties, their friendship had deepened without the slightest sign that they might re-ignite their one-time romance. They would often make the trip together to see Hannah, their dearest friend in Rowanbridge, returning with all the news for Cathy. They had even been to Paris together one Easter soon after the war, bringing back some Chanel perfume for Cathy, a wooden Pierrot puppet for Johnny and prints of Leonardo da Vinci paintings from the Louvre to decorate the classrooms.

Seamus was a great support, both emotional and practical, to Ellen and Cathy and, despite his busy practice, always found time for them. After Mrs Fitzgerald's death in 1949, Seamus had personally acted as executor of her rather complicated will, which left Cathy as the sole owner of the Academy but with some bonds held in trust for Rose and Fergus, her two other grandchildren, until they reached twenty-five. Seamus was the person Cathy went to for all financial and legal advice but he was much more than that to her, a cross between a loving elder brother and a doting uncle, not to mention a very patient driving instructor. And Cathy knew that she was the nearest thing to a daughter Seamus would ever have, the beloved child of his great unrequited love, Hannah McDermott.

Although she feared the news that Seamus would bring from his trip to Rowanbridge, Cathy was still anxious to hear it directly from his lips. She could never totally trust what her Aunt Stasia told her on the telephone and Rose seemed too nervous to say much about her mother when Stasia passed the phone over to her. But Seamus was always straight with Cathy.

Eight months ago, Hannah had been diagnosed with breast cancer. The breast had been removed without delay, along with some lymph glands. Cathy knew plenty about breast cancer and its likely progress and kept saying to her Aunt Stasia that she should be allowed to come home and see her mother. But Hannah would still not countenance it.

Hannah, however, seemed perfectly happy to see Ellen and Seamus and her elderly Aunt Lily and that really hurt Cathy. Seamus sometimes drove the three of them to Rowanbridge, but he often went alone, at least once a fortnight, returning with eye-witness reports for Cathy.

Five months after Hannah's operation, Seamus declared that she seemed to be fully recovered, other than a swollen and sore arm which prevented her from playing her violin, and that she was back working in the business whenever she could. Cathy took comfort that her mother's cancer seemed to have been caught early enough.

Just a month later and Seamus's report was less encouraging. Hannah was finding work too tiring and Seamus thought she looked 'drained'. After another month, Seamus brought back the news that Hannah was spending most of each day in bed and was getting much thinner. Ellen accompanied him on his next trip. The pair looked very grave as they shared with Cathy the state they had found Hannah in. But still Hannah would not entertain the idea of Cathy visiting her despite the pleas of Seamus, Ellen, Lily, Stasia, Rose and all the family.

'You know your mother, Cathy. She might be weak physically, but her will is like solid steel. And she always gets what she wants. I know that to my cost.' And Seamus had looked pained, remembering what might have been.

Loud squeals came from the drawing room, ending Cathy's contemplation. What on earth were they up to in there? Cathy closed her desk and went over to her small sitting area in the bay window.

'Come and read to me, Johnny, my darling.'

Johnny sat beside his mother as she put her arm around him and stroked his golden hair while he read aloud to her.

'You read beautifully, my love. You must do some practice too, before the end of the day.' Listening to her son playing the cello always aroused a mixture of joy and loss, evoking memories of her darling Daddy. She wondered what had become of her father's instrument.

The Academy front door opened and closed sharply and then there was a brisk knock at the sitting room door.

'Come on in.'

Johnny ran to open the door but Ellen and Aoife were already through it. Aoife bent down, held out her arms and Johnny jumped into them. He was really getting a bit too big for Aoife to pick up like this but neither she nor Johnny were quite ready to give up their habitual greeting.

'Now, my favourite fella, what have you been up to today?' Johnny dragged his Auntie Aoife out into the garden to show her the den he had made for beetles while Ellen flopped into a chair next to Cathy, banging her bad leg with her walking stick.

'This bloody old leg. I need alcohol right now, Cathy, to take away the ache. Bring me whiskey, girl.'

Cathy was already on her feet and pouring a generous measure topped with a splash of water just as Ellen liked it. Seamus would join her in a glass of Tullamore Dew when he arrived, but, for herself and Aoife, Cathy poured two modest glasses of gin and tonic.

'I wonder how Seamus found your mother yesterday.' Seamus had made a one-day round trip to Rowanbridge the previous day, taking chocolates and a new silk bed-jacket as offerings to his beloved Hannah.

'Well, we'll soon find out.' Cathy pointed out of the window to where Seamus was parking his Jaguar, while handing Ellen her glass of whiskey. Seamus looked grim when he entered but, with Johnny buzzing around excitedly in the company of his favourite aunties and uncle, he refrained from passing on any news until the boy had been sent off to practise in his room. Then he opened up.

'I'll be honest, Cathy, I think that was the last time I'll ever see her. She cannot have much longer to go. She's just a bag of bones. And they give her injections for the pain but she's clearly in agony. In all humanity, I'd like it to be quick now. I'm so sorry, my girl.'

'What can I do? I want to see her so much.' Cathy wailed into Seamus's chest. 'How can she leave me and not let me kiss her good-bye?' Seamus held her until her sobs eased.

No bridge was played that evening. Instead, the four of them spent the hours reminiscing about Hannah McDermott and John Fitzgerald and the many happy, hilarious, triumphant and tragic times they had all shared.

Just after half past nine, when Johnny had been put to bed and Seamus was making moves to leave, the telephone rang over on Cathy's desk. She took a deep breath before picking it up. She spoke very little to whoever it was on the other end but listened and nodded, ending with a simple 'Yes. Goodnight,' before placing the receiver down and turning to them.

'That was my Aunt Stasia. Mammy has finally asked me to come home.'

Chapter 43 – July 10th 1951

Dr O'Connor had just gone, leaving Cathy with a third spare dose of morphine which she tucked into her pocket. Father Stephen was sitting by her mother's side, saying the rosary along with her, though Hannah's voice was little more than a whisper.

A couple of hours earlier, Hannah had asked everyone to leave the room except the priest.

'I'm going to make my last confession. This could take some time, so please leave us alone for a while.'

When Cathy was allowed back into the room, she could see the oily smudges on her mother's forehead where the priest had reluctantly administered extreme unction. He seemed considerably more distressed than the patient herself.

Cathy busied herself around the room folding clothes and putting them in drawers, including the unworn silk jacket that Seamus had brought her mother two days earlier, while the low mumble of prayers went on behind her. She was perplexed by the priest sitting there bestowing absolution and dispensing sacraments, when he was as big a sinner as anyone. How did that all work then? Even though it was all a game as far as Cathy was concerned, she liked things to work by their own rules at least.

When the prayers finished, Cathy went to her mother's side. 'Mammy, Rose and Fergus and Bridie want to come up and say goodnight before you go to sleep. And Aggie too of course.'

'And Tricky.' Her mother's consideration for her strange husband of convenience remained resolute. Cathy found herself admiring her mother for that more and more.

'Everyone. Yes, of course.'

Nobody said that this would probably be their final goodnight but it was understood, as a little line formed of

Hannah's closest family; first Rose, then Bridie, then Fergus approached their mother, all wanting a tender kiss and a bony hug. Aggie blustered up to Hannah, saying very pointedly as they embraced, 'Sleep tight, Hannah McDermott, and I'll see you in the morning. Promise me that, now.' Finally, Tricky knelt at his wife's side, took her hand and kissed it fervently, saying nothing.

Father Stephen had the decency to look away while the man who had saved his reputation took his last leave but Cathy kept her eyes on the two of them. She couldn't name it but there was something very real between her mother and Tricky. Hannah eventually pulled her hand away and stroked his face. 'Bless you, Tricky.'

Then there were just the two of them left with Hannah.

'I must be off soon, Cathy.'

'Yes, of course. I'll just give you a moment then.'

Cathy stood outside the bedroom door, as the lovers said their farewells, then the door opened and Stephen rushed down the stairs.

Hannah was lying wide awake when Cathy went back into the bedroom.

'Come here, Cathy. Sit here. I don't want to go just yet. There are things to tell you and sort out. First of all - Rose. Rose is very sweet on Sam and he just as much on her. They're just great together and Sam would be such a terrific help to her in the business, but they are both very shy and I reckon they are scared to get engaged because of you. Can you set them free?'

'Good God, Mammy. I stopped having any designs on Sam McCarthy when I saw him kissing Marion Magee years ago. I have absolutely no claim on Sam whatsoever, but yes, if you think they need my blessing, I'll talk to Rose.'

'Fergus and Bridie. They have no money worries. Lucky them. But they need guidance. I have asked Seamus to step in but they need you and most of all they need your love - Bridie in particular. You don't know each other at all. I know that's my fault entirely but please will you right my wrong. Promise me you'll tell no-one else that Tricky isn't her father. For her sake mainly, but also for Tricky's dignity. He cares for her as much as any loving father should. And it would also mess up the Byrne inheritance if the secret came out.'

'I understand that completely, Mammy, though you do realise there's quite a bunch of us who now know, don't you?'

Hannah waved her hand dismissively. 'Then, your father. I want to be buried next to him. I want to lie next to him for all eternity. Stephen has promised to do that somehow. You hold him to it now. You hear? ' Hannah's voice had sunk back to a whisper. 'Your father was the most perfect man. Far too good for me. I think about him every day. You look so much like him. And you loved him so much - I just couldn't bear to see you after he had gone. Your grief was hard to watch, knowing that I had killed him, that I had made him so utterly despairing he chose to take himself away from his children – and from me.'

'He wasn't in his right mind, Mammy.'

'He absolutely was, Cathy. In his typical way, he was just putting others first. He thought he'd get out of the way so that Stephen and I could be together more easily. He didn't think I loved him. Why would he? I never told him I did. Don't you ever make that mistake. If there's someone you love, tell them every day - morning, noon and night.'

Cathy smiled and kissed her mother.

'I will. I definitely will. I love *you* Mammy.'

'Now, my angel. I want you to send me to sleep. To sleep forever. I know you can. I'm not stupid. I've seen Dr O'Connor give you that extra morphine. You must have it squirreled away somewhere. I need it tonight. But first, I want to listen to the *Harp Quartet* one last time. You'll find it in that pile.'

Cathy found the discs of Beethoven string quartets and wound up the ancient gramophone. 'Did you know that it was while playing *The Harp* together that your father and I fell in love properly with each other?'

Mother and daughter sat together, holding hands, listening intently through all four movements. As the music ended and the disc clicked through its empty revolutions, Hannah squeezed Cathy's hands. 'Now, my angel. I'm ready.'

Cathy's hand trembled as she drew three doses of morphine into the syringe. In her head, she knew it was the right and proper thing to do, taking her mother into pain-free nothingness. But her heart was hurting bitterly as she found a vein in her mother's bruised arm and slid in the needle as gently as she could.

'Thank you, my angel.' Hannah closed her eyes, as if willing herself into death. She soon fell into a deep sleep, her breathing becoming shallower and more irregular. Even so, it wasn't until nearly two o'clock that Cathy was certain her mother was dead.

Cathy gazed at the wasted body. She did her best to arrange the bedclothes neatly around her mother's corpse. Then she quietly opened the bedroom door and left. Tricky was sitting on guard, as usual.

'She's gone, Tricky. There's no need for you to stay here now. And I'm not going to wake the household. The morning will come soon enough.'

Tricky's head dropped and he made a weak gesture with his hand. Cathy crossed the landing to her own room where she drowned the pillow in tears.

Chapter 44 – July 13th 1951

L ucky to find four men as tall as each other, thought Cathy, as she walked behind Tricky, following the coffin carried by Fergus, Peter, Andrew and Seamus down the aisle of the church. At the front of the long procession was Father Stephen. Cathy held Rose's and Bridie's hands, a small bunch of hedge-picked honeysuckle in each. Behind her walked Stasia, Edmund and the rest of the apostles, Ellen, Aggie – forced by Ellen to take her place as a member of the family - Nicholas and Louisa Byrne, various schoolfriends from the Academy and then seemingly hundreds of villagers and acquaintances.

Lily had declared herself unable to cope with her niece's premature death and had stayed up in Dublin, as had Aoife and Johnny. Better for Johnny to be introduced to Rowanbridge and his relatives in happier times.

The pall-bearers set down the feather-light coffin and took their seats, Fergus next to his sisters, Peter and Andrew over the aisle with their parents and a very red-eyed Seamus in the row behind Cathy, next to Ellen and Aggie. Cathy guessed that the long arrangement of white roses on the top of the coffin must weigh almost as much as her mother's body.

Father Stephen turned to address the congregation. The man looked destroyed by grief. Cathy had wanted to get the services of another priest out of consideration for Stephen, but Stasia had insisted that it was only proper that Stephen took the service; people would think it odd otherwise.

As the bereaved husband, Tricky was sitting alone in the front pew. Cathy stared at the back of his balding head and the dandruff on the collar of his best black suit. She had not been able to rid her mind of the image that greeted her when she had entered her mother's bedroom the morning after her death. Tricky was there, lying next to her dead mother, his arms around Hannah, allowed, for probably the first time, into her bed.

Tricky had said nothing for the last three days, just helped to carry Hannah's body downstairs and arranged her on the dining room table, watching over her through the candlelit nights.

Tricky, Stephen, Seamus – even Nicholas Byrne, all these men who had been in love with her mother, thought Cathy, were here to mourn her passing. And not just men. There were plenty of women who had been captivated by her. Was her mother really so special? Had they not seen all her faults?

But none of them would get to lie next to her in death. Only her father would enjoy that privilege. When Cathy had brought up the subject of Hannah's burial next to her father, Father Stephen was well-prepared with an answer. There had been no need to emphasise his promise to her mother, no need to beg or make him feel guilty. He immediately explained to Cathy what he was planning.

Rather than exhume her father, Stephen had decided to consecrate the area of the churchyard that had hitherto been reserved for the villages' suicides - John and another couple of poor souls. There had been two days of frantic preparation. Fergus and Peter had cut back the hedges behind the plots, removed a self-sown sycamore sapling from next to John's grave where Hannah would be laid to rest and poured new gravel on the rarely-trodden path from the main graveyard.

The procession was now compacting the fresh gravel on the way to the graveside. It was all a bit of a blur really. Cathy heard soil hit the lid of her mother's deeply laid coffin. Tricky had picked up a handful of dirt to throw in as had Stasia. Cathy threw in her small bunches of honeysuckle and Rose dropped in a rose – of course. Bridie had wanted to bury her mother's violin with Hannah, but Cathy talked sense into her. Instead, she and Fergus chose to throw in some newly harvested barley from the top field. Seamus was the one to honour the musical connection and he floated in a copy of the Mozart duos that he and Hannah had played together in their teens. Then it was all over and the crowd made their way to Stasia's villa for the funeral breakfast.

******

'Another cup, Cathy?' Father Stephen held up the old brown teapot. They were sitting in quiet contemplation in his study after an exhausting day, having retreated from the Hughes's villa and the high emotion and noise of all the mourners after a couple of hours. They had had a lot to talk through and now were on their third pot of tea.

Cathy covered her cup with her hand. The clock ticked through another ten minutes of silence and then chimed nine o'clock. 'I must get home to bed. I'm on the train back to Dublin early tomorrow. Johnny will be missing me so much.'

'You called it "home", Cathy.'

'Huh! Just habit. It doesn't mean anything.' Cathy paused. 'Can I ask you one last thing, Stephen.'

'Certainly. Though I might not be able to answer you.'

'When my mother started coming to mass, was it because you and she were already lovers?'

'No, no, not at all. She was driven by a genuine yearning for God's mercy and comfort. All those lost babies, you see.'

'Yes, she must have really suffered. So, in effect, you exploited her pain?'

'Ouf. That's a low blow, Cathy. I was clearly quite, quite wrong to let my feelings lead me into such sin. I'm not sure God will ever forgive me. But what you must realise is that I had been a little bit in love with your mother ever since she had teased me at my first mass at the convent, the incident that got her expelled. Me, a newly ordained priest and none too sure of the vows I had taken, and her, with her beautiful eyes and shining hair. And that mischievous mouth, kissing the crucifix in ways that made me blush. She had plenty of devilment in her, your mother, but was also blessed with a heavenly beauty and grace that I will never forget. And so talented - not just her music. Her faith was real too, you know. Much more real than mine. She put me to shame. I simply couldn't not love Hannah McDermott, Cathy.'

'Did my father know about you?'

'Oh, I am certain he did; he was a clever man. Hannah said he was already suspicious when she fell pregnant. They had almost stopped having … intimate relations by then. And then, when Fergus was born, he must have instantly known he wasn't his and it wouldn't have taken much effort to work out I was Fergus's real father. I shall carry the burden of knowing I caused his death to my own grave.'

'Obviously what you did was very, very wrong, Father. But Daddy was also depressed by money troubles and by failing to save a young boy over in Connemara who he'd been unable to take away from the Christian Brothers. It was a poisonous combination. Give yourself a break, Stephen.'

'God will be my judge, Cathy, but it would help me survive the rest of my mortal days if you could forgive me.'

Cathy laid her hand gently over Stephen's.

'I forgive you, Stephen. I can see that you truly loved my mother.'

Their eyes met in understanding. Cathy reached down to her handbag and took out her mother's rosary.

'I thought you might like something to remember my mother by, so I've brought you this.'

Stephen took the worn wooden beads from Cathy and kissed them.

'That was a very kind thought and I shall treasure it, but I will never, ever forget your mother.' A sob broke through his fragile composure and the priest took out his well-used handkerchief again.

'What is it with Ireland though - and the church and secrets? I would bet that there are plenty of people in

Rowanbridge who suspect that you and Mammy were lovers and that you are the father of Fergus and Bridie. But there's this great conspiracy of silence: let nothing be said to discredit the clergy. It's the same back at Letterfrack School. So many people know full well that evil is flourishing there but no, better to let young lads be tortured and killed than embarrass the Catholic Church.'

'I can't explain it, Cathy, but you're right, of course.'

'And you know what's at the bottom of all this, don't you, Stephen: sex. This ridiculous notion that priests have to be celibate. It's completely unnatural and from it springs all this misery and perversion. It's against nature. I'd say it's against God, if I believed in him.'

'But what about you, Cathy? If it's unnatural for ugly old priests to be on their own what about a beautiful and clever young woman like you? It's about time you found some happiness. Why don't you come back home to Rowanbridge so that all your family can rally round and look after you and little Johnny?'

'There will always be people here that I adore, and I will always come back to see them. But I can't make Rowanbridge my home. And Dublin isn't right for me and Johnny either. I know where I want to be, and I know someone who wants me to be there. Someone my father wanted to save and who, I think, can be saved.'

'Well, you have God's blessing, Cathy, and mine – whether you want them or not.'

They took a subdued leave of each other. Cathy walked slowly back to Main Street as the last strands of light left the sky, leaving the waxing half-moon shining down on her. In her ears, was the sound of the Atlantic ocean.

BV - #0009 - 020920 - C0 - 216/140/14 - PB - 9781913425388